LITTLE,
BROWN

LB

LARGE
PRINT

A complete list of books by James Patterson is at the back of this book. For previews of upcoming books and information about the author, visit JamesPatterson.com or find him on Facebook or at your app store.

MURDER GAMES

JAMES PATTERSON & HOWARD ROUGHAN

LITTLE, BROWN AND COMPANY

LARGE PRINT EDITION

Little, Brown and Company
Hachette Book Group
1290 Avenue of the Americas, New York, NY 10104
littlebrown.com

First Edition: June 2017

Little, Brown and Company is a division of Hachette Book Group, Inc. The Little, Brown name and logo are trademarks of Hachette Book Group, Inc.

The publisher is not responsible for websites (or their content) that are not owned by the publisher.

The Hachette Speakers Bureau provides a wide range of authors for speaking events. To find out more, go to hachettespeakersbureau.com or call (866) 376-6591.

ISBN 978-0-316-27396-1 (hc) / 978-0-316-55252-3 (large print)
LCCN 2016955364

10 9 8 7 6 5 4 3 2 1

LSC-C

Printed in the United States of America

For Barbara and Will Cravens

—H.R.

PROLOGUE

THE DEALER MANIFESTO

ENTRY #1

SO YOU want to be a serial killer...

Sure, you can go around just shooting people, bang-bang, but I've found that guns, while sometimes the right tool for the job, often leave me unsatisfied. There's a lack of intimacy involved when all you have to do is pull a trigger. You hear the blast and see the carnage, the way your victim's flesh ruptures and bursts open in an instant, but you don't really feel the same adrenaline as with other, let's say more personal, methods of murdering someone.

Me? I like to mix things up. There are so many wonderful and creative ways to kill people, and I really feel as if I owe it to myself and my cause to make sure that I branch out and keep it interesting. And even when circumstances do call for a gun, I try to add a twist to it, a little something extra. Sundaes always look better with a cherry on top.

3

Still, you'd be amazed at how much satisfaction can be derived from some of the most rudimentary approaches. Stabbing someone to death, for instance. I can't think of a more personal and intimate experience. The sound that a knife makes when piercing human skin is nothing short of intoxicating. You can't help yourself sometimes. You want to hear it over and over and over.

Of course, repeatedly stabbing someone to death isn't without a downside or two. For instance, it tends to be messy. That's why I like to wear clothes that I can simply throw away afterward. No muss, no fuss. If you want to be a real stickler for hiding evidence, though, burning the clothes would be even better.

But if you're on a budget or partial to a particular outfit—you know, a certain shirt or comfortable pair of pants that you enjoy killing in more than others—remember that you want to treat the bloodstains as soon as possible with a strong prewash stain remover and let it soak in for a good hour or so before throwing the clothes in the Maytag. Also, I highly recommend an extra rinse cycle.

Another downside, or at least a potential one, is that stabbing a person to death requires a tad more preparation. It takes a little longer than simply aiming a gun, and it also puts a premium on the element of surprise. Even then, the first couple of stabs don't always do the trick. Be prepared for some resistance, depending on the size and stubbornness of your victim.

Not all folks, however, will put up a fight. We assume that people have a tremendous will to live, but it's amazing how quickly some of them will resign themselves to their fate, especially when it comes to dying in a massive pool of their own blood.

That about covers it for my first entry. If you have any questions, I'm afraid you're on your own. It's not like I have an 800 number or an e-mail address I can give out. For obvious reasons, too, I can't tell you my real name. But lately people have taken to calling me the Dealer, which I happen to like, so I've taken to it as well. There's a nice ring to it. *The Dealer*. Clean. Authoritative. Quite proprietary, too, given my methods. I'd trademark it if I could.

I mean, the best serial killers, the ones whom people tend to remember, always manage to have a good moniker, the kind of nickname that seems to suit them perfectly. Otherwise, what's the point? The shrinks will tell you that guys like me are first and foremost narcissists, but if that means taking pride in your craft and planning each and every murder with meticulous care, then I suppose there are worse things to be called.

Honestly, I'm just giving you all what you want.

A little razzle-dazzle, an escape from your dreary lives. What else are you going to talk about while sipping your four-dollar coffees and acting superior to the rest of the world?

You want me. You *need* me. And in time, you'll all discover that I'm doing you nothing less than a huge favor. Trust me.

Now, if you don't mind, there's someone else I really need to kill.

BOOK ONE

SHUFFLE UP AND DEAL

CHAPTER 1

THE LECTURE hall hushed to a pin-drop silence the moment I walked in, every conversation stopping on a dime, every pair of eyes homing in on me, watching my every move.

For the record, any professor who tells you that he doesn't get off on this bit of catnip for the ego, if only a little, is completely full of crap. We all love it.

Milking the silence a few seconds longer, I took my time unloading my shoulder bag on the table next to the lectern before slowly turning to the class with the same opening speech I've been delivering now for years. The only thing that ever changes is that the faces staring back at me always seem to look just a little bit younger every time I give the speech.

There's nothing like a college campus to make a thirty-four-year-old guy feel over the hill.

And we're off…

"Good morning, my assembled prodigies, all

you former class presidents and valedictorians, type A go-getters and relentless overachievers, and hopefully only a tiny smattering of you whose mommies and daddies knew the right people on the Yale admissions committee. Welcome to Abnormal Behavioral Analysis, commonly referred to as Intro to Psychopaths or, better yet, Your Ex-Boyfriend or Girlfriend 101. My name is Professor Dylan Reinhart; that's Dylan with a y, and, yes, my mother was a huge Bob Dylan fan. Are there any questions so far?"

Every year, someone takes the bait.

A blonde in the third row raised her hand with an easy confidence that bordered on flirtation. Clearly she hadn't done her homework on me.

"Yes? What's your name?" I asked.

"Heather," she answered. Heather with the come-hither smile.

"Thank you, Heather, but asking if there were any questions was a rhetorical question on my part. I haven't begun teaching you anything yet, so there shouldn't be anything you need to ask about," I said. "And with that we come to the first rule of this class. *Ask only what you don't understand.*"

I can be such a hard-ass sometimes.

Although I assure you it's not without a larger purpose in mind for these students. The vast majority of them have been treated like geniuses since the third grade, and the sooner they figure out they're not, the better. As a former patent-office clerk with crazy hair once said, "A true genius admits that he knows nothing." That guy's name was Einstein.

Meanwhile, poor Heather in the third row looked as if she'd just eaten a bad oyster. Don't worry, I'll make it up to her at some point.

I continued. "The textbook for this class is en-titled *Permission Theory: Redefining Abnormal Behavior,* and for those of you not familiar with the author, handsome devil that he is, let it be known that he's a bit of a narcissist who enjoys listening to the sound of his own voice almost as much as he does forcing others to listen to it."

Most of the room laughed. Those who didn't had their heads buried in their syllabi to see that, yes, I, Dylan Reinhart, was indeed the author of said textbook.

"This of course brings us to rule number two," I said. "*You will attend every class.* Your only excuse for missing a class will be your own death or someone else's, provided this someone else either breast-fed you, coached your Little League team, or routinely put a five-dollar bill in your child-hood birthday card and signed it *Love, Grandma and Grandpa.*"

A student in the first row, obviously a freshman, was typing feverishly on his laptop. I remained silent until he finally looked up at me.

"What are you doing?" I asked.

He swallowed hard and glanced at his keyboard, confused. "I was...um...taking notes," he said meekly.

"*Rule number three,*" I announced with a little added volume. "You will not take notes in this class. I repeat, you will *not* take notes. What you will do is listen. The premise of this course is to challenge the long-standing conventional thinking about abnormal behavior, and as far as I'm concerned there's nothing more abnormal than my lecturing to a roomful of stenographers." I paused, smiling. "Are there any questions?"

This time, no one raised a hand. Geniuses or not, they were all still students at Yale. They didn't get there by learning *slowly.*

"Good," I said. "Now let's get started."

But before I could, a noise in the back of the room had every head turning. It was only the door opening, nothing more.

Still, there was something different about it.

Sometimes you just know the sound of trouble even before she walks into the room.

CHAPTER 2

"SHIT!" SHE announced from the top of the aisle as she realized everyone was staring at her. Immediately she slapped her forehead. "Shit, I just said that out loud, didn't I?"

"Yes, you did," I said. "Lucky for you, I don't give two shits about someone cursing in my class." I stepped out in front of the lectern. "Welcome."

Writers can spot their own books a mile away, and she had mine tucked under her arm. "You're Professor Reinhart, right?" she asked.

"Yes," I answered. "And you are?"

"Clearly interrupting," she said.

She was either a student or someone who happened to look young for her age. I couldn't tell.

For sure, though, she was attractive. The proof wasn't so much the way the male students were staring at her but rather the female students. If you don't understand that, then you probably have no clue why women buy expensive shoes. Hint: it has nothing to do with men.

"I'm sorry, I still didn't get your name," I said.

"It's Elizabeth," she answered. "Elizabeth Needham."

"Are you a student here, Ms. Needham?" I asked.

"*At Yale?*" She laughed deeply from her gut. "You're kidding me, right?"

"Apparently I am," I said.

She looked around the room. "I mean, no offense, of course."

"I'm sure I speak for everyone here when I say none taken. But if you're not a student..."

"Then who am I? Yes, that's a good question," she said.

"Will there be a good answer?"

"How about I just sit in on the class and we'll talk afterward?"

She half tiptoed over to an empty chair in the back row. For good measure, she gave me a nod as if to say, "Carry on."

Whoever she was, she had balls.

As if the entire class were sitting midcourt at Wimbledon, they all turned their heads back to me—*whoosh!*—to see what would happen next. The ball was clearly in my court.

"Sixty-eight thousand, two hundred and thirty dollars," I called out.

Whoosh! went everyone's head back to her.

"Excuse me?" she said.

"That's the cost of a year at Yale, Ms. Needham, of which approximately forty-nine thousand dollars is for tuition," I said.

"Are you asking me to leave?"

"No, I'm asking if you have your checkbook."

Whoosh! Whoosh! Whoosh!

With that, she stood with a huff and began walking toward the door. I couldn't help feeling a twinge of guilt. My damn conscience. It's my Achilles' heel.

"I hope I didn't offend you, Ms. Needham," I said.

She stopped, raising a palm. "That's quite all right. For the record, though, it's *Detective* Needham. The reason I'm here is because I'm pretty sure someone wants to kill you."

Then *whoosh!*

She was gone.

CHAPTER 3

"GO AFTER her!" a few students shouted.

I was tempted, but I figured if someone really did want me dead there was no better place to be than in a roomful of potential witnesses.

I stayed put and delivered my lecture as planned. Okay, so maybe it wasn't the best lecture I'd ever given, and maybe I rushed through it just a wee bit. A guy can compartmentalize only so much.

I obviously needed to talk to this woman, and I knew it would take only one call after class to know whether she was still on campus.

"No," said the guy who answered the phone at the New Haven police department. "We don't have a Detective Elizabeth Needham."

I didn't think so. There was something "big city" about her. Or at least a bigger city than New Haven. That meant she traveled a distance to see me. No way she would leave without our talking.

Sure enough, within seconds I felt the vibration of a text message. *She's a detective, she flashes her badge, and the dean or some other keeper of all things confidential coughs up my cell number.*

Meet me @ Jojo's.

No address and none needed. A coffee shop that everyone on campus knows. It was close by, too.

A few minutes later, I was walking toward her at a table in the back. She had my book and some colored folders laid out meticulously, everything perfectly aligned. She was peering at me with her dark brown eyes over an over-size mug.

"Fancy meeting you here," I said, taking a seat.

Of course, the charm of Jojo's, on Chapel Street, is that there's nothing fancy about it. Wooden tables and chairs on a scuffed-up wood floor were scattered about, and some grandma-style curtains were hanging in the windows. Very college.

"How was the rest of class?" she asked. Her flashing of a wry smile would've been redundant.

"A third of the students wanted me to chase after you while another third actually thought you were a plant—you know, someone I hired. The course is about abnormal behavior, after all."

"And the remaining third?" she asked.

"Too busy wondering what grade they'll get if someone does indeed kill me before the term is over," I said.

I waited for her to tell me that she'd been a tad melodramatic; that no one really wanted to kill me. Instead she opened the folder directly in front her. It was green.

"Let's back up a bit," she said.

She reintroduced herself. Elizabeth Needham, NYPD detective second grade. I could call her Elizabeth, though.

Then she basically introduced me to myself.

I sat there listening as she quickly reduced my life to a series of bullet points, reading in a near monotone off a hand-scribbled piece of paper in the folder. At least it wasn't a cocktail napkin.

"Dr. Dylan Reinhart...Yale undergrad...PhD in psychology, also Yale...three-year research fellowship, University of Cambridge...then another PhD, this time from MIT, in statistics with a focus on Bayesian inference." She paused and looked up. "Am I supposed to know what that is? Bayesian inference?"

Maybe if you're dating Nate Silver...

"Bayesian inference is why most women shouldn't have routine mammograms until they're fifty," I said.

"And why's that?"

I nodded at the folder. "You're the one who apparently likes to do her research, Elizabeth."

"This bothers you, doesn't it?" she asked. "My looking into your background?"

"No. What bothers me is that you still haven't explained who wants to kill me. Anytime you're ready."

She closed the folder, resting her hands on top of it. No wedding ring. No jewelry of any kind. "Do you know who Allen Grimes is?"

"Grimes on Crimes?" The guy wrote a daily column for the *New York Gazette*. I'd heard about it—catchy name and all—but never read it.

Elizabeth nodded. "That's him," she said. "Two days ago, Grimes received an anonymous package in the mail. Inside it was your book."

"Is that a crime?" I asked.

I was half joking. Not Elizabeth, though.

"As it turns out, it was a crime," she said.

CHAPTER 4

ELIZABETH REACHED to her left, pulling another folder in front of her. This one was red. *Red's never good.*

"Your book came with a bookmark," she said.

She opened the folder and removed a small evidence bag. It was sealed, labeled, and just big enough for a ham sandwich. That made it the ideal size for what it was actually holding.

I leaned in, staring at it. "A playing card?"

It wasn't a question; that was clearly what it was. A playing card. The king of clubs.

"Does this mean anything to you?" she asked.

"That's silly. Why would it?"

"Yeah, you're right," said Elizabeth, rolling her eyes. "Clearly the reason I drove all the way out here from Manhattan is so I could ask you silly and irrelevant questions."

"You get the word *feisty* a lot, don't you?" I asked.

"I prefer *spirited*," she said. "What do you prefer instead of *smug*?"

"Actually, I'm okay with *smug*."

To her credit, she kept the straight face a good five seconds before she smiled. *Peace begins with a smile,* said Mother Teresa.

"No, the card doesn't register anything with me," I said. "Of course, it is pretty common for people to use playing cards as bookmarks."

"Agreed," she said. "Here's something not so common, though. In fact, it's pretty damn rare."

Elizabeth turned the bag around so I could see the back of the card. There was a dark red blotch on what was a harlequin-patterned blue-and-white background. It was blood.

"I assume you've already had it tested," I said.

"It's type AB negative," she said. "Only around 1 percent of the population has it."

"Yeah, I'd say that's rare, all right. I'd also say it was on purpose."

"You and me both," she said with a nod. "Blood type as bread crumbs."

"So where did it lead you?" I asked.

CHAPTER 5

ELIZABETH REACHED for her red folder again and took out an eight-by-ten photo, black and white. As crime scenes go, this one was particularly grisly. Even the most devout Wes Craven fan would've flinched.

"The victim's name is Jared Louden, ran a large hedge fund," she said. "He was stabbed to death—to put it mildly—six days ago in the entryway of his Upper East Side town house. No witnesses, no leads. Nothing."

I stared at the image of Louden in a pool of his own blood, his dapper-looking suit shredded from seemingly endless entry wounds. Absolutely brutal. "How many days ago did you say?"

"Six," she answered, "and since then there hasn't been another murder victim with AB negative blood in a two-hundred-mile radius."

"What about before this guy?" I asked. "Any other unsolved cases?"

"There's one from more than eight months ago. A prostitute shot to death in Queens." Elizabeth nodded at the back of the playing card. "This blood's not eight months old. The lab put it at no more than a week."

"You said the card, along with my book, was mailed, right? It wasn't delivered by messenger?"

"Yes, definitely mailed. Routed through Farley."

She assumed I knew that was the main post office in Manhattan, the James A. Farley building, a.k.a. the one with the famous inscription. *Neither snow nor rain nor heat nor gloom of night stays these couriers from the swift completion of their appointed rounds.*

"The address wasn't handwritten, was it?" I asked, speaking of inscriptions. I figured there was no chance.

"Actually, it was," she said. "But it was Toys'R'Us."

That reference I didn't know. "Toys'R'Us? As in the toy store?"

"As in writing with your nondominant hand so it's childlike," she explained. "That's what we call it, at least. Nearly impossible to trace."

"And the card itself: what was it again?"

Elizabeth spun the evidence bag around again to show me.

"The king of clubs," she said. "My first thought was a God complex. The killer thinks of himself as a king."

"Does that make me his subject?"

"He obviously identifies with you or your book in some way. But whether he loathes you or reveres you, the chances are pretty good that he wants to kill you."

"I'm sure it's a possibility, but that's a pretty big leap," I said.

"A big leap, huh?"

"Sure. Fixation disorders play out in many ways."

"You're right," she said. "Then again..." Her voice trailed off.

"What do you mean?" I asked. *What haven't you shown me?*

Elizabeth picked up the book, turning it around so I could see my author photo.

Damn.

"How's that leap looking now?" she said.

CHAPTER 6

WITH SEVENTY-FIVE miles between New Haven and the Upper West Side of Manhattan I could either suffer through the round-trip journey every week or make the best of it. I chose the latter, with more than a little help from a restored 1961 Triumph TR6 Trophy motorcycle, the same model that Steve McQueen rode like a boss in *The Great Escape*. A few hard twists of the wrist, a rev of the engine, and the world and its worries are always left behind.

Not today, though.

Keeping pace—or, more aptly, tailgating like a son of a bitch—was that picture of me on the back of my book. What was left of me, at least. My eyes had been cut out, and the rest of my face had been slashed to threads with a precision blade. Unfortunately the artist didn't sign his work, but he did manage to clip and paste a short sentence across my forehead, ransom note–style. Two words. *Dead* and *Wrong*. For good measure, *Dead* was under-lined in red ink.

Yeah, just in case everything else was too subtle, pal...

Between the countless case studies I've read and the handful of actual murder cases I've been involved with as a forensic witness, I've had both a front-row seat and a backstage pass to the ultimate freak show, the things killers do to announce their horrific intentions. Really sick and depraved stuff.

This guy going to town on my photo, on the other hand, was pretty tame by comparison. Still, for the first time, I wasn't looking at some stranger, a person I didn't know and had never met. I was looking at me.

On this day of all days, too.

"You're late!" Tracy called out from the kitchen before I'd set two feet in our apartment. "Hurry up and shower."

Normally, I would've cracked a joke along the lines of, "My day was good, thanks for asking," but that little touch of sarcasm would've only brought Tracy out of the kitchen to actually ask how my day was, and it just didn't feel like the right moment to announce that there might be some crazed lunatic out there who wants to kill me.

So instead I hurried up and showered.

"What are you going to wear?" asked Tracy, appearing in the doorway of the bathroom minutes later as I was toweling myself dry.

"Let me guess," I said, although I was hardly guessing. "Whatever you just laid out for me on the bed?"

"That depends. Were you about to throw on some old jeans and a T-shirt?"

Guilty as charged. "Yep."

"Then, yeah," said Tracy with a laugh. "What I just laid out for you on the bed."

"You do realize the whole purpose of this visit is so they can see that we'd be normal parents," I said. "How much more normal does it get than jeans and a T-shirt?"

"Do you think the gentleman interviewing us will also be wearing jeans and a T-shirt?" asked Tracy.

Rats, outsmarted again. No wonder we're together…

"Hey, how do you know it's a guy who's coming?" I asked.

"Don't you remember? We briefly met him," said Tracy. "Barbara introduced us."

Barbara was the head of the adoption agency. "Trust the process," she told us during our initial screening meeting. "It will feel like hell sometimes, but it will all be worth it."

Amen. There's nothing on this planet that Tracy and I want more than a child of our own to love.

27

It's just so dangerous to get our hopes up too much, though.

"Oh, yeah, I remember that guy," I said. "He looked like Mr. French."

"That's another thing," said Tracy. "No obscure references during the interview."

"What do you mean? *Family Affair* isn't obscure. Uncle Bill, Buffy, Jody...Mr. French? It's a television classic."

Tracy gave me "the Look." I never fared well against the Look.

"Okay," I said. "No jeans, no T-shirt, and no classic television show references. Anything else?"

Tracy came over with a kiss and a smile. "Don't get me started."

Shortly thereafter, the doorbell rang. I tucked in my button-down and straightened out the pleats on my very respectable-looking khakis before joining Tracy at the door.

Trust the process. Let the home interview begin.

Too bad it was over before it even started.

CHAPTER 7

"OH," SAID the woman. It was one measly little word.

But, oh, the way she said it . . .

She was standing in the hallway and staring at us, wondering if she had the right apartment. She quickly checked the clipboard in her hand. Once, then twice.

"Dylan and Tracy?" she finally asked.

"Yes, that's right," I said as cheerfully as I could.

Again she checked her clipboard. "Yes, well, then . . . I'm Ms. Peckler from the Gateway Adoption Agency. Mr. Harrison had a family emergency this afternoon, so I was asked to step in," she said. "You were expecting him, correct?"

"Yes, that's right," said Tracy, albeit far less cheerfully.

Shit. The fuse was lit.

Ninety-nine percent of the time, Tracy was the calm and patient one while I was the loose

29

cannon, the sufferer of no fools. But look out for that damn 1 percent of the time.

For instance when a priggish woman with a clipboard says "Oh" with just the wrong kind of inflection.

To most people it would have all the resonance of a dog whistle, but for those of us who have been on the receiving end of it more times than we'd ever care to remember, it might as well have been screamed through a bullhorn.

Still.

"Please don't," I whispered out of the side of my mouth.

Tracy turned to me. "Don't what?"

"It's the name thing," I said. "She didn't—"

"It's not my name she has a problem with," said Tracy.

"What's going on?" asked Ms. Peckler.

Bad question, lady.

"What's going on is that it doesn't matter how many times you look down at that clipboard of yours, because every time you look up I'm still going to be a dude," said Tracy.

Boom, there it was.

"Excuse me?" said Ms. Peckler.

"I think you heard me," said Tracy.

"I don't think I like what you're insinuating," said Ms. Peckler, placing her nonclipboard hand firmly against her hip.

"Then I'll ask you very clearly," said Tracy, his law school degree kicking in, as it often did when he wanted to cut to the chase. "Do you personally have a problem with two gay men wanting to adopt a baby?"

I so wanted Tracy to be wrong on this one. I wanted Ms. Peckler, all prim and proper with pearls, to set the record straight—that she didn't have time to read our case file and had assumed that Tracy would be a woman, understandably so, and that her "Oh" was nothing more than the surprise of realizing she was mistaken.

This was the Upper West Side of Manhattan, after all, the supposed tolerance capital of the world.

But it was wishful thinking, and I knew it. I heard what Tracy heard. After a few seconds of silence—which also spoke volumes—Ms. Peckler essentially confirmed it.

"What I personally think of the lifestyle choice you two have made is separate from the job I have to do," she said. "I'm a professional, and I'm insulted that you would accuse me of being otherwise."

Lifestyle choice?

Tracy turned to me again. "I don't really know where to begin with that," he said.

Nor did I. But I gave it my best shot. "You know, this reminds me of an episode of *Family Affair*..."

By then Ms. Peckler was already halfway down our hallway, heading to the elevator.

I closed the door. The sound of the latch catching—*snap!*—jolted Tracy out of the moment.

"Oh, Christ, what have I done?" he asked.

We'd been married for four years. We were a couple for three years before that and had first met almost fifteen years ago, in college. By now we could do more than finish each other's sentences; we could start them. We always seemed to know what the other was thinking, and this was no different.

But what got me was the expression on Tracy's face. It was unlike anything I'd ever seen with him. Never, not ever, had he looked so panicked, so consumed by instant regret.

Still, I could've been mad. Furious, even. *The process.* We'd already devoted so much time and energy to it. Stacks of paperwork. Endless phone calls to government offices. On the surface it seemed crazy that Tracy couldn't overlook the ignorance of one person. It was all a dog and pony show anyway, this in-home interview.

Yet I wasn't mad. Far from it. If anything, I was more convinced than ever that Tracy and I were ready to be parents. Good parents.

"What you've done is the same thing we would've taught our child," I said. "Always stand up for yourself."

CHAPTER 8

"I KNEW you'd call," said Elizabeth.

I knew I would, too. "For the record, though, that was by far the worst attempt at reverse psychology I've ever seen," I said. "And I've seen them all, Detective."

Elizabeth looked over at me, sitting in the shotgun seat of her unmarked Ford sedan. We were driving through Central Park late the next morning via the 65th Street Transverse, below Sheep Meadow. "It couldn't have been that bad," she said.

She was right. I was there with her, after all, even after she'd told me at Jojo's that it was best if I didn't strap on my junior detective badge and get too involved with the investigation. She could always follow up with me if she had any more questions. I could advise her from the sidelines.

Of course, she knew all along I wasn't a sidelines kind of guy.

Hence my calling her first thing that morning.

Had it not been the weekend, though, my first call would've instead been to the head of the adoption agency, Barbara Nash, to discuss the disaster of the in-home interview that never even made it into our home. Most Manhattanites have their cell numbers printed on their business cards. Barbara, a transplant from Montana, didn't. I was fairly certain that wasn't an oversight.

"There it is," said Elizabeth, pointing.

As fast as you can say "Sherman Hemsley," we'd crossed over to the Upper East Side, arriving at Jared Louden's town house on 68th Street near the corner of Fifth Avenue.

"Must be nice," I said.

Elizabeth nodded. "Yeah. Swanky neighborhood."

"No—I meant the parking." She'd pulled directly in front of a hydrant. "Nice perk."

"That's nothing. I also never pay for coffee at the doughnut shop," she deadpanned. "On the flip side, I have to interview grieving loved ones on a weekly basis, and approximately once a year someone shoots at me."

"So you're saying it's a toss-up?"

She smiled at my sarcasm. "Actually, the free coffee is pretty nice."

"Has anyone shot at you yet this year?"

"No, but it's only September. Plenty of time left on the calendar," she said, cutting the engine.

I followed Elizabeth up the steps of Louden's impressive town house, quickly reminding myself of what she'd told me. The guy had been killed right inside his front door, the same door we were about to knock on…the same door we were asking his wife, Emily, to open for us. No wonder the woman looked as if she were standing in a minefield when she greeted us in the foyer. I could still smell the bleach used to clean up her husband's blood.

"Thanks for agreeing to see us, Mrs. Louden," said Elizabeth.

"Correction: I only agreed to see you," she said before pointing at me. "Who's this?"

"I'm Dylan Reinhart," I said, extending my hand. Mrs. Louden ignored it.

"Dr. Reinhart is a professor of psychology at Yale," added Elizabeth. "He's assisting in the investigation."

Elizabeth had essentially invoked the Jewish mother trifecta on my behalf: doctor, professor, and Ivy League. But Mrs. Louden ignored that, too.

"As I explained on the phone, I've already told the other detectives everything I know," she said. "And as you can see, I'm very busy here."

Every room off the foyer was stacked with boxes, loose sheets of Bubble Wrap strewn on the floor. It was side 1, song 1, of my favorite Billy Joel album, *The Stranger.* Mrs. Emily

Louden was "Movin' Out." Hardly a surprise given the circumstances.

"I understand," said Elizabeth, "and I can only imagine what an incredibly hard time this has been for you. The reason Dr. Reinhart is here with me, though, has to do with your husband's murder, something you should know."

Mrs. Louden put a hand on her hip and quickly looked me up and down with more shade than a solar eclipse. "Is this the guy who did it?" she asked. "Because if he's not, I'm not interested."

"Mrs. Louden, if you could simply—"

She cut Elizabeth off cold. "Now, you bring me the guy who did do it. Then I'll be interested," she said. "*Really* interested."

CHAPTER 9

IT WAS Dr. Elisabeth Kübler-Ross, the Swiss-American psychiatrist, who famously introduced the five stages of grief in her book *On Death and Dying*.

Stage 1 was denial. Stage 2 was anger. They were followed by bargaining, depression, and, finally, at stage 5, acceptance.

But Mrs. Emily Louden was nowhere near stage 5. She was locked and loaded on stage 2. Angry as hell.

Still, Detective Elizabeth Needham had a job to do.

Elizabeth finished explaining to Mrs. Louden about my book being sent to Allen Grimes at the *Gazette* and the playing card with her husband's blood on it. Did the king of clubs mean anything to her?

No, she answered. It didn't.

"Your husband's blood type," said Elizabeth. "Did you know that it was rare?"

"I didn't know it at all," said Mrs. Louden.

"What about your husband's doctors?" asked Elizabeth.

"What about them?"

"I'm assuming he had a primary care physician. What other doctors did he see?"

"Don't you think that's personal?" asked Mrs. Louden.

"I think it's very personal," said Elizabeth calmly. "But if we're going to make a list of the people who would have knowledge of your husband's blood type, that's where we start."

"Well, I'm afraid I can't help you."

"Can't or won't?" asked Elizabeth.

"Does it really make a difference?"

"Not that I want to, Mrs. Louden, but I can easily get hold of your husband's medical records without your permission," said Elizabeth.

"Then that's what you'll have to do," she said. "Now, if you don't mind... *get the hell out of my house.*"

I could tell that Elizabeth had no intention of doing anything that remotely resembled leaving. Not yet. All the more reason why I got an earful thirty seconds later out on the sidewalk.

"For Christ's sake, rookie, just because someone tells you to get the hell out of her house doesn't mean you do it!" said Elizabeth.

Rookie?

"We weren't getting anywhere," I said.

"That's the point," she said. "That's why we needed to keep her talking."

"To tell us what? The names of his doctors? Anyone could've known Louden's blood type," I said. "It's not only his doctors; it's anyone who worked for his doctors. Or it could be a blood-lab technician or anyone who worked with that technician. Are we really going to interview each and every one of those people?"

"Have you got a better idea?" she asked.

"Not yet, but I will."

"*You will?* Oh, that's just great, Reinhart. When exactly do you plan on having this better idea? Please—the suspense is killing me. When will you know?"

"When he wants me to know," I said.

"What does that mean?"

"Think about it." I walked to the curb to hail a cab.

"Wait: where are you going?"

"I've got lunch plans," I said.

CHAPTER 10

"I'LL TAKE a pound of the drunken spicy shrimp boil, one big-ass pork plate, a skirt steak with extra chimichurri sauce, an order of curried succotash, some crispy coleslaw, and a side of roasted whipped sweet potatoes with spicy nut topping," I said. "Oh, and let's add a couple of slices of your chocolate icebox pie."

"Anything else?" joked the woman scribbling my take-out order at the Dinosaur Bar-B-Que up on 125th Street in Harlem. She looked like Lauryn Hill during her days with the Fugees. Great hair, beautiful eyes.

"No—that oughta do it," I said with a wink. "Thanks."

Tracy had gone to bed devastated and woke up devastated, blaming himself for ruining our chances of becoming parents. The mission now was to cheer him up with his favorite comfort food, and there was only one way to go about it. Shock and awe.

Lunch in hand, I walked two blocks north into the offices of Harlem Legal House, which was actually just a guitar shop that had gone out of business a few years back. It was small and run-down, but on the plus side the acoustics were excellent.

"Is he with anyone?" I asked Miss Jacinda, the receptionist who doubled as mother hen to all the staff members. Some of them were working attorneys volunteering on the weekends, while others were law school graduates who weren't currently practicing. Or, as in Tracy's case, never did practice.

"Yeah. He's got someone with him, but go on back," said Miss Jacinda. "They should be finishing up any minute." She leaned forward over her desk, her deep voice dropping to a whisper. "Is our guy okay?"

"Is it that obvious?" I asked.

"Only to me, sweetheart," she said. "He's still smiling, but there's pain in those baby blues."

Pushing seventy, with every one of those years spent in Harlem, Miss Jacinda was more on the ball than anyone I'd ever met. You can't teach intuition.

I lifted the bag from Dinosaur's, one of the corners already soaked with some leaking barbecue sauce. "Let's hope it's nothing that a few thousand calories can't fix," I said.

I made my way back to Tracy's office, somewhat glad that he was with a client. He hates when I do this, but I always eavesdrop a bit outside his door, listening to how good he is at helping people who really need his help. There's never an insincere moment, never a false note.

If only casting directors felt the same way.

Ladies and gentlemen, may I present Tracy McKay, the most genuine struggling actor in all of New York City.

Which is not to say he never gets work. He does. There have been commercials, the occasional off-Broadway play, a two-week stint as the "handsome stranger" on a soap opera. They've all paid, and in the case of a few national spots, paid very well. They just haven't led to his big break yet, let alone a role that has some real meat on it. He truly deserves it. Thankfully, when I tell Tracy how talented he is, I actually mean it. Half the battle for him now, though, is remaining as convinced of that as I am.

"Is it too late to apply to Juilliard?" he's joked more than once.

For sure, not many head shots out there have Columbia Law School listed on the back. Then again, not many gay men went there because their parents were perhaps *too* accepting of their sexuality.

It almost sounds like a brainteaser, but that's what happened. Tracy caught the acting bug when we were at Yale together as undergrads. He squashed it, though, to pursue law. He thought he would be pleasing his parents. What he was really doing was overcompensating.

Tracy's parents—born-and-bred Iowans who aren't exactly your Brie-eating, Chardonnay-sipping, *Utne Reader* readers—were so supportive and accepting of his coming out in high school that his biggest fear became disappointing them with his career choice.

"Besides, it doesn't get any less original than an unemployed gay actor in Manhattan," he told me during his senior year. He was going to go to law school and become a lawyer. His father is a lawyer.

So what changed his mind?

Six words from his father, ultimately. Not unlike Miss Jacinda at the front desk, Mr. McKay could tell that his son wasn't truly happy after graduating from law school.

"I love you no matter what," he told Tracy. Six beautiful words.

Of course, then there's what my father said when I told him I was gay after college. *"Are you sure?"* he asked.

Thanks, Dad.

But that's a whole other can of therapy.

CHAPTER 11

"THAT'S NOT very polite, you know," said a little voice. "You're eavesdropping."

I turned around outside the door to Tracy's office, totally busted. Then again, the kid looked to be around six or seven. If he could believe in Santa Claus, what else could I make him believe?

"I'm not eavesdropping," I whispered.

"You are, too," he whispered back. "I caught you!"

Okay, so maybe he did. "It's not what you think," I said.

"Yes it is," he insisted. "And my mother says it's rude."

I was getting schooled by a pair of mini Air Jordans and cargo shorts, although it was the T-shirt that mostly caught my eye. On it was a picture of Questlove, the drummer for the Roots—or, if you happen to be really, really white, "that drummer" for the *Tonight Show* band.

Either way, it was pretty cute. The kid and Questlove had almost matching afros.

"Who's your mother?" I asked, still whispering.

"In there," he said, pointing at Tracy's office. That figured.

"What are you doing out here?"

"I had to go to the bathroom."

"Are you going to tell on me?" I asked.

He shook his head. "Mom says I shouldn't do that, either, because no one likes a tattletale."

"You've got a smart mother."

"Yes, he does," came another voice. Christ, busted again.

I turned to see the kid's mother standing next to Tracy in the doorway of his office.

"Ms. Winston, I'd like you to meet my husband, Dylan," said Tracy.

"Oh," said the woman.

However, this "oh" was the exact opposite of the one we got out of Ms. Peckler, from the adoption agency. This was, *"Oh, isn't that nice?"* No two ways about it.

She extended her hand. "Nice to meet you, Dylan," she said. "I see you've met Miles."

"I'm named after Miles Davis," the kid said proudly as he offered up a fist bump. "He played the trumpet."

"Boy, did he ever. Like nobody else," I said. "Did you know I'm named after a musician, too? His name's Bob Dylan. Do you know who that is?"

"No," said Miles.

"You will one day; trust me," I said. I turned back to Tracy and Ms. Winston. "Sorry for interrupting. We were trying to whisper."

"It was more the smell," said Tracy with a nod toward the bag in my hand.

"Is that Dinosaur's?" asked Ms. Winston. "It's got to be, right?"

"Yes, and there's plenty of it," I said. "Have you eaten lunch yet?"

"Thanks for offering," she said. "We actually have a lesson to get to."

"I play the trumpet, too," said Miles. "I'm not as good as Miles Davis yet, though."

"That's what the lessons are for," I said. "Right?"

"Yeah, and lots of practice in between. Sometimes I like to play in front of my window in our apartment and pretend that the whole world is watching me," said Miles.

"Maybe one day it will be," I said. You never know.

Tracy walked Miles and his mother out as I waited in his office. I was emptying the bag from Dinosaur's when he returned.

"So are you trying to cheer me up or just put me in a food coma?" he said, staring at the feast laid out on his desk.

"It is a lot, isn't it?"

"No, it's perfect," he said. "I really appreciate it. Thank you."

"I was worried," I said.

"I know you were. But this place is the best cure for feeling sorry for yourself," he said. "Miles and his mother? They might be homeless in a week. Their landlord thinks he found a loophole in their rent-controlled status."

"Did he?" I asked.

"I don't care if he did. I'm going to close it," said Tracy.

That wasn't the lawyer speaking; that was the former Academic All-American lacrosse player who played his last three games as a senior with two cracked ribs. Always determined, never deterred. That was Tracy.

"So do you want to make the call to the adoption agency on Monday morning or should I?" I asked as we began eating.

"None of the above," said Tracy, popping a spicy shrimp into his mouth.

He had a different idea.

CHAPTER 12

TEN HOURS later and more than a hundred blocks south, Bryce VonMiller—black sheep son of famed restaurateur Aaron VonMiller—was coked out of his mind, something he hadn't been for years. Cocaine, after all, was the pay phone of drugs. Still around but barely ever used.

Instead Bryce's usual party drug of choice was Ecstasy, and lots of it, although he wouldn't have been caught dead—or, even worse, caught by an undercover narc—calling it that.

Bean, blue kisses, white dove, thiz, hug drug, disco biscuits, Skittles...

Proper slang was a badge of honor for the twenty-three-year-old regular of the Manhattan club scene, but it wasn't enough to stay current. You had to stay ahead.

Same for the drugs themselves. Bryce had been one of the first in the city to try the concentrated form of Ecstasy, called Molly. He was always on the lookout for the next big thing, the latest high.

Tonight, though, he was going decidedly retro with some good old-fashioned blow, inspired by the recently opened White Lines, a 1980s throwback club in SoHo. Saturday was their masquerade night, but it wasn't about wearing masks. Instead the theme was the classic eighties B movie *Masquerade,* starring Rob Lowe, Meg Tilly, Kim Cattrall, and Doug Savant, the actor who played "the gay guy" on *Melrose Place.* Dress up as any one of them and the fifty-dollar cover charge was waived.

Grinding on the dance floor with a mixture of Tillys and Cattralls, Bryce thought he looked pretty damn fetching in his tight shorts and polo shirt, the same outfit Rob Lowe wore throughout most of the movie. It was the hair, though, that was key. Feathered just so, it was longer than what Lowe sported in *Oxford Blues* but not quite as long as his *St. Elmo's Fire* look.

"I'll be right back," Bryce lied to some random Tilly he'd been making out with under the dozen or so mirrored balls hanging from the ceiling, which looked like the Liberace solar system. After a DJ mash-up of Duran Duran's "The Wild Boys" and "Girls on Film," it was time to look for trouble elsewhere.

Sweat dripping down his cheeks, Bryce strolled

into the Leather Room, toward the back of the club, which had been renamed the Junk Bondage Room for the night. With images of Ivan Boesky and Michael Milken—both with and without his toupee—projected on the walls and ceiling, Bryce watched for a minute as a naked S and M couple took turns hitting each other with horse whips while sucking on cherry-flavored Ring Pops.

Ho-hum.

After a shot of absinthe at the bar, Bryce slipped a Benjamin to the man working the velvet rope of the VIP Room, but there was only a collection of Eurotrash sprawled on the sofas. For most of these shiny-shirt-wearing clowns, an eighties bar was a contemporary setting.

Quickly Bryce was out of there, a waste of a hundred dollars.

Then again, it wasn't like it was his money. It had been earned by his father, who got it by wildly overcharging tourists and self-proclaimed foodies for Wagyu beef sliders and "fresh" Miyagi oysters FedExed in from the Karakuwa Peninsula. *Domo arigato,* suckers!

Finally Bryce ended up in the men's room for the least likely reason that any guy at White Lines ever ended up in the men's room: he actually had to take a piss. Before he could, he was approached by a guy wearing black Ray-Bans and a shoulder-length blond wig.

"Hey," said the guy.

"Hey, yourself," said Bryce back.

He knew most of the dudes in the neon-lit bathroom were there for one of two things—getting high or giving head. Bryce just didn't know which of the two this guy was leaning toward.

"Pulp?" the guy asked.

Pulp?

Clearly he wasn't talking about orange juice. It was a drug. But Bryce had never heard of it before. *How could that be?*

No matter. For the first time that night, Bryce VonMiller was genuinely interested in something. Intrigued.

"Tell me more," he said.

CHAPTER 13

"IN HERE," said the guy, motioning to the last stall. *Step into my office...*

Bryce followed him, any reservations subdued by the rush of the unknown—and, he hoped, an even greater rush after that. It had a nice ring to it, he thought. Concise and catchy. Pulp. *All the kids are doing it—but not before I do it first.*

"Who are you supposed to be, by the way?" Bryce asked the guy, eyeing his wig and sunglasses, which all but obscured his face.

"Michael Caine," the guy answered.

Huh?

"Not exactly seeing it," said Bryce with a chuckle. "Besides, he wasn't in *Masquerade*."

"Yes, I know. He was in a different movie from the eighties. I liked it much better."

Bryce was about to ask which movie when the guy opened his palm to reveal a small syringe, half the size of a crayon. An orange crayon. The liquid loaded in the barrel was bright orange.

"What's up with the color?" asked Bryce.

"Pulp," said the guy. "Like with orange juice." *Get it?*

Bryce got it. He just wasn't buying it, not yet. "I don't do needles," he declared with a wave of his hand.

"Neither do I," said the guy. "This doesn't go in your veins. It's like a B12 shot...only much, much better."

"So it's a boost, like coke? Because coke I have."

"Believe me, you don't have anything like this. Clean and quick, the ultimate jolt of adrenaline."

Bryce did a double take on the guy. He knew where B12 shots went. Was this some perv pulling a bait and switch? "You're not just trying to get me to drop my pants, are you?" he asked.

The guy ignored him. Instead he rolled up the sleeve of his black T-shirt. Clearly the issue was trust. How do dealers flush out narcs?

"Like this," he said, casually flicking off the needle cap. He jammed the syringe into the meat of his upper arm, pressing hard on the plunger.

Clean and quick, all right. No sooner had the orange liquid disappeared into his skin than he threw his head back against the metal panel of the stall, his face laced with euphoria.

Sold, thought Bryce. "How much?" he asked.

"First one's free," said the guy, reaching into his pocket.

He handed over another syringe that looked identical to the first and watched as Bryce mimicked the way he had flicked off the needle cap.

"Pulp," said Bryce with a confident nod.

"Yeah, Pulp," the guy echoed. "Enjoy."

CHAPTER 14

BRYCE PLUNGED the needle into the meaty flesh of his upper arm, eyeing the bright orange liquid as it quickly drained from the syringe. The roller coaster was climbing that first big hill. The ride was about to begin. Pure anticipation. The rush. The euphoria.

The pain?

Bryce's knees suddenly buckled as he stumbled backwards, banging his head hard against the stall. Reaching out, arms flailing, he tried to steady himself, but the feeling was nothing short of agony in every muscle, every fiber. There were lightning bolts shooting out from his spine, a fire raging through his insides. His arms, his legs— everything hurt all at once.

His eyes begged. *Make it stop! Please, please make it stop!*

Then, as quickly as it came, it did exactly that. It stopped. The fire extinguished. The pain gone.

Two seconds later, though, he would've done anything to get it back.

Move! yelled Bryce's brain to the rest of his body. Do something. Say something. *React!*

Only he couldn't. He could see and he could blink, but nothing more. From head to toe, he was frozen. Paralyzed.

Michael Caine smiled. He reached into his pocket, removing another needle and syringe. Only this one was bigger. Much bigger.

"Have you read your Bible, Bryce?" he asked, flicking away an air bubble in the cartridge after removing the cap. The liquid was clear, not orange. "No, of course you haven't, have you?"

Bryce tried desperately again to move as he stared at the long needle. *He knows my name. How does he know my name?*

Michael Caine shrugged. "To tell you the truth, I'm not much for religion," he said. "But I do like the Bible. I like what it says about right and wrong and the nature of sin. Are you a sinner, Bryce? You are, aren't you? I know you are."

Bryce screamed, if only in his head, as the tip of that long needle edged closer to him. *Where is he going with it?*

The more he stared at it, the more the answer became clear right before his eyes.

His left eye, to be exact.

Bryce tried desperately to move again. He tried

to fight back. Or escape. Or something other than what he was doing, which was nothing. The most his body would give him was a tremble, a sort of low-rumble seizure that did little more than make his heart race even faster. A harbinger of things to come. We all have to die some way, right?

Michael Caine shook his head. "C'mon, hold steady for me, Bryce," he said, annoyed. "Don't fight it."

But cooperation was hardly to be expected, so he jammed the palm of his free hand against Bryce's forehead, pinning him flat to the stall so he could peel back the eyelid enough to expose the orbital socket. Even the most thorough of coroners wouldn't think to look there.

"This is going to sting a bit," he said, aiming the tip of the needle north of the pupil before plunging it into the sclera, otherwise known as the white of the eye.

As he pushed down on the syringe he counted to five.

One one thousand, two one thousand…

CHAPTER 15

THERE WAS no need to check the caller ID.

I'd love to say that was deductive reasoning of the highest order, but it was really more like a gut feeling as I reached for my phone in the darkness, the ring waking only me and not Tracy, who pretty much could sleep through the apocalypse.

I knew who was calling at three in the morning, and worse, I knew why.

"So much for one and done," said Elizabeth, letting out a sigh. "Sometimes it sucks to be right, doesn't it?"

Aaron VonMiller was the first guy I saw when I stepped out of the cab twenty minutes later in front of White Lines in SoHo. I'd never heard of the club.

I recognized VonMiller from the myriad articles written about him, especially the one in *New York* magazine a year or so back. He was on the cover, a big close-up photo of him with his unruly salt-

and-pepper hair, playfully scrunching his face to keep a fork wedged between his upper lip and nose, as though it were a mustache. The guy was a partner in nearly a dozen wildly successful restaurants in Manhattan. A few in Vegas as well.

But there was nothing playful about VonMiller now. He was screaming at a cop who was blocking him from the entrance to the club. *"That's my son! That's my son in there!"* He was living a parent's absolute worst nightmare in the middle of the night.

I shot a text to Elizabeth as instructed.

I'm here.

Within seconds she was walking out of the neon-purple doors, finding me on the sidewalk among the crowd of onlookers.

"Nice bed head," she said, motioning for me to follow her.

She led me past the velvet ropes, now strung with yellow police tape, and into the club, which looked like the last days of Studio 54. Totally eighties and—save for the requisite police and EMTs—totally empty.

That changed when we turned a corner toward the bathrooms. Gathered by a cigarette machine that had been reconfigured to dispense condoms was a group of "kids" being interviewed by a detective, or so I assumed that's what he was, his rumpled Men's Wearhouse suit being the first clue.

The kids, who looked barely out of their teens, were clearly potential witnesses. Less clear, though, were their outfits, or whatever it was they were wearing. *Was this supposed to be a costume party?*

"Don't ask," said Elizabeth after we walked by them.

Two cops were flanking the entrance to the men's room, one fidgeting with his phone. The other shot Elizabeth a look: *What gives?* "How much longer?" he asked her. "We really need to move him."

"Just one more minute," she said without breaking stride.

That generated another look from the guy—a series of them, actually—all aimed at me. *Who the hell are you? What the hell took you so long to get here?* And *Can you hurry the hell up?*

Granted, I may have been reading a little too much into a single arched eyebrow.

"This way," said Elizabeth as we entered the bathroom. "He's in the one on the end."

As we walked toward the last stall, the only sound I could hear was in my head. *That's my son! That's my son in there!* Somehow it didn't seem right that I, a total stranger, got to see Aaron Von-Miller's dead son before he did.

Then again, nothing seemed right about anything I was about to see. Except that I was meant to see it. That's why I got the call from Elizabeth, who was "third-wheeling," as she put it, on homicides across all precincts.

The killer was talking to us again. *To me.*

Without a word, Elizabeth stepped back so I could have a full view inside the stall, and for a few seconds I stared at Bryce VonMiller's lifeless body crumpled on the floor, arms and legs askew. If I didn't know better, he could've just been passed out.

But I knew better. So did Elizabeth.

"Where was it placed on him?" I asked.

CHAPTER 16

"IT WAS sticking out of his pants, the right front pocket," said Elizabeth. "It's been bagged and logged. Eddie's got it."

"Who's Eddie?" I asked.

"That's me," came a voice from the doorway.

Eddie was the detective in the Men's Wearhouse suit. As he walked toward me under the glare of the bright white neon lights mounted on the bathroom walls, it became evident that he was also Eddie of the Hair Club for Men. His plugs looked as natural as Mike Huckabee at a tea dance in Provincetown.

"Eddie, this is Professor Dylan Reinhart," said Elizabeth, making the introduction. "Dylan, this is Detective Eddie Molson."

"Like the beer," he said, shaking my hand.

In his other hand was the evidence bag, exactly like the one Elizabeth had showed me in New Haven at Jojo's. The difference was the playing card inside. There was no repeat of the king of clubs. Our killer had placed the two of hearts in the pocket of Bryce VonMiller's pants.

"Anything from the Brat Pack out there?" asked Elizabeth.

Eddie rolled his eyes. "They'll barely admit to having been in the bathroom," he said. "They all knew of VonMiller—the kid had a rep—but the card didn't mean anything to them."

Although I could hear what Eddie was saying, I was listening more to his body language. The slouched shoulders, the pinching of his brow. Not to mention the way he stole a peek at his watch after our introduction. I wouldn't expect the guy to be daisy fresh on the graveyard shift, but he still had a job to do. Tired was one thing. This guy was simply going through the motions.

"Did you only question them as a group?" I asked.

You would've thought I just insulted his mother. *"Excuse me?"* he said.

"They're kids," I explained. "Last I checked it's still not cool to tell cops anything."

Eddie chuckled. "Last you checked, huh?"

"I'm simply saying that one-on-one might work better."

"Yeah, you're right," he said sarcastically. "Do you know what also might work better? Water-boarding. Perhaps we should do that, Professor. One-on-one, of course, not as a group."

I glanced over at Elizabeth, who was content to simply watch from her perch in Switzerland, albeit with a noticeable smile. Fellow detective or not, Eddie had led with his chin. All bets were off.

"I'm sorry you're offended, Detective Molson, like the beer, but I was simply making a suggestion," I said. "Perhaps you couldn't hear me clearly from where you're phoning it in tonight."

Eddie looked like a nine on a standing eight count.

"Christ, where'd you find this guy, Lizzie?" he asked.

Elizabeth winced. She clearly hated being called Lizzie. "Yale," she said. "Or was it MIT? Professor Reinhart has a PhD from both, so I can't remember. He was also in *Forbes* magazine's "30 Under 30" issue a few years back, but I suspect the dimples had more to do with that than anything else."

So much for Switzerland. And so much for Eddie.

"Hey, go at it, Professor," he said, pointing out to the hallway. "Go interview each and every one of those spoiled brats about their little dead friend in here, the club king."

Wait.

"What did you just say?" I asked.

"I said, you can go interview—"

Elizabeth had heard the same thing. "No—the last part...what did you call him?" she asked.

"The club king," he said. "That's what one of the kids called him. I asked if VonMiller partied a lot, and they told me he was always at all the clubs."

"Well done, Eddie," I said.

"What'd I do?" he asked.

"You asked the right question," said Elizabeth.

He was still confused. "You messin' with me?"

"Not at all," she said.

"Does this mean you don't want to do the one-on-one interviews?" he asked hopefully.

"No, but you don't have to bother asking about the two of hearts," she said.

"I didn't know why I was asking about it in the first place," he said. "What's it supposed to mean?"

"I'm not sure," said Elizabeth.

But that wasn't entirely true. She and I both knew what the two of hearts meant.

We just didn't know *whom* it meant.

CHAPTER 17

THE COPS had all left. So had Eddie.

During the one-on-one interviews, one of the kids "suddenly" remembered hearing something from the direction of the last stall. At the time, he didn't think too much of it. "A lot of crazy stuff happens in these bathrooms," he said. "People are weird."

This from a kid who had pink eyebrows, a double-pierced tongue, and a tattoo of Bea Arthur on his neck.

As for Bryce VonMiller, he'd been wheeled out and taken to the morgue, his father having finally been allowed to see him before he was zipped up in a black body bag. I'd watched for a moment before turning away.

And that was that.

Nearly two hours after she'd first called me, Elizabeth and I were the only ones on the sidewalk outside White Lines, the last of the onlookers having long since dispersed.

"Where are you going?" she asked.

"Home," I said. *Is that a trick question? Where else would I be going?*

Without another word she hit a speed-dial button on her phone. "Where are you right now?" she asked the person on the other end.

I was trying to figure out who that could be at nearly five in the morning and how the answer to her question could be anything besides "In bed."

Of course, I really should've known.

"Christ, I'm starving," announced Allen Grimes, practically hip-checking me as he slid into our booth fifteen minutes later at the Marigold Diner in Greenwich Village. Not only was he up and awake, it was pretty obvious that our intrepid crime reporter hadn't been anywhere near his bed yet. Or if he had, it wasn't to sleep. The guy literally had lipstick on his collar.

Elizabeth summed up Grimes on the ride over. *His driver's license says he's fifty, his libido thinks he's twenty, and his liver is convinced he's Keith Richards.*

"Allen," said Elizabeth, "this is—"

"Yeah, I know," said Grimes, thrusting his hand at me. "Nice to finally meet you, Professor. Or do you prefer 'Doctor'? I'm not ashamed to say that I understood only half your book."

"Not to worry," I said. "The other half was just made-up bullshit."

He laughed loudly, the smell of alcohol, tobacco, and a way-overmatched Altoid blanketing my face. "Actually, that's probably the half I understood!"

He laughed some more as a waitress came over with a menu, but he waved it off, already knowing what he wanted. A Western omelet and a whiskey.

"It's after four," said the waitress in a monotone, barely glancing up from her order pad. "I can't serve you alcohol."

Grimes took a fifty out of his shirt pocket, placing it under the saltshaker. "That's for you if you change your mind, sweetheart."

Elizabeth cocked her head at Grimes as the waitress walked away. "You're kidding me, right?"

"What are you going to do, Detective? Arrest her?" he asked.

"You'd like that—an instant column," said Elizabeth. "The only thing she's coming back with is your omelet."

Grimes elbowed me in the ribs. "Tell her, Dr. Professor. Tell the pretty detective what you and I both know. Human behavior is more pliable than a bowl of mashed potatoes. And nothing whips it up better than the almighty dollar."

Before I could admit that the guy had a point, the waitress returned with a coffee cup. Quickly and smoothly, she set it down in front of Grimes while swiping the fifty from underneath the saltshaker.

We all leaned over, peering into the coffee cup. It wasn't coffee.

"Cheers," said Grimes, taking a sip of his whiskey. He wiped his mouth and grinned. "Now, what do you two have for me?"

CHAPTER 18

GRIMES WAS the newsman, but Elizabeth knew enough not to bury the lede. "We have a real live serial killer," she said.

"I thought we already knew that," Grimes shot back, unimpressed. "Isn't that what you told me?"

"No, I told you that's what it *could* be," said Elizabeth. "Now I'm convinced. Do you know who Aaron VonMiller is?"

Duh, said Grimes's face. *Do I live in this city?* "You can't throw a rock without hitting one of his restaurants."

"So I've been told," said Elizabeth. "Clearly I don't eat out enough. In any event, his son was murdered a couple of hours ago at White Lines."

Immediately Grimes reached for his cell.

"Don't bother," said Elizabeth. "There's no missed text from anyone on your payroll."

Still, Grimes checked anyway. Sure enough, there was no text. "How did you know that?" he asked.

"Because right now the three of us are the only ones who know that the VonMiller kid was murdered," she said. "Everyone else will be reading later today that it's a suspected drug overdose."

Watching Grimes creep forward in his seat while hanging on Elizabeth's every word was...well, a bit creepy. The guy undoubtedly lived for this sort of stuff.

"So it wasn't an overdose?" he asked.

"Actually, that's exactly what it could've been. We'll wait on toxicology for that," said Elizabeth. She reached for a few of the single-serve grape jellies from the jelly caddy hugging the wall. She neatly lined them up next to one another, as if she were missing her color-coordinated folders.

"Stop yanking my chain!" Grimes practically yelled.

Everyone within earshot—which was pretty much everyone in the diner—turned to look, but he couldn't care less. He wanted answers, and Elizabeth was making him wait. On purpose. A little revenge, perhaps, for the fifty-under-the-saltshaker stunt.

"You remember the bookmark, right?" asked Elizabeth.

"Of course," said Grimes. "The playing card."

"Yeah, but which playing card?" asked Elizabeth.

Grimes gave her his *duh* face again. "The king of clubs," he said. "So what?"

"So VonMiller's son was known for his partying, always on the scene," said Elizabeth. "In fact you might say he was the king of..."

"Motherfucker," said Grimes. "The killer was announcing his next victim."

Elizabeth nodded. "Tipping his hand, you might say."

"Damn, I like that," said Grimes, jabbing his index finger at her. He quickly pulled out a tiny digital voice recorder from his jacket, hitting Record. "The killer is tipping his hand, playfully declaring his next victim with..."

Grimes stopped and stared at Elizabeth. She nodded a second time, as if she'd been waiting for him to catch up.

"Motherfucker," he said again. "That's how you know it was murder. Our guy left a card behind on the kid, didn't he?"

"The two of hearts," said Elizabeth. "Stuffed in VonMiller's pocket."

Grimes turned to me. He could barely contain himself. "Tell me you've already figured it out," he said. "Who's the next victim? Or is it two victims? A couple, maybe? No, wait. It's much better if you don't know. No one should know. That's a much better story. The whole city should be wondering." He raised his recorder again, speaking in a hushed tone. "The two of hearts...who will it be? Who will the killer...no, no, no...who will the *dealer* kill next? Yes, that's who he is...the Dealer!"

It was as if someone had pulled a string on his back; Grimes was rambling on, an endless stream of consciousness, totally absorbed in the moment.

So much so that he never saw it coming.

The real reason Elizabeth had called him.

CHAPTER 19

FASTER THAN Sugar Ray Leonard in his prime came her right hand, swiping Grimes's recorder. "Hey!" he barked. "What the hell are you doing?"

"It's what you're not doing," she said. "You're not writing about this yet."

"The hell I'm not." He tried to swipe back the recorder, but he looked more like George Foreman against Muhammad Ali. Too slow.

"I need you to wait," said Elizabeth.

"For what?" asked Grimes.

Elizabeth pointed at me. That was my cue.

"There are two types of serial killers," I said. "Those who want to get caught and those who *really* want to get caught. On the surface it seems like our guy is just seeking publicity, that he wants to be famous. You're a reporter, and he sends you that package. He's chosen you as his messenger. *But what's the message?*"

Grimes shot me a look, basically the opposite of his *duh* face. He didn't quite follow.

"It's a game," chimed in Elizabeth. "Catch me if you can. If he only wanted publicity he would've flat-out told you about his first victim. Instead he sent you two clues. He knew, though, that there was only one thing you would do with them. Go to the police."

"So how do you factor in?" Grimes asked me. "If my role is so clear, that is."

"I'm not sure yet," I said. "Presumably he's out to prove me and my book either right or wrong. We're still trying to figure that out."

"And that's the problem," said Elizabeth. "We need more from this guy than he's giving us— clues, hints, anything—and the best way to get that is to make him think we're not as smart as he thought, that we haven't caught on."

"In other words, that the game hasn't started yet," said Grimes.

By George . . .

"You got it," I said. "With any luck, he'll give us a little more than he intended."

"And game over," said Elizabeth.

"But according to Dr. Professor here, this guy wants to be caught," said Grimes. "Won't he eventually just, you know, play to lose?"

"It doesn't work like that," I said.

"Then enlighten me," said Grimes.

"Do you really want a lecture on the subconscious?" I asked.

"No. What I really want is to break this goddamn story in Monday's paper."

"Okay, let's assume you're right for a second," I began. "Our guy allows himself to get a little careless down the line. Like Son of Sam, he gets a parking ticket. Or he steals a car and gets nailed for it, like Ted Bundy. Or hell, let's say he does the ridiculous and turns himself in. Maybe it's even as early as next week. But what if it's not? What if it's next year? Because here's all I know at this point. The king of clubs? The two of hearts? He's still got fifty cards left in his deck."

With a glance, I handed the discussion back to Elizabeth. It was sort of like good cop, bad cop, except I was actually no cop.

"Allen, you can break the story Monday and never get anything more from me on this or anything else ever again," she said, folding her arms on the table. "Or you can give us a couple more days, still break the story, and then be the guy who knows everything first."

I eyed Grimes carefully. He could've chosen to go apeshit over Elizabeth's threat, but she'd managed to say the one word that was like all the whiskey in the world to a guy like him.

"*First*," he said.

"*First*," she repeated.

"I'm going to hold you to that, Detective," he said.

"You won't have to," she assured him, sliding his recorder across the table. She swung her legs out of the booth and stood. "Enjoy your omelet."

CHAPTER 20

I WASN'T sure if Elizabeth was aiming for a dramatic exit, but she didn't look back as she walked out of the diner. Presumably I was supposed to follow her. Grimes, however, had me pinned into my seat in the booth. He wasn't moving.

Instead, "Be careful, Dr. Professor," he said.

"Careful about what?" I asked.

"She hasn't told you, has she?"

"Okay, I'll bite," I said. "What hasn't she told me?"

"Well, you're the expert on human behavior, so you might want to ask yourself this," he said. "Of all the detectives I could've called after getting that package, why did I call her?"

"Because she's good at her job?" I said. It wasn't a question.

"You're right: she is good at her job. Good enough, though, to be the youngest detective second grade in the city, not to mention the prettiest?"

"What exactly are you suggesting?" I asked. "That she slept her way to a promotion?"

"No. Elizabeth's too smart for that. But she *is* in bed with someone," he said, taking another sip of his whiskey. "Do you follow politics by any chance? There's a big election coming up here in the city, and it's going to be a tight race. A very tight race."

"So I've been hearing," I said.

"Even if you don't follow politics, how could you miss all those damn TV and radio ads, right? I'm already sick of them."

"I know what you mean."

"Do you, though?" he asked. "Do you really?"

"Okay, so I don't know what you mean," I said. "Apparently you've taken a course in cryptic bull-shit that I somehow missed."

Grimes smiled, tilted his coffee cup of whiskey at me, and promptly polished off the rest of it in a single swig. "I like you, Reinhart," he said.

I couldn't say the feeling was mutual. At least not yet. The guy did have a certain charm about him, though.

"Thanks," I told him. It was the best I could offer.

"Just remember what I told you, okay?"

"What did you tell me?" I asked.

"To be careful," he said. "Sometimes you think you want to know things only to find out you really don't."

I wasn't about to ask what the hell that meant, because I knew he had no intention of explaining. Instead he slid out of the booth and made a bee-line for the waitress, who was standing by the register.

"Ix-nay on that omelet, sweetheart," he said, handing her a twenty. "I've lost my appetite."

CHAPTER 21

THE TWO cops camped out in the otherwise empty lobby of the Excelsior Hotel on the Upper West Side barely looked up from their newspapers as Elizabeth walked by them. They knew who she was. It wasn't her first time there. It wouldn't be her last.

Although had they thought about it, they might have at least asked if she was expected. It was very early in the morning, after all.

But they hadn't thought about it, and they didn't ask. Further proof, perhaps, that their guard duty assignment wasn't exactly a reward for being the best and brightest on the force.

Ding.

The elevator opened in front of Elizabeth, revealing the man she'd woken up only minutes before with her call from outside the hotel.

"This better be good," he said, walking toward her. He was wearing a hastily assembled outfit of jeans and a Harvard sweatshirt. "What is it that you couldn't tell me over the phone?"

Elizabeth glanced over her shoulder, making sure they were truly alone. They were. "I need to see him," she said.

"Do you know what time it is?" asked Harvard.

"Yeah, it's roughly a few minutes past I don't give a shit," she said. "Wake him up."

He hesitated. She knew what that meant. Men and their vices...

"He's not alone, is he?" she asked.

Harvard hesitated again, weighing his options. There weren't any. He was one of the most gifted liars in the city, the Botticelli of bullshitters, but never to Elizabeth. It's how she found out about the charade in the first place.

"No, he's not alone," he said.

Elizabeth smiled all too knowingly. "I'm curious," she said. "Is there anything you *wouldn't* do for him?"

"It's called loyalty, Detective," he said. "It wouldn't hurt you to show a little more of it."

"I'm here, aren't I?"

Harvard frowned. That was one of the things that really pissed him off about Elizabeth. She had an answer for everything. Of course that was also why his boss liked her so much. She was always thinking ahead.

"Why don't you tell me whatever it is you were

going to tell him, and I'll relay the message later?" he said.

"Or," said Elizabeth, "you could do what I asked you to do in the first place and wake him up."

"What if I don't?" he asked.

"Then I'll go wake him up myself," she said. "If I can't win Powerball or marry Jake Gyllenhaal, my next wish in this world is having you and your skinny Ivy League ass try to stop me."

Ding.

The elevator doors opened immediately after Harvard hit the Up button. It was his turn for the all-too-knowing smile. "Just making sure," he said.

"Of what?" asked Elizabeth.

"That you're the right man for the job." He stepped back, allowing Elizabeth to step on the elevator. Ladies first.

"You already woke him, didn't you?" she asked.

Harvard loved to play games.

"Right after you called me," he said, following her onto the elevator. He punched the button for the penthouse. "You wouldn't be here unless it was important, right?"

CHAPTER 22

HARVARD DIDN'T say another word during the entire ride up to the top floor. Nor did he say anything when he led Elizabeth down the hallway to the largest suite in the hotel, the door of which was slightly ajar.

"Good morning, Detective Needham," said the man wearing the lush waffle-knit white robe. He was sitting on the couch, drinking coffee from the kind of bone china they don't exactly sell at Pottery Barn. Behind him was one of the best views of Central Park that money can buy—exactly what the man had thought back when he ruled commercial real estate. In fact he liked the view so much he bought the entire hotel.

"Good morning, Mr. Mayor," said Elizabeth. "Sorry to wake you."

"No, you're not," he said, motioning for her to sit down. "What do you have for me? The sun's not even up, and already you're here to ruin my day."

It was more like save his ass, and they both knew it. The mayor simply liked to razz her a bit. It was how he flirted at arm's length.

Elizabeth waited until he set down his coffee before she launched right into it, a recap of the evening in bullet-point fashion.

The murder of a club kid most likely disguised as an overdose.

Bryce VonMiller as the king of clubs.

And proof that the killer, who had now killed twice, intended to kill again.

"The two of hearts, huh?" asked the mayor. "Who else saw it?"

"I think the important question, sir, is who else knows what it means," said Elizabeth. "Besides the people in this room, that's Reinhart and Grimes."

"*Grimes?*" said Harvard. "You freakin' told Grimes?"

"Of course she did," said the mayor. "Feed the lion and he forgets he's in the cage." He turned back to Elizabeth. "Isn't that right, Detective?"

She loved it when the mayor put Harvard in his place. His Honor didn't do it very often, but when he did it was a thing of beauty. Not that she ever let on.

Still, if you're going to wear that crimson sweatshirt in public, you pretentious prick, you gotta know you're asking for it.

"Nothing's going in his column for now," said

Elizabeth, assuring the mayor. "But Grimes is definitely rattling that cage."

"What about the professor?" he asked.

"What about him?" she asked back.

The mayor shrugged slightly under his white robe. "Has he been helpful?"

"Sure," she said. "Right now, though, we're all just trying to figure out the rules of the game."

"In other words, it's too early to tell," said the mayor. "Is that what you're saying?"

Whatever sixth sense Elizabeth possessed kicked in like a mule with that last question. *Too early to tell* was not what the mayor wanted to hear, for reasons as obvious as the huge stack of polling data on the coffee table in front of him. The first Tuesday in November was less than two months away, and his support for reelection was slipping, not gaining traction.

For the man wealthy enough to buy almost anything, this was the one thing he couldn't afford. A serial killer terrorizing the city. Not now.

"What I'm saying is that the original plan is still the best plan," said Elizabeth. "We buy enough time to end this story before it ever becomes a story."

For once, the mayor seemed more concerned about someone other than himself. At least it appeared that way.

"I'm not complaining," he said. "Not yet. I was

only asking about the professor. Tell me more about him."

"What would you like to know?" asked Elizabeth.

"His private life," said the mayor. "What has he told you about himself? Anything?"

"Do you mean the fact that he's gay?" she asked.

The mayor reached for his coffee. "Did he tell you that?"

"No. It's never come up," she said. "But it's hardly a secret."

"What about something that is?" asked the mayor. "Has he told you anything in confidence?"

That sixth sense of a mule kicked hard again in Elizabeth's gut. *Is he testing me? Trapping me?*

All she knew was that he was obviously leading to something.

"No," said Elizabeth. "Suffice it to say there's been no pillow talk. Nor have we braided each other's hair yet."

The mayor smiled, reminded again why he liked this detective so much. Then he reached for an envelope sticking out of a folder next to the stack of polling data. He handed it to Elizabeth.

"For all the things we know about Dylan Reinhart, it turns out there's one thing we didn't know," he said. "Until now."

BOOK TWO

EVERYTHING'S WILD

CHAPTER 23

I COULD hear the early morning traffic creeping and honking its way down Fifth Avenue twenty floors below as Barbara Nash sat down behind her desk. Like a disapproving parent, she shot a glance at Tracy and me.

"You really should've made an appointment, gentlemen," she said slowly.

Perhaps showing up unannounced first thing Monday morning and camping out in the waiting room was not the best strategy for currying favor with the head of the city's largest international adoption agency.

"I apologize, Barbara. It was my idea," said Tracy. "But I think we're owed an apology as well."

That was Tracy at his most sincere but also clever best. Before anything else, he wanted to learn what, if anything, Barbara had been told about our home interview debacle. Had she already spoken to Ms. Peckler? Were we dealing with a clean slate? Or would Barbara now be looking for "our side of the story"?

Something told me it was the latter.

"You think I've got a homophobe working for me, huh?" asked Barbara.

You had to admire her bluntness. That was sort of her thing, really. A job requirement. The world of foreign adoption was like no other, and she'd been quick to make that clear when we'd first met. Messy politics. Conflicting regulations. Bribes and handouts. And one law above all others: Murphy's. Anything that can go wrong will go wrong. For instance, a seemingly innocuous home interview.

So yeah, despite being a Montana transplant, Barbara acted every bit the native New Yorker, direct and to the point. She had to.

"To be honest, I hate the word *homophobe* almost as much as I hate the word *homo*," said Tracy.

"Then what are you accusing Ms. Peckler of being?" asked Barbara.

"The wrong person for the job," he said.

"She's been working at the agency for eleven years. That's longer than I've been here," said Barbara.

"Are you condoning her behavior?" asked Tracy.

"I wasn't there," she said.

Tracy began to explain our side of the story when Barbara cut him off. "I think I already know what happened," she said.

"You mean, based only on what she told you," said Tracy. The subtext being, *Don't we get a turn?*

Barbara folded her arms. "I'm curious," she said. "Your intention is to adopt a baby from South Africa. Were you aware that gay couples were forbidden to do so in that country for decades?"

"Yes, but they changed their policy," said Tracy.

"In other words, they saw the light," said Barbara. "Is that really what happened, though? Did key government officials suddenly wake up one morning and become more accepting of gay couples?"

"Someone there had to," said Tracy.

"But not all of them, right? Or maybe it was none of them; maybe it was simply a matter of someone new coming along, one person," she said. "Did you ever consider that?"

I'd been the dutiful listener up until that point, content to let Tracy do the talking. It was now clear, though, that he was preaching to the choir. Barbara had tipped her hand when referring to Ms. Peckler's eleven years at the agency. *That's longer than I've been here,* she'd made a point of saying.

"Barbara," I said, cutting in, "is it possible that Mr. French didn't run it by you first?"

"Mr. French?" she asked.

"The man who was supposed to conduct our home interview but couldn't at the last minute," I said.

Barbara smiled. "Wow, *Family Affair*...I used to love that show," she said. "Edward sort of does look like Mr. French, doesn't he?"

"If I had to bet, he went to Ms. Peckler on his own and asked if she could fill in for him," I said. "Right?"

"Yes," said Barbara. "I only found out after the fact."

I turned to Tracy. He got it now. "In other words, Ms. Peckler wouldn't have been your choice," he said.

"No," Barbara answered. "She wouldn't have been."

This was excellent news. The next step seemed obvious.

"Thank you," said Tracy.

"For what?" asked Barbara.

"Allowing for another home interview, I'm assuming," he said. "With the person you would've chosen."

Barbara unfolded her arms, leaning back in her chair. Her expression almost made the words redundant. "If only it were that simple," she said.

CHAPTER 24

HE RARELY, if ever, yells or screams. Instead, when Tracy's mad, his temples throb. I mean, they *really* throb. It's as if all his anger is pounding on the inside of his skull, looking for a way out.

For the first time, I thought his head might actually crack open.

"Where are you going?" I asked.

Tracy couldn't even walk. Out on the sidewalk, less than fifty feet from the entrance to Barbara Nash's office building, he peeled off and sat down on a bench outside a pastry shop. Or maybe it was a deli. I didn't really bother to look. I was too busy staring at those temples.

"We should sue," he said. "In fact that's exactly what we should do."

But Tracy never confused mad with foolish. No sooner had the words left his mouth than he admitted what we both already knew. We couldn't sue. It was torture for him to say it. "They're not denying us the right to adopt, are they?"

No, Barbara and her agency weren't.

Instead they were postponing us. Six months, to be exact. That's how long we had to wait before we could be granted another home interview, and it had nothing to do with how busy the agency was. This wasn't about the calendar. As Barbara explained it, this was all about "checks and balances."

The so-called process we were supposed to trust also required the trust of everyone else within the agency. The person conducting the home interview had to be given a certain autonomy. He or she couldn't fear having a recommendation overturned simply because Barbara might disagree with the assessment. That was the balance—the balance of power.

The check was that Barbara could ultimately allow another home interview after a suitable waiting period.

Suitable, that is, to everyone except us.

"I don't think I can wait another six months," said Tracy. "Or six days, for that matter."

"I know," I said. "I just don't know the alternative."

"Maybe another agency?"

"Start from scratch? That would take even longer than six months."

Tracy fell silent again. We were both hurting, but I knew his pain was worse because of the guilt. The more he sat there blaming himself, the more I racked my brain for something—any-thing—to give us some hope, a little optimism. I had nothing.

It was a helpless feeling. It was also all too famil-iar, I realized.

And suddenly, that was something.

God, how much I still miss her...

CHAPTER 25

"MY MOTHER," I said.

Tracy turned to me. He'd been staring down at the ground, his body moving only to blink. He knew I almost never talked about my mother. Not in earnest, at least. Although I could tell an entire lecture hall full of students that she named me after Bob Dylan, they would never know about the cancer that took her life when I was thirteen.

"When she went back into the hospital for the second time, when everyone except me knew that she'd never be coming home again, she asked my father and brother to leave the room one day when we were visiting," I said. "She wanted to talk, just the two of us. She told me how much she missed cooking my favorite meal, this elaborate noodle casserole that had chicken and sausage and something like five different cheeses. It truly was my favorite. Anyway, she handed me a list she'd written."

Tracy smiled. "A grocery list."

"Yes. Every single ingredient. My father drove me to the market and gave me money, but he had strict instructions from my mother that he had to stay in the car. I had to do all the shopping on my own and bring everything to the hospital, where she'd arranged to use the kitchen in the doctors' lounge. My mother wanted to cook for me one last time. How could they say no?"

"Of course not," said Tracy. "They couldn't."

"But that wasn't the real reason," I said. "That wasn't why she was doing it. The list, making me buy the food—even letting me prepare some of the casserole when she told me she was getting too tired—it was all about giving me the chance to do something I hadn't been able to do the entire time she'd been sick. *Help her.* I was only thirteen. She was going to die soon, and there was nothing I could do about it. She couldn't tell me everything was going to be okay; she would've never lied to me like that. She knew how helpless I felt, and she figured out a way for me to help her. Not save her life, not make her awful pain go away. It was simply so I could make her smile for one night as she watched me eat that casserole."

Tracy stared at me for a moment. His forehead was smooth, those temples quiet. "Thank you for that," he said finally.

"There's always something that can be done. It will come to us," I said. "Don't worry."

CHAPTER 26

ELIZABETH IS acting a little different; I can tell. I just can't tell why. Not yet . . .

She squinted at me from across her spotless desk that afternoon in the First Precinct, her home base, not too far from City Hall. She wanted to trust me but wasn't sure. "What are you not seeing?" she asked.

"I don't know. I'll know it when I see it, though," I said, handing her back a copy of the autopsy report on Jared Louden, our murdered hedge-fund manager.

The cause of death was never in doubt. Multiple stab wounds.

Elizabeth was still squinting. "Do you think the medical examiner missed something?"

"Not necessarily," I said.

"Then what is it?" she asked.

"Nothing," I said.

"I don't believe you."

"Fine. Don't believe me."

"Seriously," she said. "What aren't you telling me?"

"Better yet," I said, "why are you nagging me about this?"

She blinked. "Did you really just use the word *nagging* with me?"

"I'm sorry. Would you prefer *busting my balls?*"

"Hey, you two, get a room," came a man's voice from behind two tall stacks of paperwork on a nearby desk.

Elizabeth leaned back in her chair so she could see the guy, a fellow detective. "Sorry, Robert," she said before turning to me again. Her squint was gone, but there was still something in her eyes. Again, she'd been looking at me a little differently ever since I'd arrived at the precinct.

"Listen," I said. "Louden's already dead and buried. The question is whether there's anything he can still tell us about his killer."

"I get that," she said. "I can't have you holding back on me, that's all."

Holding back?

"I'm not," I said. Although I couldn't help tacking on a slight chuckle.

"What was that for?" she asked.

I glanced over at the other detective, Robert— or at least what I could see of him over the files, which was basically the top of his forehead and his receding hairline. My concern was what I couldn't see. His ears.

"Later," I told Elizabeth.

"No, now," she insisted. "And don't worry about Robert; he knows more about me than my shrink…if I actually had one."

I still hesitated.

"Hey, Robert, you still there?" she asked.

"Yeah," came his voice again from behind the files. He sounded like Abe Vigoda from his *Barney Miller* days. Drier than rye toast.

"When's the last time I had sex?" she asked.

Robert snap-answered. "Eight months ago."

"What foods give me gas?"

"Wheat bread, hummus, and potato chips."

"Why don't I speak to my father?"

"Because he cheated on your mother," he said. "That's why you have trust issues."

Elizabeth cocked her head at me, spreading her arms wide. *Satisfied?*

More like entertained, but it was the same difference. She apparently had nothing to hide.

"It was something Grimes said to me," I explained. "Right after you bolted from the diner. A warning. He was telling me to be careful around you."

"Why?" she asked.

"He more than implied that your rank on the

force wasn't entirely your doing, that you had some help," I said. "I think his exact words were...you were *in bed* with someone."

Immediately the girl who had nothing to hide raised a finger to her lips. *Shh.*

"Hey, Robert?" she called out.

"Yeah?" came his voice.

"Go smoke a cigarette," she said.

CHAPTER 27

"SURE," SAID Robert without the slightest hesitation. "That sounds like a great idea."

I watched as he promptly rose up from behind the file stacks, not once making eye contact with me before turning and walking away.

"Does Robert sit and roll over, too?" I asked once he was out of earshot.

"Yes, and he's fiercely loyal to boot," she said. While I was joking, she was making a point. "For a guy who knows so much about me, including intimate details about my personal life, he sure seemed fine with my telling him to get lost for a few minutes. Do you know why that is?"

As a matter of fact I did. "Because there are some things a person doesn't want to know, and he trusts you to know the difference on his behalf," I said. "I believe the term is *plausible deniability*."

Elizabeth rolled her eyes. "I should've known

better than to ask a psych professor," she said. "What exactly did Grimes say to you?"

"I told you," I said. "You're in bed with someone."

"He didn't name names?"

"No, and I didn't ask him to."

"He wouldn't have told you anyway," she said. "He's enjoying the thought of you and me having this conversation way too much. He probably fed you lines, too, like why he came to me instead of any other detective."

"As a matter of fact..."

Elizabeth glanced around, making sure no one else could hear her.

"Plenty of other places we could go," I offered.

"We're fine," she said. Still, she leaned in a little closer. I could smell her perfume, a hint of jasmine. "Three years ago, I was put on the mayor's security detail. It had been only guys up until that point—an all-boys club—and it was determined that the optics of that weren't good. That was the pretense, at least."

"Pretense?" I asked.

"It was true that the detail had only been men prior to me, but let's just say fixing a gender imbalance wasn't the primary concern," she said.

"What was?"

"That's the part you shouldn't know."

"Then why even mention it?"

"Because you asked."

"Only because of what Grimes told me," I said. "So it's the mayor? Grimes thinks I need to be careful because of your connection to him?"

"Actually, Grimes doesn't really think that. He just wanted to see how much you know."

"About what?"

"Exactly," she said. "*Plausible deniability.* You didn't know."

"Only now you're going to tell me, right?"

CHAPTER 28

IF I'D leaned in any closer, Elizabeth and I would've been bumping foreheads.

"I was the first *detective* Grimes called," she said. "But I wasn't his first call."

"Who was?" I asked.

"Beau Livingston," she said. "The mayor's chief of staff."

"Why?"

"Crime reporters, by definition, are a pain in the ass for a mayor, especially one who advocated making the city safer."

"Advocated?" That word didn't begin to describe it.

During his initial run for City Hall, Mayor Edward "Edso" Deacon made Rudy Giuliani look like Neville Chamberlain in his effort to combat crime. Deacon's reelection campaign, backed by his own immense fortune from commercial real estate, had been no less relentless. The only problem was that the statistics weren't exactly in Deacon's favor. Far from it. Crime hadn't dropped at all since he took office.

"Yeah," said Elizabeth, bobbing her head. "*Advocated* isn't really the right word, is it?"

"His ad blitz was more like an all-out assault."

"More to my point," she said. "The mayor didn't want a guy like Grimes running wild in his column with every crime story he could get his hands on. Politically, it was too risky."

Suddenly the idea of plausible deniability was looking good to me. Was Grimes right? *Do I truly want to know all this?*

"If you're about to tell me that the mayor bought off Grimes, don't tell me," I said.

"No, it's not like that," she assured me. "Besides, you could never silence a guy like Grimes, not for money. What you can do, though, is call on him first at press conferences, let him be photographed with you on the golf course, and make sure that when unnamed sources from the mayor's office are giving quotes, it's his number they're dialing."

"And in return?" I asked.

"Grimes treats Deacon with kid gloves," she said. "That, and when a strange package shows up on his desk in the middle of a reelection campaign with your book and a bloody playing card in it, he calls the mayor's chief of staff."

"Who in turn gets you assigned to the case without its actually being a case yet," I said. "It's not public."

"Not yet, at least," she said. "As you saw first-hand, though, even Grimes has his limits when it comes to this arrangement."

"Which leaves you stuck in the middle."

"Stuck I'm okay with. *Compromised* is something else," she said.

She didn't need to elaborate. So far what was in the public's best interest was aligned with the mayor's interest. Meaning it didn't serve anyone to have the public panicking about a serial killer on the loose. Not yet. But if the murders continued . . .

"You're getting a lot of pressure from the mayor to catch this guy," I said. "Before it gets out of hand."

"More than you could possibly imagine."

"Then we've got a medical examiner to go see," I said.

"So you *do* think he missed something?"

"It's a hunch," I said.

She reached for her blazer on the back of her chair. She was up and ready to go. Meanwhile, I hadn't moved.

"What are you waiting for?" she asked.

"Who else knows?"

She flinched. It was all I needed. That's why she was acting different around me.

"Excuse me?"

"Never mind," I said. "Let's get going."

CHAPTER 29

THE FORENSIC biology laboratory on East 26th Street, part of New York City's Office of Chief Medical Examiner, reeked of antiseptic. And that was *outside* the building.

Inside, there was even more of a reason to hold my nose.

"Does he have a badge?" asked Dr. Ian Wexler.

That was his welcome to me when Elizabeth introduced us, straight past a hello and a handshake and directly into a massive attitude. It was classic Freudian displacement. He didn't like a detective questioning his work but couldn't kick Elizabeth out. I was the next best thing.

"No, Ian, he doesn't have a badge," Elizabeth said calmly. "I told you he's a professor assisting the investigation."

"If he doesn't have a badge, he can't be in here," he insisted.

The "here" was the autopsy suite, where Wexler

was setting up a full body X-ray on a cadaver. It was the second dead body I'd seen in as many days, and there was no shaking the horrible feeling that there were more to come.

For sure this room could accommodate them. There were at least half a dozen other examination tables—slabs—along with a series of deep-basin sinks and hanging scales that could've easily been mistaken for the kind you see in the produce section of your local supermarket. Although these particular scales were never going to be used for weighing bananas.

"C'mon, Ian, play nice," said Elizabeth. "He doesn't need a badge."

Wexler stared at her. Then he stared at me. Up and down, a real good once-over. I figured maybe I could break the ice.

"Badges? We ain't got no badges...I don't have to show you any stinkin' badges!" I said.

"Yeah, ha-ha," said Wexler, stone-faced. Not even a hint of a smile. *The Treasure of the Sierra Madre.* Overrated movie, if you ask me."

But it was enough for him to drop it. "What did you want to talk about?" he asked.

"Jared Louden," said Elizabeth.

"The hedge-fund guy," said Wexler, nodding. "Did you read the report?"

"We did," said Elizabeth.

"Then what is there to talk about?" *In other*

words, My shit don't stink, and neither do my autopsy reports.

It was as if we barely had the doctor's attention as he resumed fiddling with the X-ray machine. Whatever caused the death of the elderly man on the table in front of us—his otherwise naked body covered only by a small towel across his midsection—it wasn't from an external injury.

As opposed to Jared Louden.

I chimed in again. I was, after all, the one who led Elizabeth here. "You wrote that he died from multiple stab wounds," I said.

Wexler, now shaping up to be a first-ballot inductee into the Asshole Hall of Fame, managed to combine sarcasm, condescension, arrogance, and mild amusement into a single chuckle. "Did you reach another conclusion, Professor?" he asked.

"No, but I was curious as to *how many* stab wounds there were," I said.

"You saw the accompanying photos in the report. There were too many to count. Mr. Louden was practically shredded."

"That's the thing," I said. "The photos you included only show certain sections of his body, not all of it. You photographed all of him, though, correct?"

"Of course," said Wexler.

"But you didn't bother to count the stab wounds?"

Wexler glared at me. If looks could kill I would've been toes-up on one of his other slabs.

"No, I didn't *bother*," he said, beginning to lose his cool. "Again, there were too many to count...and I really don't like what you're suggesting, Professor."

In that case, Doc, you're really not going to like what's coming next...

CHAPTER 30

I MUTTERED a few words under my breath. Loudly enough for the doctor to hear something, but not loudly enough to know what it was.

"What's that?" asked Wexler.

"Three hundred and fifty-two," I repeated.

He could hear me just fine now. He simply didn't know what the hell I was talking about.

"That's how many dimples there are on a Titleist Pro V1 golf ball," I explained in response to his blank stare.

"Listen, Professor—"

"Four thousand five hundred and forty-three," I continued, cutting him off. "That's the number of words in the US Constitution. One thousand seven hundred and ten? That's the number of steps to the top of the Eiffel Tower when it was first built."

"Are you trying to impress me?" asked Wexler. "Or just piss me off?"

"I'm trying to get you to do your job," I said.

"Telling you whether Jared Louden died of thirty versus forty or fifty stab wounds—that's what this is about?" he asked.

"Not exactly."

"Then enlighten me."

"I'm a professor, not a magician, but I'll do my best," I said. "Louden is stabbed to death seemingly *countless* times, yet the wounds are spread out over his entire body. What's more—at least as far as I can tell from the pictures you included in your report—every wound is distinct. Not a single one overlaps another, and that can't be a coincidence. Meaning the killer *wanted you* to count how many times he stabbed Louden. Because that's your job. He's trying to tell us something."

"Which is what?" asked Wexler.

"That's my job," I said. "So if it's okay with you, let's go have a look at all the photos you took—the entire body."

"Now?" asked Wexler. "In case you haven't noticed, I'm in the middle of something."

"I'm sure this gentleman won't mind," I said, nodding at the slab. "It's not like he's going anywhere." Then I really persuaded him. "It's not like I'm going anywhere, either, until we do."

Wexler pursed his lips, the exasperation making his face look sunburned against the white of his smock. "I'll be right back," he said.

He left the room, heading for an adjacent office. Elizabeth waited until he was gone.

"You should apologize," she said.

"To Wexler?"

"No—to the poor soul lying on the table here," she said. "You pretty much used a dead guy as your straight man."

"Comedy is not pretty," I said. "Steve Martin."

"Christ, is there anyone you don't quote?"

"Yeah, Hitler and weathermen," I said. "So I wasn't too hard on Wexler?"

"No: you were definitely brutal," she said. "For some reason, I don't mind your arrogance as much as his."

"That should be a Hallmark card."

Her laugh was cut short by the ring of her cell. Her eyes narrowed as she saw who was calling. Not good, I could tell.

"Hello?" she answered.

I heard the sound of a man's voice on the other end but could understand nothing of what he was saying. As for Elizabeth, she wasn't saying anything. Just listening.

Meanwhile Wexler returned with a file in hand. No sooner did he open it than Elizabeth ended her call.

"We've got to go," she announced.

"What about the photos?" asked Wexler. "Don't you want the count?"

"Fifty-two," I said.

"Excuse me?"

"That's the number of wounds, if I had to guess," I said. "In fact I'm almost sure of it."

CHAPTER 31

I'D HEARD about Tribeca 212. It was the current "it" hotel in lower Manhattan, complete with a ridiculously over-the-top lobby that looked like a cross between a Salvador Dalí painting and the Korova Milk Bar from *A Clockwork Orange*. Throw in the feng shui–inspired rooms and the rooftop pool heated by solar panels and you understand why so many save-the-planet A-list actors were meeting in its all-vegan, gluten-free restaurant for their *Vanity Fair* interviews.

In short, you either loved the place or wouldn't be caught dead there. In a manner of speaking, at least.

"Tenth floor, room 1009," said the cop standing guard by the waiting elevator.

"Thanks," said Elizabeth, pocketing her badge as we stepped on.

Instead of pumping out Muzak all the way up to the tenth floor, the overhead speaker was treating us to a recording of one of Che Guevara's protest speeches.

Elizabeth shook her head slowly. "In case you were wondering, this is why so many people hate liberals."

Ding.

There was no need to follow any signs as we stepped off the elevator. Just follow the commotion. Thirty feet down the long, mirrored hallway to our left were the hotel manager and the detective who had called Elizabeth. The two guys were toe-to-toe, mano a mano. Another cop was the lone spectator.

The manager, with his perfect head of hair, was angrily demanding to know why it was taking so long to remove the bodies. The detective was shouting back at him to calm down while surely entertaining thoughts of what Tasering the guy might do to that perfect coiffure.

"You must be the manager," said Elizabeth, immediately inserting herself between the two. "I'm Detective Needham."

"Oh, great, another detective," said the guy, rolling his eyes.

"I know, I apologize for the delay," said Elizabeth. "It's my fault. My fellow detective here was merely doing what I'd asked. Tell me, is there a back exit to the hotel, perhaps an alleyway?"

"Yes," said the manager. "There is."

"Wonderful," she said. "Would you prefer we take the bodies out that way or would you rather we parade them through the front, where all the photographers and news vans are?"

Elizabeth flashed a smile, sweet as honey. I'd yet to hear her sound so polite. Meanwhile, the manager softened like last week's banana.

"Um. I mean, of course I would prefer the back exit," he said. "Speaking on behalf of the hotel, I would really appreciate your not going out the front."

"Of course you would," she said. "But I had to check because, you see, I'm the one who makes that decision. Now, can I ask you a favor in return?"

"Sure," said the manager. "Anything."

"Get the hell out of my face before I change my mind," she said.

Again, Elizabeth smiled at the guy.

I was really starting to like her.

CHAPTER 32

ELIZABETH TURNED sharply, walking through the open door of room 1009. I followed right behind her, as did the detective who was first tangling with the manager. He was chuckling to himself.

"You're so sexy when you're a bitch, Needham," he said. "Will you go to the prom with me?"

Elizabeth quickly introduced me to Detective Eric Monroe, a chunky man with a double chin, two-day stubble, and easily twenty years on the force who would probably be the first to admit that his crack-wise demeanor was little more than a coping mechanism for all the dead bodies he'd seen.

Here were two more.

Although it was safe to assume he hadn't seen anything quite like this.

Ditto for Elizabeth. *"Jesus,"* she muttered under her breath.

It wasn't that the couple on the bed had each been shot multiple times at close range, bits and chunks of their brains and entrails splattered across the sheets. Or that the sheets themselves were so stained with blood that barely an inch of white remained.

That wasn't it. Not even close.

"You said to leave the bodies untouched until you got here," said Monroe. "Just pictures and perimeter evidence so far."

"Thanks, Eric," she said. She leaned toward him, dropping the volume on her voice. "The report of death?"

"I was slightly delayed calling it in," he said with a wink. He was referring to the medicolegal death investigator. "MDI is currently on his way here, though. There's only the responding officer out in the hall so far and our two forensic friends here."

Monroe turned to the two guys who had all the mannerisms—if not quite the looks—of their CSI counterparts on TV. They were standing next to some weird credenza made of driftwood, busy labeling samples they had already bagged. I assumed they were waiting for the okay to get started on the bodies. Among other things, they would collect sample DNA and make an official tally on all those bullet wounds.

Also, they'd be checking for signs of a struggle. Was the couple forced into their pose, as it were, or had the killer somehow managed to enter the room undetected? These were the things the investigator from the medical examiner's office would be working to know as well. When he finally arrived, that was. By "slightly" delaying the report of death, Monroe had bought Elizabeth a few extra minutes, time that she very much wanted.

Monroe spun around back to the bodies on the bed. "So are they who you think they are?" he asked.

Elizabeth nodded, even though she'd never seen the couple before and didn't know the first thing about them. Same for me.

But we both knew exactly who they were.

The two of hearts.

CHAPTER 33

"WHO FOUND them?" asked Elizabeth.

"Room-service kid," said Monroe. "The door was propped open on the safety latch. He knocked repeatedly and ultimately came in."

"Where's the kid now?" she asked.

"Staff lounge, along with the cleaning lady who arrived after hearing him yell for help. I already took statements from them both. They didn't see anyone or anything strange prior."

"What did they order?" I asked.

"*Huh?* Oh, you mean the couple," said Monroe. "I'll have to check with room service. Why do you ask?"

"He thinks maybe it was the killer who placed the order," said Elizabeth. She turned to me. "Right?"

"It's a possibility," I said. "The killer left the door open, didn't he? He wanted the bodies discovered sooner rather than later."

Elizabeth stepped closer to the bed, her eyes

taking everything in. The couple, completely naked. The man propped up against the headboard, legs spread. The woman, lying on her stomach, her head between his legs.

And, lastly, the only reason Elizabeth and I were there in the first place.

"Whoever pulled the trigger," said Monroe, "he sure as hell has a sick sense of humor."

"Are you referring to the position they're in or the position of that playing card?" asked Elizabeth.

"Both," said Monroe. "Although who's to say he actually choreographed them? It's possible they somehow didn't hear him come in."

"Caught in the act, as it were," said Elizabeth.

"Even more caught than that," said Monroe.

"What do you mean?" Elizabeth pointed at the wedding rings, a huge diamond on the woman's hand and a titanium band on the man's. "They're married, aren't they?"

"Yeah," said Monroe. "Just not to each other."

He glanced at the small pad in his hand, reading off the names he'd written down, courtesy of their driver's licenses. Rick Thorsen and Cynthia Chadd. Two different last names with different addresses and pictures of different kids in their wallets. This definitely wasn't a married couple.

"That explains the blow job," I said.

Monroe laughed. I clearly was beginning to develop a coping mechanism, too.

"That reminds me," he said. "Our first officer on the scene wants to know how much detail he should put in the report."

Elizabeth folded her arms. "You mean he wants to know if he should really write that the female victim was found with the penis of the male victim still in her mouth?"

"Well," said Monroe. "When you put it like that..."

"Tell him he can limit the details," she said.

Monroe nodded. "That's what I thought. Besides, a picture's worth a thousand words, right?"

"Yeah...about those pictures," said Elizabeth, turning to the CSI duo by the credenza. "Can I see them?"

"Sure," said the younger of the two. Much younger.

The older one, though, traded glances with Monroe. They both had been around the block pretty much the same number of times. The exchange happened quickly, but I caught it. So did Elizabeth.

"Sorry, Needham, I can't do it," said Monroe.

Can't do what?

CHAPTER 34

ELIZABETH TILTED her head in disbelief. I couldn't help thinking there was a little playacting involved.

"Are you serious?" she asked. "You can't show me the photos?"

"You know what I mean," said Monroe. "I can't do what it is you want me to do."

"Which is what, precisely?" she asked.

Monroe took a step toward her, his easy laugh suddenly a distant memory. "I didn't ask you the question; I didn't make you lie to me," he said. "The only reason you're here is because of that nine of diamonds wedged between that dead woman's ass cheeks. We all know it, but I didn't ask you to explain what it means. So don't ask me to make that card disappear like some magic trick."

"I would never do that," said Elizabeth.

Except her heart wasn't in it. Monroe had called

her on the carpet, and instead of a full-throated defense of her integrity, the best she could offer up was some pallid denial. In that moment it was as if I were inside her head, hearing her say the very words to herself that she'd said to me earlier.

Stuck I'm okay with. Compromised is something else.

Monroe, satisfied, rested his hands across his protruding gut. But not before throwing her a lifeline.

"You're right. My apologies, Needham. Of course you would never do that," he said.

I'm not sure how long the room would've remained silent after that, but the sound of Monroe getting a text made sure none of us would ever know. He glanced at his cell.

"MDI just arrived," he said.

Elizabeth nodded. In a minute or two, the investigator from the medical examiner's office would be walking into the room. She didn't want to be there when he did.

After a few steps toward the door, though, she stopped and returned to the side of the bed for one last look. She then took a picture, a close-up of the nine of diamonds.

Watching her, I could only think of the nickname Grimes had come up with at the diner. The Dealer.

This is all a game to you, isn't it? A sick, perverted,

and twisted game that's only getting started. Are you really going to play every card in the deck? It's what you want us to think, right?

I wasn't sure. I wasn't sure of anything, not yet. Except for one thing.

The Dealer officially had the upper hand.

CHAPTER 35

"OKAY, I'VE got some bad news and some bad news," said Elizabeth twenty minutes later down in the lobby. "Which one do you want first?"

"Definitely the bad news," I said.

She'd been off grilling the hotel manager and his perfectly coiffed hair about their security cameras while I questioned the member of the kitchen staff who took the room-service order. Our rendezvous point was the lobby, which had been kept clear by the police, save for the few guests actually there in the afternoon who had come down from their rooms looking for answers. *Why are there so many cop cars and news vans parked in front of the hotel?*

Elizabeth let out a sigh. "The security cameras are nonoperational."

That was bad news, all right. "How is that possible?" I asked.

"Long story," she said. "Apparently it involves a

certain movie star who was here with a woman who wasn't his wife."

"This place is just hook-up central, isn't it?"

"More than we know," she said. "Turns out someone on the security staff tried to sell footage of them in the elevator to TMZ and the movie star got wind of it. TMZ couldn't buy the footage because it was stolen property, but the star threatened to sue the hotel anyway. Next thing you know, the owners had the cameras in all the public areas disconnected."

"That's a bit of an overreaction, no?"

"Or a stroke of marketing genius," she said. "It seems word got around to some of the hotel's high-end clientele, presumably the horniest ones."

"Do you think—"

"That our killer knew he wouldn't be recorded? It's possible."

"I'm afraid to ask," I said. "What's the other bad news?"

"The room-service guy," she said. "Right after he yelled for help he somehow decided to snap a picture and post it on Instagram."

"Christ, please tell me it wasn't a selfie," I said.

"No, but the damage is done."

I knew exactly what she meant. As soon as that picture went viral—and there was no doubt it would—all bets were off. So, too, was any agreement with Grimes. I could see his headline now. CITY IN PANIC! WHO WILL BE THE NINE OF DIAMONDS?

The mayor was really going to love that.

"What about the room-service order?" asked Elizabeth. "Anything?"

"At first, nothing," I said. "The order was Champagne and strawberries, and it was definitely a man who ordered it."

"That doesn't mean it's our guy, though. We don't even know for sure that he's a he."

"We do now," I said. "The woman who took the order remembered that the guy first asked for steak and eggs. But it's a vegan restaurant, so no steak and no eggs. Still, why order that in the first place?"

"Because he simply forgot," said Elizabeth.

"I thought the same thing, and then it dawned on me."

"What?"

"*Me,*" I said. "From the start, this guy's wanted me involved in the investigation. He knows my background studying serial killers and wants to show me that he knows. So he tries to order steak and eggs. In fact I bet he knew all along that it was a vegan restaurant."

Elizabeth shot me a blank stare.

"*Steak and eggs,*" I repeated. "That was Ted Bundy's last meal."

"Okay, let's put aside how weird it is that you

know that," she said. "What does it mean? Is he actually telling us anything?"

"I'm not sure, but at least it's not bad news," I said. "He's talking to me, and as long as he does there's no telling what else he might—wait; what are you looking at?"

She was squinting up at the mezzanine balcony, which hung over the lobby like one of Salvador Dalí's clocks.

Something had caught her eye. Make that some*one*.

"*Get down!*" Elizabeth yelled.

CHAPTER 36

I HAD around six inches and sixty pounds on her, but Elizabeth took me down faster than a house of cards in a hurricane. We crashed to the floor, her arms wrapped around me, the wind knocked entirely out of my lungs as I landed with a horrific thud on my back. *Is that one of my ribs that just snapped?*

The only way I thanked her for saving my ass was that I cushioned her fall. Chivalry is not dead...and neither were we.

Not yet, at least.

The shots continued, bullets screaming past us. Even louder were the screams of the guests in the lobby who had come down from their rooms. To think they wanted to know about the commotion *outside*.

"This way!" said Elizabeth.

She'd rolled off me onto her stomach and into a crawl, quickly heading toward the shelter of a nearby couch. I fell in line behind her on my hands and knees, trying my best to keep up and keep low. Never had ten feet looked so far away.

More shots. They were relentless, one after another. Each getting closer. Too close. Right before my eyes a glass coffee table exploded, the shards raining down on top of us.

He had us lined up now; crawling wasn't going to cut it.

Change of plans.

"Run!" shouted Elizabeth.

We both pushed off the floor, sprinting the rest of the way. Screw going around the couch, we hurled ourselves over it. No points for style, but we were still breathing.

More like gasping. The adrenaline felt like a clamp on my throat as we plastered ourselves against the back of the couch.

"You all right?" asked Elizabeth, reaching for her semiautomatic. It was a Glock 19, one of the first guns my father taught me how to shoot.

"Yeah," I said. "You?"

"Just peachy."

"Did you see him?" I asked.

"I saw his hand...and the gun," she said. "That's it."

That was enough for me. "Thanks," I said.

She checked her clip. "Yeah, well, you're no good to me dead, Reinhart."

"A simple 'You're welcome' would've sufficed."

The shooting had stopped, but that didn't mean it was over.

"Give me your shoe," she said.

I hesitated. *My shoe?*

"Hurry!" she said.

Shoe first, ask questions later. I pulled off one of my loafers, handing it to her.

"Ferragamo," she said, glancing at the label on the insole. "Nice." She promptly tossed it high over her shoulder as though it were a piece of trash.

No, check that. As though it were a clay pigeon.

Faster than you can say "Pavlov's dog," the shot rang out. First movement and an itchy trigger finger will do it every time.

He missed, though. The only sound after the shot was my shoe hitting the ground on the front side of the couch.

"Quick, give me your other shoe," said Elizabeth, sticking out her hand.

Seriously? "Are you *trying* to let him hit it? Why does he get a do-over?" But I knew what she was doing. Better my shoe than her head. "Here," I said, giving it to her.

She launched it even higher this time, quickly turning to take a peek over the back lip of the couch. The only sound, though, was my second shoe hitting the ground unscathed.

"Shit," said Elizabeth. Translation: *He was gone.*

The next second, she was, too.

CHAPTER 37

ELIZABETH PEELED around the couch, running toward the stairs leading up to the mezzanine. There was no stopping her. Or what followed.

Irony was the only word for it. The sudden silence in the lobby had acted like the mother of all starter pistols. Welcome to all hell breaking loose, part 2.

My view from behind the couch was of the front entrance, the double doors now bursting open as cops with their guns drawn split off left and right, high and low. Most of the hotel guests remained hiding behind whatever cover they'd found, and those few who ventured out into the open were quickly barked at to take cover again lest the shooter have thoughts of opening fire for a second time.

If only anyone knew where he was.

"Mezzanine!" I shouted.

Every hand on every gun immediately swung up

to the overhanging balcony. I stood and turned, thinking I'd see Elizabeth still heading up the stairs, but she'd already disappeared.

So had the shooter. *It has to be the Dealer, right?*

"Clear!" yelled two cops in unison after reaching the mezzanine. They were echoed by another at the elevator bank and still another by the entrance to the hotel's restaurant. Everywhere was clear.

Except nothing was clear. There was no Elizabeth. No Dealer. No idea where they were.

I went about gathering my shoes in front of the couch, the seat cushions now tufted with bullet holes. That was it, though, for my immediate to-do list. All I could do was wonder if there was something more I could be doing. *Should* be doing. Sitting on my ass didn't feel right.

Where the hell are you, Elizabeth? This whole thing doesn't feel right.

Suddenly every gun was swinging wildly again, no two in the same direction. A loud crashing noise had come from somewhere beyond the lobby, but where? And what was it, exactly? It wasn't a gunshot; it was more like something falling hard to the ground. Real hard.

I craned my neck trying to trace the sound, which was nearly impossible given the size of the lobby. It was too cavernous, too much like an echo chamber. Everyone was clearly thinking the same thing.

Including the hotel manager. I'd seen him pop up from his hiding place behind the front desk as though he were the target in a game of whack-a-mole. His hair looked as if it had been through a wind tunnel.

That's all I needed, though—one glance at the guy to remind me of Elizabeth shutting him down earlier in the upstairs hallway. In a matter of seconds, she'd given a master class on human behavior.

Human beings are pretty simple once you figure out what they want.

What does the Dealer want right now?

CHAPTER 38

I MADE a beeline to the front desk. "Where is it?" I asked the manager. More like demanded. "Where's that back exit?"

You would've thought I'd asked the guy to tell me the square root of pi he was blinking so rapidly.

"The back exit!" I repeated.

"Down the stairs behind the elevators," he finally answered.

Instinct and nothing more had me heading toward those stairs on my own. I would've kept going, too, if my brain hadn't kicked in.

Never bring a knife to a gunfight? Hell, Dylan, you're not even bringing anything.

I didn't get very far. The police had every path into and out of the lobby covered, and those not standing guard were talking into their radios or interviewing hotel guests, who were finally allowed out from hiding.

"Hey, excuse me," I said, approaching a cop underneath the mezzanine balcony. He was wrapping up his questioning of a Wall Street type in a slick suit who had the look of a guy who would later be in a bar bragging about his near-death experience to anyone willing to listen. I could almost see the overpriced IPA in his hand.

"Yeah?" said the cop, although he couldn't have sounded less interested if he tried. He was far more concerned with whatever he was checking on his phone.

"I need your help," I said. "I'm here with Detective Elizabeth Needham, and she's now—"

"What did you say your name was?"

"I didn't," I said. "What I'm trying to tell you is that the guy doing all the shooting is probably looking for a way out of here, and there's a—"

"Back exit. Yeah, we know," he said. "We've got men out there already."

"Okay, but what about between here and there?"

"What about it?"

"This guy isn't an idiot," I said, "and he's not just going to turn himself in."

"Idiot or not, he ain't a magician. We've got every door covered."

"No, as a matter of fact, we don't," came Elizabeth's voice.

I turned to see her halfway down the stairs from the mezzanine, the look on her face making my question all but redundant. "No luck, huh?"

"I lost him in the stairwell," she said. "He nearly took my head off with a fire extinguisher when I looked up over the railing."

The officer immediately went for his radio. "Suspect headed for the roof," he announced.

Easy there, Dick Tracy. Elizabeth leaned in a bit so she could read the cop's nameplate. "He's not headed for the roof, Officer Jenkins," she said.

"Did he use that back exit?" I asked.

"No," she said. "He didn't use any exit."

"Then where the hell is he?" asked Jenkins. "*Where did he go?*"

CHAPTER 39

IT WAS way too early the next morning.

"You don't have to be here," said Elizabeth.

"He asked," I said. "He wanted you to bring me, right?"

"Yes, you were *summoned*," she answered, tacking on some air quotes. "But he's the mayor, not the king."

"Are you sure he knows the difference?"

The reception area outside Mayor Deacon's office suggested the Taj Mahal rather than City Hall. Trump's Taj Mahal, that is. The curtains were red velvet, the chandelier was dripping crystal, and the walls were painted with gold leaf.

"Trust me, the mayor knows the difference," said Elizabeth. "Kings don't have to get elected."

Or reelected, for that matter.

Edso Deacon, the former air force pilot who went on to amass untold wealth in Manhattan commercial real estate, won his first term as mayor on a two-pronged promise. As a slogan, it was everywhere.

Deacon: Tough on crime, tough on poverty.

After the election, Deacon indeed made good on his campaign promise to do more for the poor. He spearheaded a host of programs that were shown to make a difference.

Crime, though, was another story. As in the cautionary tale about all political honeymoons. They always end.

Deacon's programs to fight crime were eventually seen as ineffective. There were no results to tout, no statistics to point to. In fact murders and violent crime were actually up since he had been elected.

The press had taken notice. *A lot* of notice. One story after another centered on Deacon being the mayor of a dangerous city—although not for much longer if things didn't change.

While Deacon's approval ratings dipped, a former district attorney with a winning smile started shaking hands at a lot of subway stops. Tim Stoddart's formal announcement that he was running came at the very site where two cops had been gunned down while on a stakeout. The triggerman was a prisoner who had been furloughed. To hear the former DA's stump speeches you would've thought Deacon was Willie Horton himself.

So Deacon would be damned if some serial killer

was going to be the death of him come November. He wanted a second term at all costs, according to Elizabeth, and until he got it he was hell on wheels.

Now I was about to witness his wrath firsthand.

A minute later, Deacon's secretary stepped out of his office. I expected her to turn to us, announcing politely that the mayor would see us now.

Instead she didn't even glance our way, walking straight back to her desk. I couldn't help noticing that she'd left his door open.

"Elizabeth!" came Deacon's booming voice. *"Get your ass in here!"*

CHAPTER 40

"SO, THIS is him, huh? Our 'catcher in the rye,'" said Deacon, eyeing me up and down. He was grinning, but he wasn't happy.

Clever reference, though, Your Honor. J. D. Salinger's signature novel motivated Mark David Chapman to kill John Lennon, or so Chapman claimed.

Elizabeth formally introduced me to the mayor, who immediately motioned for the two of us to have a seat on the couch along the wall. But not before I met the only other person in the room, the mayor's chief of staff. He introduced himself.

"Beau Livingston," he said, giving me the sort of firm handshake and direct eye contact they teach you in a job-interview workshop. "That's definitely an interesting book you wrote."

"Thanks," I said. "Apparently you're not the only one interested in it."

Oops. I'd pretty much teed it up for the mayor.

"So when the hell are we going to catch this ass-hole?" asked Deacon, although it was clear that by "we" he meant Elizabeth and me.

We'd barely sat down, but we were already in the hot seat.

"I'm doing everything I can," Elizabeth answered respectfully but firmly. There was just a trace of edge and a hint of push-back in her voice. Suffice it to say she wouldn't have been in the room, let alone been Deacon's "personal" detective on this, if she didn't know how to hold her own against him.

"Everything you can, huh? Well, you're sure as shit about to get a lot more help, aren't you?" he said, pointing at the newspapers spread atop the coffee table in front of us. Naturally, Grimes's front-page story in the *Gazette* was on top. Too many of the hotel staff knew about the playing card left behind—or, rather, left "in the behind," as Grimes blithely wrote in his article—for him to hold off any longer. Not to mention the photo the room-service kid had snapped. As predicted, it spread on Reddit faster than the Zika virus.

Now the whole city knew about the Dealer, and everyone with a badge was about to be on the case. FBI badges, too, if the victims began to pile up. Surely that was the last thing in the world the mayor wanted.

Deacon folded his arms, flashing that unhappy

smile again. "So much for nipping this fucking thing in the bud, huh? What a bullshit wish that was."

The mayor might have been an air force man, but he had the whole cursing-like-a-sailor thing down pat. Listening to him, I could picture the wholesome campaign ads featuring him and his wife with their two adorable little daughters eating cotton candy at a street fair.

In fact everything about the guy seemed to be a study in contrasts. For all the profanity, Edso Deacon sort of looked like Mister Rogers. And whereas the reception area was all glitz, his actual office was bare-bones and purely functional.

"What's the latest from the hotel?" asked Livingston, whose chief-of-staff duties surely included keeping the mayor focused. "Do you really think this guy had a room there?"

At the hotel, I had assumed the Dealer would be desperate for an exit. His way out, however, was a door the cops couldn't cover. It was the door to his room.

Cunning bastard.

Tribeca 212 had hundreds of rooms. Safety in numbers. It would've been nearly impossible to search them all while keeping people from coming and going. We didn't even know what he looked like—not the slightest clue.

"We're working off a registered guest list," said

Elizabeth. "We're doing background checks, checking credit cards and alibis, but . . . " Her voice trailed off.

"What?" asked Livingston. "What is it?"

"Yeah, what the fuck is it?" asked Deacon.

They were both staring at Elizabeth. Not for long, though, once I loudly cleared my throat.

"It's a waste of time," I announced. "That's what it is."

CHAPTER 41

IT WAS only right that I jump in, since I was the one who'd convinced Elizabeth that our time was better spent elsewhere. Of course convincing the mayor and his chief of staff of that would be a little trickier. The hot seat was only getting warmed up.

"*A waste of time?*" asked Livingston. His eyebrows were so raised they were practically part of his hairline.

Ditto for Deacon. "What the hell are you talking about—a waste of time?"

Easy now, Dylan. These aren't your students, and this isn't your classroom...

"Perhaps *waste* is too strong a word," I said. "But if we're going to catch this guy, it won't be by doing what he expects us to do. His escape plan from that hotel was to stay put. He most likely went back to his room, remained there a bit, and then reemerged with other guests. Just another face in the crowd."

"Yeah, only we're not talking Yankee Stadium," said Livingston. "This is a crowd of, what, a hundred or so people? And we know he's one of them."

"Is he, though? There are a lot of ways to check into a hotel as someone else," I said. "Maybe he paid cash and used a fake ID. Maybe he used a stolen credit card. Or maybe it's something we haven't thought of yet. The point is, he already has thought of it."

Livingston wasn't sold. "Are you sure you're not giving this guy too much credit?"

"If anything, I'm still underestimating him," I said.

"What if you're wrong, though? How do you explain it to the family members of the next victim, this nine of diamonds, whoever he might be?" said Livingston. "Go ahead, tell them we didn't track down and triple check every person at that hotel because we assumed the killer knew we would."

"I sure as hell can't do that," said Deacon.

"Maybe not, but in the meantime you've managed to turn a whole bunch of innocent people into potential suspects," I said. "Detectives will comb through their lives, and the backlash will be inevitable. The words *right to privacy* will suddenly haunt you in the media, and the whole tone will become personal, because that's what people always do: they make things personal. Headlines will scream that the NYPD and especially the mayor are being outsmarted by a serial killer."

Deacon blinked a few times. "Are you calling me stupid, Dr. Reinhart?"

"No," I said. "I'm calling you a candidate."

"So what's the alternative?" asked Livingston. "Wait around until the next dead body turns up?"

Deacon and Livingston were forgetting something. "It's not like I don't have skin in the game," I said.

"What, your book?" asked Livingston.

"I was thinking more about the back of my book. The author photo," I said.

I waited for that spark of recognition to ignite their eyes. Together the mayor and his chief of staff would nod and realize that out of everyone in the room, I was the only one who had a target on his back.

But the spark never came. Or the nods.

"What's so funny?" I asked Livingston.

CHAPTER 42

HE WASN'T actually laughing. It was worse. It was that Livingston wanted to laugh and knew he shouldn't. The result was somewhere between a canary-eating grin and whatever you call that look people give you right before they tell you that your fly is open.

"Yeah, about your author photo," said Livingston. "Sorry about that."

Elizabeth took the words straight out of my mouth. *"Sorry about what?"* she asked.

Meanwhile, Deacon less than subtly turned to look out the window behind his desk, as if by not actually watching Livingston explain what he'd done he couldn't be held accountable.

Mark Twain had it right. Politicians and diapers must be changed often, and for the same reason.

"Naturally, when Allen Grimes showed me the envelope containing your book and that bloody playing card, we wanted your help," said

Livingston. "We enlisted Elizabeth, and off she went to ask you. All I did was increase the odds that you would say yes."

At that point, it would've been redundant of him to elaborate. I was already picturing him getting all arts-and-craftsy with my author photo. He must have used an X-Acto knife not only to slice up my face but also to cut up a magazine and pull out the letters that spelled *Dead Wrong* across my forehead. Nice touch underlining *Dead* with that red pen, too. A real thorough job.

The worst part? The thing that really pissed me off?

It was clever.

Although Elizabeth hadn't quite gotten that far yet. To look at her was to know exactly what she was thinking. She wanted to kill Livingston with that same X-Acto knife.

"Are you kidding me? Do you know how fucked up that is?" she said to him, her cheeks burning red.

Apparently only Mayor Deacon himself was allowed to swear like that in his office. He spun around from his conveniently long stare out the window. "Cool it," he warned her.

All that did was redirect her anger.

"You okayed this?" she asked the mayor.

"First off, I didn't okay anything," he insisted, each word more clipped than the next. "Second, you don't get to ask me that."

"But I do," I said.

While Deacon was as politically savvy as they come, even the best of them lead with their chins from time to time. This was one of those times. Whatever hold the mayor had on Elizabeth, it didn't extend to me. I was a free agent. If he didn't realize it, his chief of staff certainly did.

"Dr. Reinhart, I hope you can understand that we simply couldn't afford your turning us down," said Livingston, coming to his boss's rescue. "I know how tempting it is to be upset. What you should be is relieved."

"That's really how you're going to spin this?" I asked.

"I'm serious," said Livingston, doubling down. "If you really think about it, it never made sense. This guy clearly wants us to guess his next victims. Why would he so overtly announce you as a target?"

"That's brilliant," I said. "Did you major or minor in psychology?"

"Actually, the psych department at Harvard sucked when I was there," he shot back.

The only thing worse than a Harvard guy is a guy who goes out of his way to tell you that he went to Harvard.

"Yes, you're right. It's my fault that I couldn't figure out what you'd done," I said with all the sarcasm I could muster. "Instead of a deranged serial killer slicing up a picture of me, it was actually you. To think I couldn't tell the difference."

Since I didn't have a mike in my hand to drop, I did the next best thing. I stood up to leave.

"Mr. Mayor, good luck catching your serial killer," I said. "And good luck in November with your reelection."

Then I walked out.

CHAPTER 43

ELIZABETH RAN after me, the pounding of her heels echoing up and down the hallway outside Deacon's office as I headed for the stairs. I could almost picture her timing the sprint, staying behind a few extra angry seconds to give the mayor and Livingston a little more grief while still leaving herself enough time to catch up to me. Advanced multitasking.

"Dylan, wait!" she called out. "Wait!"

I didn't wait. But only because I wanted to get the hell out of the building. When I'd first walked in, it was City Hall. *The* City Hall. When I walked out, it was just another building in the city. Not even.

I stopped on the sidewalk when I got to Park Row. Then I turned around and waited.

"I know," I said the second Elizabeth reached me.

"You know what?" she asked, catching her breath.

"I know you obviously had no idea what

Livingston had done, and I know how sorry you are nonetheless," I said. "I also know what you're going to tell me now, so go ahead."

"You can't just walk away," she said.

I watched her jaw tightening as she braced for an argument, most likely kicked off by some snappy retort on my part, like "I just did."

But I was all out of snappy, at least for the day. Besides, if there's a curse to studying human behavior it's that you always start with yourself. I knew it wasn't in me to walk away, not a chance. I couldn't abandon Elizabeth.

"Do you really think I'd do that to you?" I asked.

"No, I really didn't," she said. Then, of all things, she leaned in and kissed my cheek.

"What was that for?"

"Proving me right," she said, "and not leaving me hanging."

"I am leaving you, though."

"*Wait—what?*"

"Only for a couple of days," I said. "I'm back Thursday night."

"But—"

"Don't worry. The nine of diamonds—whoever he or she is—will still be alive when I return."

"How can you be so sure?" she asked.

"Because I saw it on the news," I said. "Which means the Dealer has, too. This is everything he wants."

"Publicity."

"No," I said. "*Fear.* It might be September, but it's about to be the summer of Sam all over again in this city, and our guy is going to milk it for a bit now that he has everyone's attention. In fact he was probably wondering why it took so long for Grimes to break the story. No wonder he put that nine of diamonds where he did."

"Not to sound like Livingston," she said, "but what if you're wrong? What if he's killing that nine of diamonds right now?"

"Trust me; he's not."

"I don't trust anyone, in case you haven't noticed," she said. "What if I need to reach you? Can I call your cell?"

"Sorry: no cell phones."

"What do you mean?"

"There are two rules where I'm going, and that's the first," I said. "No cell phones."

"What's the second rule?"

"No food."

"*No food?*"

"You can't bring food, and you can't buy any once you're there."

"You're kidding me, right?"

"Nope."

"Where exactly are you going?" she asked.

CHAPTER 44

"YOU'RE LATE," said my father.

That's what I arrived to—his very first words to me. Never mind that I'd been driving in a rented Jeep Cherokee since the crack of dawn and that I hadn't seen him for almost a year, since the last time we went hunting.

No hello, no handshake, no hug.

No surprise.

I dropped my gear, glancing at my watch. Noon on the dot. "The hell I'm late," I said. "Isn't that right, Diamond?"

My father's vizsla, unequivocally the coolest dog in the world, came jumping over to me, landing his front paws on my waist, as he always did. As I always did in return, I gave Diamond's golden-rust coat a vigorous working over, watching his tail whip back and forth to the point of being a blur.

Leave it to a breeding stock that first arrived the

United States from behind the Iron Curtain to be my father's emotional surrogate.

"So you found it all right, huh?" asked my father.

"The last couple of turns were a little tricky," I said. "GPS only gets you so far in these parts."

So did the roads themselves. Rendezvous was an off-the-grid cabin half a mile beyond the end of a dirt road. The last stretch of pavement was at least five miles before that. I wasn't sure I had the right spot until I saw my father's old—*very* old—Jeep Commando parked in a small clearing.

Usually we'd be meeting at a hunting preserve in New Hampshire near where my father retired, in Concord, but my calling him out of the blue required ad hoc measures. The start of grouse season was still a few weeks away in the Granite State, so my father called in a favor from a friend who owned four hundred acres an hour north of Bangor, Maine. The private land was exempt from the state's hunting regulations, thanks to a grandfather clause. We were good to go, just the two of us, all four hundred acres to ourselves.

Still, safety first. Hunting gospel: be seen or be dead.

"Here," said my father after lugging my duffel into the cabin. He tossed me a bright orange pinny. "Wear it."

There was a joke to be made, something about not having an excuse to shoot one another now.

But I held my tongue. This trip had a larger purpose, after all.

"Dad, what are you doing?" I asked.

The second I put my arms through the pinny, my father reached for the small sling bag that I've used since I was a teenager to carry my ammo and shooting glasses. It was almost like he planned it that way, waiting until my hands were occupied so I couldn't stop him.

"Just making sure," he said, poking around inside the bag. "Remember when that Milky Way mysteriously found its way in here?"

"Yeah, I remember," I said. "I also remember that I was fifteen at the time."

"Rules are rules." He handed me back the bag. "All clear."

"Are you sure? You could frisk me, too," I said.

The prohibition against food was the crazier of his two rules, for sure. Although for the purist—and, if anything, Josiah Maxwell Reinhart was a purist—it made sense. Kill only what you intend to eat.

And if you don't kill anything, you don't eat.

No exceptions. Including contraband candy bars, I learned as a kid. "Hunger makes a man focus," he told me then.

I stared at him now. His short-cropped hair was graying at the tips. Other than that, he was winning the fight against aging. Kicking its ass, actually. No sag beneath the chin or anywhere else. Still sturdy as hell.

Just as stubborn, too.

"How's your friend?" he asked.

"His name is Tracy, Dad, and he's a little more than a friend," I said. "I know you got the wedding invitation."

He mumbled something in return. I couldn't hear it, and I was pretty sure I didn't want to.

Instead I wet my finger, checking the breeze. Hunting for grouse meant heading into the wind so the scent would blow toward Diamond.

"So," I said, propping the same 20-gauge Remington against my shoulder that I've been using since my Milky Way days. "Are we going to stand around talking like girls or are we going hunting?"

My father smiled. It was genuine, no trace of his trademark smirk.

"We're going hunting," he said.

CHAPTER 45

MY FATHER and hunting have a lot of things in common. First and foremost, they both require a lot of patience.

For nearly two hours, we walked in silence amid the dense poplars—mostly bigtooth aspens and quaking aspens—with Diamond leading the way. It was good exercise, but it wasn't dinner. From time to time, Diamond even turned back to us and cocked his head as if to say, "Not a single whiff— what gives?"

The only good news was that I didn't have to wait out my father's state of denial as long as I'd thought. He knew there was more to this outing than my suddenly having a hankering for ruffed grouse. Plenty of restaurants serve the bird in Manhattan, although "those lefty idiots down there," as my father calls them, mistakenly refer to it as partridge.

No, my father definitely knew I had something to discuss with him. In person.

Finally he gave me his version of putting his arm around me and asking kindly what was on my mind.

"Oh, for Christ's sake, son, spit it out already," he said.

I gave him the background, quickly and in bullet-point style, as he was used to. It was everything from the initial package Grimes got with my book and the bloodstained card to my meeting in the mayor's office.

But this wasn't about the Dealer. This was about me. Maybe my father, too.

"She knows," I said.

"Who? The detective?"

"Yeah—Elizabeth. She didn't say anything, but she didn't have to."

I expected any number of reactions. Anger was one. Doubt was another. I could almost hear him calling out my arrogance, reminding me that having a doctorate in psychology didn't mean that I could read people's minds.

Instead I got the reaction I least expected. Ambivalence. "Okay, so maybe she knows," he said. "So what?"

"So everything," I said. "That would mean—"

"Yeah, that Deacon told her." My father shrugged. "He's not exactly the mayor of

Podunk, and he's a billionaire to boot. Besides, you were surely the first suspect, right? A guy like Deacon would take his vetting of you very seriously."

"By vetting, do you mean hacking?"

"It's possible. It's not like a State Department official would ever have a private e-mail server in her closet or anything," he said. "Point is, classified just ain't what it used to be."

"What do you suggest I do?"

"What you do with any leak," he said. "Seal it."

My father suddenly stopped, motioning at Diamond, who had gone birdy. The dog was rigid as a rock, having picked up a scent.

Sure enough, there it was, twenty yards ahead of us. *Bonasa umbellus*. The ruffed grouse.

A fat one, too. They don't spook as easily. The young, lean grouses tend to flush at the sound of a leaf falling, not to mention the snap of a twig. The bird was perched on a low branch of one of the few sugar maples that were mixed in with all the aspens. Dinner, here we come.

On my father's nod I raised my rifle, lining up the shot. It was mostly clean, only the hang of another small branch in the way. Quickly I looped my index finger around the trigger.

When I was a boy and my father first taught me how to shoot, he repeated the same words over and over. "Ready and steady, son…ready and steady."

I could hear him now in my head. I could see him, too, out of the corner of my eye.

Then I watched in horror as he fell to the ground.

CHAPTER 46

THE SHOT wasn't mine.

It came from the other side of the sugar maple, the laughter that followed it removing any doubt. *Laughter?*

I was sure that's what it was as I dropped my rifle, running over to my father. He'd rolled onto his side next to a low stretch of bramble and was reaching for his left leg, directly above the knee. Blood was oozing from two small holes in his briar pants—holes caused by pellet spray from a 3.5-inch magnum shell, if I had to guess. That's as large as they come for a 12-gauge. Too large if you value skill.

Hunters hunt. Others simply fill the air with lead.

Whipping off my belt, I tied it around my father's thigh above the wound. "Are you—"

"Yeah, I'm okay," he said.

"Well, hell, that's good news," came a voice from behind me.

"Shit, yeah," said another.

I turned to look at the two guys, probably in their late twenties. One was big, the other even bigger. Together, it was as if John Steinbeck had replaced George with another Lennie in *Of Mice and Men*.

The only difference? Steinbeck's Lennie seemed to be a hell of a lot smarter than these two.

You just shot someone, you idiots. You might want to put the beers down…

Idiot number 1 shook his head and laughed, the same laugh I'd first heard. Only now it was the most annoying sound on the planet. "You picked one hell of a place to be standing, old man," he said.

Is that supposed to be an apology?

I really didn't know where to begin. My father did, though.

"You picked an even worse place to be shooting from," he said.

"This is private property," I added, although I immediately regretted it. It made me sound like a city boy, not the tone I was going for. Not with these two. Idiot number 1 was actually wearing overalls.

"Private, huh? Do you two own it?" asked Idiot number 2, convinced that we didn't.

That got the first one laughing again, his large gut sloshing around underneath those overalls. He clearly hadn't missed a meal in his life. "Yeah," he said. "Show us some paperwork."

"They can't because they ain't got any. They're not even from around here. You can tell."

"Yeah. Where you from, old man?"

Go ahead, call him old man one more time…

My father was a lot of things. Conversationalist wasn't one of them. "You two are poaching, and you know it," he said calmly. Then the switch flipped. *"Now stop fucking around."*

The way he punched each word, raising his voice, immediately set off Diamond. There's no breed more loyal than a vizsla.

Diamond began barking more loudly than I'd ever heard him before, showing his teeth while edging toward the two idiots. Things were beginning to spiral out of control.

"If you don't shut that dog up, I'll shut it up for you," said Idiot number 1.

I called to Diamond, but he kept barking. He answered to my father, not me, and my father wasn't about to call him off. He'd been shot, and he was pissed. He was also something else. Ready.

It was as if he knew what was about to happen next. An asshole with a beer in one hand and a pump-action shotgun in the other was about to make the sort of mistake he'd been building to-ward his entire misbegotten life.

The second that can of beer dropped from his hand, I knew it, too.

His gun was raised. He was aiming at Diamond.

CHAPTER 47

MY FATHER immediately sat up, lunging for the old-school Winchester 101 lying by his side. He pulled it toward him so fast it could've been on a string. Every muscle in his neck went taut. His voiced dropped, and the terms couldn't have been clearer.

"You shoot that dog, and I shoot you," he announced. Just like that, neither idiot was laughing anymore.

But they weren't backing down, either.

"You ain't gonna shoot me," said Idiot number 1. "Not a chance."

My father whistled. "Down, Diamond!" he said.

Diamond immediately stopped barking, backing off. Now there was no reason for anyone to shoot anyone. Simple as that.

If only.

"I don't fuckin' like nobody pointing a gun at me, old man," said Idiot number 1.

The second he pivoted, his double-barrel lined right up with my father's chest, was the second I was doing the math. Two of us, two of them. Except my gun was ten yards away from me. As dumb as these two guys were, they still knew that two is greater than one.

"Easy there," said Idiot number 2, raising his gun as I glanced over at mine. Somewhere in between he tossed his beer to free up his trigger finger.

All I could do was stare at my father. *Now what?*

In return, all he could do was stare back at me. *And laugh?*

His was louder than that of either of the two idiots. Hell, it was louder than the two of them put together. A real deep, guttural laugh that echoed throughout the entire woods.

Josiah Maxwell Reinhart had gone batshit crazy.

Or so it seemed to the two idiots now looking at one another. Make that three idiots, because I couldn't figure out what the hell my father was doing...until he finally stopped and asked me a question.

"So you're telling me she knows, huh?"

I blinked. *"What?"*

"The detective back in New York," said my father. "Are you sure she knows?"

Seriously? You're bringing that up now?

Yes, it was exactly what he was doing, as sure as

he'd incited Diamond to start barking in the first place. He never intended to defuse the situation. Instead he was expediting it.

"Yes," I said. "I'm sure she knows."

"In that case, why don't you let these guys know, too?" he said. "For the both of us."

CHAPTER 48

I STOOD up from my father's side, my palms raised. "Guys," I began, "I don't how this got out of hand so quickly. On behalf of my dad here, I apologize. He's been shot. It was clearly an accident, but you can understand his being a little bent out of shape. There's no need to make a bad situation worse, though."

I turned to my father, motioning for him to hand over his gun.

"Hell, no," he said.

"C'mon, Dad. Enough is enough. Clean out those barrels and hand me the gun."

My father's tortured expression made it clear that surrendering his gun was the very last thing in the world he wanted to do. Finally, though, he nodded and cycled out the rounds, one shell after another. For good measure, he let me know exactly how he felt about having to do it.

"You pussy," he said.

And just like that, both idiots were laughing again. *Perfect.*

I took my father's Winchester, its walnut stock etched with an American eagle, and held it out in front of me as if it were on a platter. Walking toward the two, I watched as their arms went slack. They could still do the math, and it was even more in their favor. Instead of two against one it was two against none. My father and I were unarmed.

They were standing around six feet apart, and the closer I got to them the bigger they looked. Of course, the bigger they are . . .

"*Fallaces sunt rerum species,*" I said, breaking out the Latin. The appearances of things are deceptive.

"What?" they both asked in unison. They had no idea what I was saying.

They had no idea, period.

Faster than a New York minute, I closed my fist around both barrels of the Winchester, whipping my hips around with my arm straight and locked for maximum torque. Exactly as I'd been trained.

The weight of the stock, solid black walnut, did all the work from there as it traveled head-high toward Idiot number 2. Ear-high, to be exact. If you really want to incapacitate a guy, don't hit him in the face. Hit him in the ear—right smack against the auditory meatus, otherwise known as the ear canal. He won't just feel the pain as he crashes to the ground, he'll also hear it for the rest of his life.

One down, one to go.

My back was turned to Idiot number 1. I could feel the breeze of him coming at me, though. He was armed, but self-preservation is a primal instinct and tends to negate everything except the purest form of combat. Simply put, he wanted to kill me with his bare hands.

Instead what he got was Newton's second law of motion, courtesy of my spinning back around with the butt of the Winchester leading the way. I lodged it into his massive gut, knocking the wind clear out of him. His knees buckled but didn't give as he loaded up to swing at me with everything he had. The one thing he didn't have, though, was balance.

Grabbing the straps of his overalls, I dropped and barrel-rolled him over my head, slamming him hard to the ground using all his momentum. To make sure he stayed there, I swung my forearm down on his Adam's apple, a maneuver that, when done properly, can make a guy wish he'd been hit in the ear instead.

Two down, none to go. Done and dusted. All within six seconds.

"You've lost a step," said my father.

"You wish," I said.

He smiled and pulled out Diamond's long leash from his vest, cutting it into two strands with his hunting knife and tossing them to me.

As I tied up the idiots I glanced over at my father as he was reaching into one of the other pockets on his vest.

"You're kidding me," I said the second I saw what he was taking out. So much for the no-cell-phone rule. "All these years?"

"Just in case," he said.

He called the police, giving them our coordinates, courtesy of Google Maps. He then reached back into the same pocket after announcing that dinner might be a while, if we were going to have any at all. "Here," he said, tossing his other contraband to me.

It was the best Milky Way bar I'd ever had.

BOOK THREE

DEALER'S CHOICE

CHAPTER 49

"MAY I have a volunteer?" I asked, kicking off the class from behind my lectern.

I held back a smile as I watched a grand total of zero students raise their hands. I might as well have asked if someone were willing to strip naked and dance a polka in front of everybody.

Finally a hand went up in the last row. "Thank you," I said to the young man wearing a Yale hoodie. "Now, as they say on *The Price Is Right*...come on down!"

The young man sidestepped out of the row, then made his way down to me. Since it was only the second class of the semester, I explained that I hadn't committed everyone's names and faces to memory yet.

"It's Edward," he said. He awkwardly put out his hand to shake mine, which got a laugh from the entire class. That made my segue all the better.

"Edward, I have a simple proposition for you,"

I said. "I'll give you an A for this course if within the next five seconds you punch me as hard as you can in my stomach."

The class laughed again. They thought I was joking. Right up until I turned to Edward and spread my arms wide as if to say, *Take your best shot*.

Of course he did no such thing. As I began counting, "One one thousand, two one thousand..." Edward looked to be suffering from an acute case of rigor mortis. He froze. The question quickly switched from whether he would actually punch me to whether he was actually still breathing.

"Relax," I told Edward after reaching the count of five. I turned to the class. "Quick, someone give me a reason why he didn't do it."

Almost every hand shot up now. I pointed at students around the room as though I were giving a press conference on speed.

"He didn't believe you," said one.

"He was afraid he'd get suspended," said another.

"He's a pacifist," said a third.

"Good. Very good," I said. "Now, what if the proposition were different? What if I told Edward that I would *fail him* if he didn't punch me? Would that change anything?"

A collective "Nooooo" echoed throughout the

class. I resumed my pointing at students for reasons why.

"He wouldn't believe that, either," said one.

"He'd be afraid *you'd* get suspended," said another.

"Okay, fair enough," I said. "But what if I change the proposition yet again? This time, I hand Edward a suitcase filled with a million dollars in cash. He gets to keep it if he hits me. What's more, I have the president of the university on hand to tell him that there will be no risk of any disciplinary action from the school. What does Edward do now?"

"Swing away!" someone yelled.

"If he doesn't, I will," joked another.

"Exactly," I said. "So what does this tell us about human behavior? *It's context-driven.* Meaning that changing the circumstances will often change the resulting behavior. Thou shalt not kill, right? Unless of course it's in self-defense or during a war or, more controversially, an act of capital punishment. Put another way, we can be motivated to do almost anything depending on the circumstances. Normal behavior, therefore, is when we collectively believe that the circumstances justify the behavior. Likewise, abnormal behavior is when we don't. But how much does behavior actually tell us about the circumstances? *Can we ever really judge behavior simply by the behavior itself?*"

With that I promptly turned to face young Edward again in his Yale hoodie.

I then punched him in the stomach as hard as I could.

"Welcome to permission theory, class."

CHAPTER 50

"HOW MUCH did they all freak out?" asked Tracy, pouring two glasses of our go-to red, an Artesa Cabernet. Hands down, it was our favorite vineyard during our trip to Napa years ago.

We were hanging out in the kitchen after I got back from New Haven. I'd already changed into the home uniform: jeans, bare feet, and my Stones T-shirt.

"On a scale of one to ten, it was a solid eight and a half," I said. "The collective gasps were louder than last year, although not quite as loud as the year before. That class was like *Spinal Tap;* it went to eleven."

"What about the kid?" asked Tracy. "Was he believable?"

"Best one yet," I said before raising my glass. "Cheers once again to the Yale School of Drama."

Every year the dean sends over one of his most promising male students, and every year the kid doubles over after I hit him. But he's really just taking a bow. Always smiling, he pops right up and lifts the bottom of his hoodie to reveal a body protector, the kind boxers wear when sparring.

Can we ever really judge behavior by the behavior itself?

Lesson learned. Most often, we can't.

"You know what I love the most?" said Tracy. "You always swear the class to secrecy afterward so they don't spoil it for future classes, and they always keep their promise."

"That's one of those counterintuitive things about human nature," I said. "One person with a secret is more likely to reveal it than a whole group."

"Did Freud say that?"

"No. Reinhart did."

Tracy shook his head. "Never heard of him."

"Yeah. Me, either," I said, reaching for our stack of take-out menus. "So what are we in the mood for? Pizza? Chinese? Sushi?"

I should've known better. Tracy certainly did. He pulled out the drawer next to the dishwasher, grabbing the birthday gift he gave me after we first moved in together. Dinner a-go-go, he called it.

From day one, we could never decide what we wanted for takeout, so Tracy took the spinner from an old Twister game he found at a flea market and wrote the names of all our favorite restaurants in the colored circles ringing the dial.

Best. Gift. Ever.

"Chinese it is," I said after the spinner settled on "Han Dynasty."

I was about to phone in our usual order (mu shu pork, chicken with broccoli, and two spring rolls) when Tracy pointed over my shoulder. "Hey, turn it up," he said. "Have you been following this?"

Our small TV in the kitchen was on, the sound muted. I grabbed the remote next to me and hit the volume.

"What is it?" I asked.

Once again, I should've known better.

"This serial-killer story really exploded while you were in Maine with your dad," said Tracy. "It's crazy, right?"

At least I'm pretty sure that's what he said. All I could really hear was the voice of my conscience. *You still haven't told him yet?*

I stared at the TV, watching the five o'clock local news. On one side of the split screen was the anchor talking about "a series of murders linked to playing cards and all linked presumably to one killer. They're calling him the Dealer."

On the other side of the screen was a wide shot of the pressroom at City Hall. The podium was empty, but every single seat in front of it was taken, as was every inch of wall space along the sides. It was standing room only, and even through the TV you could almost smell the blood in the water.

"Mayor Deacon's press conference is scheduled to start any moment now," continued the anchor. "According to reports, one of the main questions will be: When did the mayor first know about this serial killer now terrorizing the city?"

Right on cue Deacon appeared from stage right, squaring up behind the podium. At least he had the courtesy not to be late to his own funeral.

Of course, as much as that was the vibe, the truth—Deacon's version of it, at least—was going to be different. It was sure to be convincing, too. Deacon was, after all, a gifted politician. He never went anywhere near a microphone without knowing exactly what he wanted to say.

Better yet, without knowing who was going to let him say it.

"A hundred dollars he calls on Allen Grimes for the first question," I said.

Before Tracy could even respond, Deacon parted the sea of shouting voices among the press corps, his index finger landing directly on Grimes. "Yes, Allen, go ahead," he said.

Tracy turned to me, stunned. "How the hell did you know that?"

"Funny you should ask," I said.

CHAPTER 51

COLTON LANGE, ace closer for the New York Yankees, hated being a celebrity, especially when he was home in Manhattan, where he was raised. The relentless attention, life under a microscope...it sucked.

He even hated the supposed perks—people always buying him drinks and picking up his tab in bars and restaurants. *Bullshit.* Nothing was ever free.

Damn right he was complaining. Why the hell did people think they could stop him on the street simply because they rooted for him on the mound? The endless picture and autograph requests...the unsolicited critiques whenever the team lost a few games in a row...he had to put up with all of it. And he hated it.

But there was one thing Colton Lange hated even more about getting recognized all the time.

It made it almost impossible for him to buy his heroin.

"Wait here; I'll be back in five minutes," he told the Uber driver, a kid in his twenties who was gripping the steering wheel of his Prius so tightly that Lange, even through his dark sunglasses, could see the whites of the kid's knuckles.

"I don't know, man," said the kid. He was wearing a lumberjack-plaid shirt and a knitted hat, the de rigueur outfit of a Brooklyn hipster. He was also nervous as hell.

This wasn't Brooklyn. It was Harlem. At two in the morning.

"You don't know *what?*" asked Lange from the backseat, the edge in his voice confirming that he knew exactly what the kid meant. Moreover, he couldn't give a rat's ass.

"This neighborhood," said the kid, craning his neck. "I'm just saying."

Lange smiled underneath the fake mustache he sported when making his late-night junk runs. The mustache was added to the disguise back in the pre-Uber days, when cabbies still managed to recognize him despite the sunglasses and the do-rag he wore over his blond hair. Post-mustache, his record was perfect at remaining unrecognizable. Lange truly was incognito.

This kid, on the other hand, was as obvious as they come. Like so many of the other drivers before him, he'd never actually set foot in the 'hood. Of course that's why Lange always listed a "safer" destination when ordering the ride, only to announce the change of plans when the car arrived.

"C'mon, don't be a racist," Lange would then say when the driver hesitated. They *always* hesitated.

The racist line, though, worked every time. As did the thing Lange did with the hundred-dollar bill to make the driver wait for him. He'd seen it in a movie.

"Here," he said to the kid, ripping the bill in two and offering him half. "You get the other half when I return."

The drivers might have been young, idealistic liberals, but they were also money-loving capitalists. God bless America.

"Okay," said the kid, eyeing half of Ben Franklin's face in his hand. "But make it quick."

Lange guaranteed him he would. After all, he had this routine down cold.

It wasn't always the same dealer, but it was the same alley behind the same Chinese restaurant, which was lit by nothing more than the light from whichever rundown apartment overhead had a lamp on. Most of the time, there'd be a couple of dealers hanging out behind a rusted Dumpster. Other times there'd be only one. Tonight was one of those other times.

"Hey," said Lange, approaching the guy. He was barely more than a silhouette.

The guy said nothing. They always said nothing.

Lange asked for a "pillow," which was slang for a bundle of ten glassine bags, each one containing a hundred milligrams of heroin. Usually Lange would buy less, if only to stave off the temptation of doing more than he could function on—i.e., so much that he could no longer throw his ninety-eight-miles-per-hour fastball or his devastating 12–6 curve—but the team had an extended West Coast road trip coming up, and he had to make sure he was covered.

Again, the guy behind the Dumpster said nothing.

That wasn't the problem, though. It was that he also *did* nothing. No reaching into his pocket, no holding up one finger to confirm the price, which Lange was putting at a hundred dollars. Cheap as that was, he'd still be overpaying. Not that he and his eighty-million-dollar contract really cared.

"Problem?" asked Lange.

"As a matter of fact . . ." said the Dealer.

CHAPTER 52

LANGE STOOD perfectly still in the darkness, unsure of his next move. How big of a problem could it be? Maybe it wasn't one at all. Maybe this guy was just messin' with him.

"Do you know who I am?" asked the Dealer.

Lange didn't. The only thing he knew was that he'd never scored from him in the past. The other dealers were always younger, more like the kid's age back in the Prius. This voice was older.

Lange squinted to get a better look at him, something more than the silhouette. Best he could see were the whites of his eyes, not a single other feature on his face. The reason why became clear as Lange leaned in a bit. The guy was wearing a ski mask.

"There's been a mistake," said Lange.

"No," said the Dealer. "No mistake. This is fate."

"Who are you?"

"I'm a closer, too."

Tingle was too delicate a word to describe the feeling that shot up Lange's spine. *Shock,* though, was too strong. *I'm a closer, too?* In Lange's world, that line was a purpose pitch. A brushback. Something to get the legs jumpy and the mind racing. A reason to be scared.

But fear was always what the other guy felt, not Lange. He was the badass, the unflappable one. Standing sixty feet and six inches away from home plate, he still got right up in your face with his famous death stare while notching another save.

Only Lange still couldn't see shit.

It occurred to him, however. Forget about disguises: if he couldn't see this guy, then this guy couldn't see him.

Yet he said *closer,* didn't he? No way that was a coincidence.

"How do you know who I am?" asked Lange.

"It's so much worse than that," said the Dealer. "I also know what you've done. The real story. Not what you made everyone else believe. This moment? You and me? This has been a long time coming."

The urge to run overtook Lange in a heartbeat, but faster still was the Dealer's hand. He jabbed the stun gun under Lange's nose, the jolt dropping the baseball player to his knees. It was a nifty bit of foreshadowing.

Stun guns and real estate share the same mantra:

location, location, location. Aim for the nostrils, with all those nerve endings, and a stun gun does more than merely stun.

Lange yelled out in agony, grabbing his face, the pain unlike anything he'd ever felt. He couldn't fight back. He was helpless.

The Dealer was only getting started.

His hands still covering his face, Lange couldn't see the bucket rising over him. He heard it, though. The liquid sloshing about.

Then he felt it—cold at first, as it drenched his entire body. Then some of it seeped past his fingers and into his eyes, which immediately began to burn like hell. Some of it got into his mouth, too, but by then he already knew what it was. The smell was unmistakable.

The Dealer lit a match and tossed it, the gasoline igniting Lange into a giant flame. He then grabbed a milk crate, turning it upside down on the ground to make a chair for himself so he could watch as well as listen.

Human skin hisses like a rattlesnake when it burns.

CHAPTER 53

IT'S NOT easy getting a cab to take you to Harlem at four in the morning. The first guy I flagged told me he was at the end of his shift and Harlem was too far away. The second guy didn't even bother to lie. He lowered his window, asked me where I was going, and simply shook his head no before driving off.

I'd seen enough.

I walked two blocks to the place where I garaged my motorcycle, handing a five-spot to the late-night attendant—a new guy—who pulled it around for me from a couple of levels down. He swung his leg off the bike and gazed at all the original Triumph parts, restored to perfection. He wasn't the first to say it, and he wouldn't be the last.

"Man, I should be tipping you," he said.

Around three blocks away from the address Elizabeth had texted me, there was no longer a need to check the street signs. The slew of cop cars with their cherries flashing was tantamount to a giant neon sign. DEAD GUY HERE.

"You a Yankees fan?" asked Elizabeth, breaking away from a fellow detective once she saw me.

"Mets, actually," I said. "I don't follow minor league teams."

I could tell that joke in my sleep and practically was. Serial killers are murder on the circadian rhythms.

Of course Elizabeth wasn't making idle ESPN chitchat. Nor was there going to be anything amusing about what I was about to see. That much I knew, no matter how tired I was.

"He had one of those fancy aluminum wallets, like a cigarette case. Otherwise we'd be waiting on dental records," she said as she led me around a corner, under some police tape, and down an alley that put all other alleys to shame on the fear-for-your-life scale. Were it not for all the cops around, I'd sooner be walking the streets in Kabul.

We reached the end of the alley, the portable floodlights creating an almost surreal mix of glare and shadows. I'd taken just enough chemistry back in high school to know that that wasn't smoke still rising off the victim. That was the heat of his charred corpse mixing with the chill of a September night. Good old-fashioned steam.

I stared at the remains only because I had to. It's why I was there.

You want me to see them all, don't you? You want me to see what you're capable of, the power you have. You want me to see that yes, you're holding all the cards...

I turned to Elizabeth. "You mentioned the Yankees?"

"Driver's license from the aluminum wallet," she said. "It's Colton Lange."

Lange was the best Yankees closer since Mariano Rivera. Homegrown, too. Came up through the organization. He had somewhat of a bad-boy reputation after a few scrapes with the law, barroom fights and such. As long as the radar gun kept lighting up in the high nineties, though, no one in the city seemed to care.

I'm a Mets fan, so it's not like I knew all his stats. Or even his jersey number. But I did now.

"The nine of diamonds," I said.

Elizabeth nodded. "Nine's the only number he's ever worn."

There were a ton of questions that needed answers, not the least of which was what the hell Colton Lange was doing in an alley in Harlem in the middle of the night. Although there was some low-hanging fruit in terms of guesses.

But my head was elsewhere. It was as if I could feel the suction between my ears, the Dealer pulling me deeper into his game. It was like an undertow. A riptide.

Who's next?

"Do you have it?" I asked.

It sure as hell wasn't on Lange, not anymore. Was it ever? Did he actually wait and watch him burn—wait until the flames died out—before placing his next card?

"He pinned it to Lange's chest with one of those fancy cocktail toothpicks," said Elizabeth. "You know, the kind that look like little swords."

"Yeah, I've seen them," I said. What I didn't know was why I hadn't seen the card yet. *Why aren't you showing it to me?*

"This one's a little more problematic," she said.

Elizabeth told me which card it was.

I immediately knew what she meant.

CHAPTER 54

LINGERING NEAR a dead body was one thing. Loitering was another.

After eyeballing the area around Lange's body to make sure the Dealer hadn't left anything else behind besides his calling card, I told Elizabeth I'd meet her back out on the street.

"Good idea," she said.

It was a simple reply, but the subtext spoke volumes. She still had some work to do, only it wasn't anything that would be showing up in the police report. In fact, that was the point. The "good idea" was that I not be a part of it.

Instead I had my own job to do. One thing. *Think.*

Almost all serial killers choose their victims in one of two ways: randomly or very, very carefully. The reason boils down to a single word: motive. When the victims are unrelated—when there's no real link between them beyond, say, physical characteristics such as sex and age—the motive tends to be about the act itself. *Killing.*

But when there's a link, something seeded deeper among the victims, the motive goes beyond the act of killing and becomes about the result. *Death.* In some way, shape, or form, the victims are being judged.

Or so I wrote in my book. The same book the Dealer surely read before mailing it off to—

"Well, if it isn't Dr. Death," came a voice over my shoulder.

I'd been leaning against my bike, as good a place as any to block out the world and get lost in my thoughts. But there was no mistaking Allen Grimes. His voice matched his persona, loud and obtrusive.

"*Dr. Death?* How much do I have to pay to make sure that nickname doesn't show up in one of your columns?" I said.

"I'll get back to you with a figure," answered Grimes, not missing a beat. "It's true, though. Anytime there's a dead body these days, there you are."

"And here you are," I said. "I could say the same thing."

"Yeah, except I actually get paid to be here. It's my job," he said. "This is my business."

"Business has certainly been good for you lately, huh? A serial killer with a clever hook, tailor-made for the papers, and of all reporters he reaches out to you with a special package in the mail," I said. "If you ask me, you couldn't have it any better *if you had planned it all yourself.*"

Grimes stared hard into my eyes.

A horde of cops and EMTs were shuffling about, and half the neighborhood had gathered along the perimeter trying to see what they could see. But all Grimes could see was me.

There's a moment in human behavior, a few telling seconds, when a person is trying to figure out if you're being serious with him or not. In Grimes's case, it made him look constipated.

"You fuckin' with me, Doc?" he asked finally.

I smiled. "I don't know. Am I?"

CHAPTER 55

"YEAH, YOU'RE fuckin' with me," decided Grimes, nodding his head.

I could tell he still wasn't sure, but that same persona of his wasn't about to let indecision get in his way. Besides, he had that job of his to do.

"Do you know that I never work at home?" he said, lighting up a cigarette. "Not once have I ever written a column from the comfort of my own couch. Do you know why?"

"I will as soon as you tell me," I said.

"It's because comfort and crime don't mix, that's why. To write about crime, to really understand it, you need to be out here breathing it," he said. "Do you know what I mean?"

"Behold the turtle. He makes progress only when he sticks his neck out," I said. "James Bryant Conant."

"Who?"

"Never mind."

"Fine," he said. "Only now tell me what I really want to know."

I stifled a yawn and played dumb. I knew exactly what he wanted. "Tell you what?" I asked.

"C'mon," he said, making quick work of his cigarette. "I know you know, and soon enough I'll know, too. The new card, the next victim…help me speed things along."

"You're going to have to get that from Elizabeth," I said. "Although I don't know if she'll—"

"Yeah, yeah, yeah…I know, she's pissed," he said. "I couldn't sit on the story any longer; you know that."

"Maybe she's forgiven you," I said.

"Fat chance. That girl's like G.I. Joe with the kung-fu grip when it comes to grudges," he said. "That's why I'm asking you. I did try to give you the heads-up about her and the mayor, remember?"

"Yeah, I remember," I said.

"So you'll tell me?"

"Nope."

Grimes sighed. Swing and a miss. "At least give me this," he said. "Was Lange up here buying drugs? He had to be, right?"

"Are you asking because you're guessing or because you've heard rumors about the guy?"

"Both," he said. "But I don't write sports. I did once arrange an interview with him, though. He'd

been busted for going Sean Penn on some pa-
parazzo, so suddenly he was in my wheelhouse. I
told his agent that it was Lange's chance to tell his
side of the story."

"And did he?"

"He was supposed to. We agreed to meet at the
King Cole Bar, and I stared at that damn Maxfield
Parrish mural for more than an hour waiting for
him. Then he calls me and says he changed his
mind."

"You must have been pissed," I said.

"What can I tell you? The guy was a real
prick...and now he's dead. Maybe he had it coming," he said.

I stared at Grimes for a split second, roughly the
same amount of time it takes for a few synapses to
fire. *Eureka.*

"Wait—where the hell are you going?" he asked.

Before he could light another cigarette I'd already grabbed my helmet, strapping it on.

"Tell Elizabeth I had to go home," I said.

I should've been dead tired as I rode off into the
sunrise. Instead I was wide awake, stoked.

A killer idea will do that to you.

CHAPTER 56

ELIZABETH MARCHED straight past me when I opened the door, never mind that it was her first time in my apartment. She had her case file in one hand, a bag from Dunkin' Donuts in the other, and an immediate question for me. Actually, two questions.

"Glazed chocolate or vanilla frosted?" she asked first, holding up the bag.

"Glazed chocolate," I said. A no-brainer.

She handed me my doughnut and hit me with the second question, her real one. "Why'd you take off on me last night?" she asked.

Last night was only five hours earlier, but who was counting?

At least she looked as if she'd gotten a few hours of sleep. I looked exactly like the number of hours I'd gotten. Zero.

"I was in a hurry to make sure," I said.

"Make sure of what?"

"Assholes."

"Excuse me?"

"All the victims," I said. "They're all assholes."

Elizabeth took a bite of her vanilla frosted. "So are half the people in this city," she reminded me.

"I know, but this isn't a coincidence."

"Even if it isn't, what are you suggesting? The Dealer personally knows all his victims?"

"It was a possibility at first," I said. "Now it's highly unlikely."

"How do you know?" she asked.

"Step into my office," I said.

I led her across the living room toward the extra bedroom that Tracy and I had converted into an office. We shared it, complete with two desks.

"Nice place," she said, looking around as we walked. "Where's your better half?"

"It's weird for you to say 'husband,' isn't it?"

"Hold on a minute...*you're gay?*"

"Very funny," I said. "Tracy's at the gym."

Simultaneously we glanced down at our half-eaten doughnuts. *The gym?* All we could do was chuckle.

"How's he handling all this, by the way? I mean, you told him, right?"

"Not at first," I said. "I think that's why he was a little mad. Then he immediately called our life insurance company and tripled the policy on me."

"Smart guy," she said. "Seriously, is he okay with your helping with the investigation?"

"He understands, given that my book's involved, but we're talking about a serial killer, so obviously he's a little concerned for me. Maybe even very concerned."

We reached the office, Elizabeth stopping dead in her tracks. Her jaw dropped. "That makes two of us," she said.

CHAPTER 57

FUELED BY a couple of twenty-ounce Red Bulls and an overzealousness that academics politely call intellectual curiosity, I had basically turned the office into one big bulletin board, every inch of all four walls covered with everything I could possibly find online about all the victims. This was the drill-down stuff, the things that wouldn't necessarily show up in their case files, all of which I'd read multiple times without seeing any connection. I'd been googling for hours on end, nonstop, and the result was one big giant collage of papers, each one taped to any flat surface there was, windows included. The Internet and a printer can be a dangerous thing.

"Okay, so maybe I got a little carried away," I said.

Elizabeth shot me her deadpan look. "No— Carrie on *Homeland* got a little carried away," she said. "This is..."

Her voice trailed off. She didn't quite know what this is.

"Thorough?" I offered.

That was one word for it. But there was a method to my madness, and it went by a different word.

"Wait: this is your Bayesian thing, isn't it?" asked Elizabeth.

I overlooked the way she pronounced *Bayesian,* as if it were something you needed to get vaccinated against. The point was she'd clearly done some googling herself. Bayesian inference: a modeling approach that updates the probability of an event or a hypothesis based on ongoing evidence and observations.

"Very impressive," I said.

"Yeah. Just don't quiz me on it."

What I gave her instead was more of a review session of what I had so far, walking her around the room as we finished our doughnuts.

It was a lot to chew on.

All the victims had a raised profile; they were "known" to a certain extent. Colton Lange was the only household name, but Jared Louden was certainly famous in the world of finance. As for the kid, Bryce VonMiller, he had more boldface mentions on Page Six in the *Post* than Lange and Louden combined. That's what being the bad-boy son of a renowned restaurateur and dating a constant stream of models and budding actresses will get you.

Even those two of hearts—cheating hearts, as they were—had some notoriety. Both were star editors at Knopf, the publishing house, working with some of the most highbrow authors.

"They acted like it, too," I said. "In every article and profile written about them they came across as arrogant, stuck-up snobs. That's when I was sure about there being a connection between all the victims."

"But you're not saying—"

"No. This isn't vigilante justice against jerks. Here's what I *am* saying. We start with two theories. The first is that the Dealer is killing indiscriminately. The second is that he's choosing his victims specifically and with good reason, at least in his own mind. Then we update the probability of both theories with everything we've learned since that package arrived on Grimes's desk— names, sexes, ages of the victims, locations of the murders, occupations...all the things you'd typically see in a police report."

"In other words, everything about the victims on the surface makes the killings look random," she said. "Except for the ways in which he kills them, of course. Each one had to be planned well in advance."

"Right. Only he still wants us to think the

victims are chosen at random," I said. "So what does he do?"

"*The cards,*" said Elizabeth. "He uses them as if they're dictating the action, leading the way on who he decides to kill. Almost like it's the hand he's been dealt."

"And the more creative he gets—the nine of diamonds, for instance—the less it looks as if there's any real motive tying it all together."

"Okay, so what's the motive?"

"We don't know yet," I said. "But he hasn't killed a nun or a child or someone who's been named teacher of the year. That's not by accident."

"Maybe not. It doesn't get us any closer to catching him, though, does it?"

"Actually, it does," I said. "That's the problem."

"I don't follow," said Elizabeth.

"You're not supposed to," I said. "Not you, not Grimes, not anyone but me. I'm the one he chose. Everything I've been able to figure out so far is because he wanted me to."

"Is that really a problem?" she asked. "You said so yourself. There are two types of serial killers. Those who want to get caught, and those who *really* want to get caught."

"Yeah, but do you know where I first said that?"

She nodded. *Now* she was following. "Your book."

"That's right," I said. "He's playing us. Not only

that, he's probably got an endgame. Which means there might be one thing worse than not catching this guy."

"What would that be?"

"Catching him."

CHAPTER 58

I DON'T know if Sun Tzu said it first, but it was Michael Corleone who definitely said it best. *Keep your friends close, but your enemies closer.*

As for who said it the loudest, my vote was for Mayor Deacon. When I walked into his penthouse suite at the Excelsior Hotel on the Upper West Side, he didn't have to say it at all.

It was that obvious.

Not that Deacon viewed me as his outright enemy. It's that I clearly wasn't his friend, especially after I walked out on him in his office at City Hall. I was now somewhere in between; a guy who could help him but also hurt him. A wild card.

Did you really go digging around in my past, Mr. Mayor? Yes, of course you did.

All the more reason why he wanted me in the room.

"Thanks for doing this on a Saturday," Deacon said to me without the slightest hint of irony. Only half an hour earlier, with Elizabeth still at my apartment, he screamed into her phone that he needed to see the two of us immediately. *And don't you dare take no for an answer from that son of a bitch Reinhart,* he added.

I was standing ten feet away from Elizabeth when he called, and I could still hear him perfectly.

What we were doing on a Saturday—the "this"—could best be described as an emergency campaign strategy session. It was pure bunker mentality, albeit in five thousand square feet of luxury with a full kitchen, a media and conference room, and sweeping views of Central Park.

Since Grimes broke the story on the Dealer, Deacon's poll numbers were down three points. His challenger, Tim Stoddart, the former DA, was now within the margin of error. In every one of Stoddart's campaign stops he was talking about the Dealer and how his killings were emblematic of Deacon's failure to curb crime.

As we sat down in the sunken living room of the penthouse suite, the focus was on one thing and one thing only. Containment.

The Dealer's latest card had added a wrinkle, to put it mildly. All bets were off.

"Who else knows?" Deacon asked Elizabeth, who was sitting to my right on the L-shaped couch, where Beau Livingston was also sitting.

The mayor's chief of staff was Deacon's proverbial Siamese twin.

Of course the mayor wasn't really asking Elizabeth to name all the people who knew about the card that was pinned to Colton Lange. What he really wanted to know was: Who were the ones, if any, he couldn't keep quiet?

"Mr. Mayor, are you sure this is the best strategy?" asked Elizabeth.

Deacon didn't mind the question so much, barely raising one of his thick eyebrows, but Livingston immediately became unhinged. Strategy was his thing, not hers, and he'd be damned if he was going to let her challenge him on it.

"Do you know what I'm sure of, Elizabeth?" said Livingston, cutting in with all the subtlety of a chain saw. "I'm sure that the blacks in this city hate that we brought back zero tolerance and challenged the court's ruling on stop-and-frisk. I'm also sure they think this administration has been silent on racial profiling. But what I'm *really* sure of is that there's only one thing worse than a serial killer terrorizing this city on the mayor's watch. And that's a racist serial killer."

"Who's being a racist?" asked Elizabeth. "The nine of diamonds was a baseball player. For all we know, the jack of spades could be a farmer."

"Yeah, because that's what this city's known for, *farmers,*" scoffed Livingston. "Wake up, Detective.

'A spade' doesn't mean 'a gardening tool' in Harlem any more than 'a hoe' does."

"I'm afraid Beau's right," said the mayor. "Besides, who's to say we can't change the game on this cocksucker?"

That was the strategy. There was no hiding the fact that Colton Lange was the nine of diamonds. People were bound to figure that out. The question was whether those same people really needed to know that the next victim was the jack of spades. The police could simply go public with another card or no card at all.

In other words, take the deck right out of the Dealer's hands.

"There's just one problem, gentlemen," I said.

The words had barely left my mouth when everything but the fire alarm went off in the room. Two of the mayor's aides were hightailing it into the suite as both Livingston's and Elizabeth's phones lit up. He was getting a text; she was getting a call.

And I was getting ready to hear the news.

He's killed again.

CHAPTER 59

WE WERE heading back to Harlem. Fast.

The "we" was everybody. Me, Elizabeth, the mayor, his entire detail, and key staff members, including Livingston. It was a speeding caravan of black Ford Explorers and sedans, lights flashing, as the traffic moving north along Madison Avenue parted like the Red Sea.

"Crazy, right?" said Elizabeth from behind the wheel. She and I were bringing up the rear, the whole spectacle playing out in front of us.

"That's one word for it," I said. "Leave it to Livingston to turn dead bodies into a photo op for his boss."

As crass and calculated as it was, I knew what the guy was thinking. The Dealer had changed things up with this one. Broad daylight, out in the open—and an open invitation to the entire neighborhood, as well as the media, to come have a look. If they all were going to be there, the mayor needed to be there, too.

Boy, were they ever all there.

The intersection of Madison Avenue and 112th Street, in East Harlem, looked like a block party, albeit one that was being covered by every single news outlet in the city. Satellite trucks lined one curb, police cruisers another. A few ambulances were scattered in between. And everywhere you looked, people. Lots and lots of people.

Murder really knows how to make a place come alive.

"C'mon, let's go," said Elizabeth. She'd parked and bolted from the car so fast that I wasn't sure she'd even turned off the engine.

I fell in line behind her as we wove through the crowd, catching up to Deacon and Livingston, who were being greeted by the top cop himself, the police commissioner.

I couldn't remember his name, but I knew his face from TV, along with that "shoot 'em" thing he did during press conferences. When calling on reporters, the commissioner wouldn't simply point at them. Instead he made a gun gesture with his thumb and forefinger, then flicked his thumb as if pulling the trigger. It was like he was acting out some revenge fantasy on the media.

Now here he was, live and in person.

"Who are you?" he immediately asked me.

Livingston did the honors. "Hank, this is Dr. Reinhart, the professor who——"

"Yeah, the book. Lucky you," he said, shaking my hand. "Hank Saxon."

Shoot-'em-Up Hank quickly briefed the mayor and the rest of us on what was known. There were four dead, all members of the same gang and all shot multiple times while walking along 112th Street.

"Where's the card?" asked the mayor.

The commissioner glanced knowingly outside our circle. We were set apart from the crowd, thanks to a few barricades, but you could feel the countless eyes upon us—or, more specifically, on the mayor.

"It's in my pocket," answered Saxon. The subtext being that he wanted to keep it there and not on display.

"Of course," said Deacon, nodding. "Fuck if I need to see it anyway. A joker, huh?"

"Yeah, a joker…jammed into the mouth of one of the victims," said Saxon. "I've already had someone check, too. It's the joker from the same Bicycle deck he's been using—linen stock with a black core layer."

"Was the card bent at all?" I asked.

"Bent?" asked Saxon.

"Folded? Creased? Anything but pristine?" I asked.

"It looks brand new. No prints, either—just like with the other cards," said Saxon. "Ah, screw it...here."

The commissioner reached inside his suit jacket, removing a small evidence bag containing the card. It was exactly as advertised—brand new, from the same kind of deck.

The joker.

CHAPTER 60

IF YOU wander into a pots-and-pans convention somewhere, you'll quickly think the whole world revolves around pots and pans. Point being, people always steer a conversation to the things they care about most.

"Do we have the names of the victims yet?" asked Livingston.

What Beau Livingston cared about most in this world was his boss's reelection. Maybe even more than his boss did.

"Only two of them were carrying ID," said Saxon. "The first was Tyrell Burke."

"Is there a middle name?" asked Livingston.

The commissioner squinted at the question momentarily before glancing at the pad in his hand. "Melvin," he said. "His middle name was Melvin."

Livingston exchanged glances with the mayor. Their minds were easier to read than the first line of an eye chart. *Tyrell Melvin Burke? That's not even close to a Jack.*

"What about the other one?" asked Livingston.

Saxon checked his pad again. "Lawrence Tack," he said. "That came off a credit card he had on him. No middle name yet."

"Tack?" I asked. By then I'd already stolen a peek at Saxon's notepad. A doctor with the yips had better handwriting than he did. "Are you sure that's a *T*?"

Saxon looked again. "My bad...that's a *J*, not a *T*," he said. "The kid's name was Lawrence Jack."

"*Jack?*" repeated Livingston.

"Yeah," said Saxon. "Actually, he's the one who had the card in his mouth."

I looked over at Elizabeth. She knew what I was thinking. No wonder she looked away.

If the police commissioner, the highest official with the NYPD, had actually known that the Dealer had pinned the jack of spades to Colton Lange's burned-to-a-crisp corpse, this would've been his "Aha!" moment. But Saxon said nothing. *He hadn't been told.*

"Hank, you mentioned there were four victims total?" asked Livingston.

"Yes," said Saxon. "We got them out of here to the morgue right before you arrived. Thought it best to be quick, given the crowd."

"Four kids gunned down in broad daylight,"

said the mayor. "How many witnesses were there?"

Saxon again glanced knowingly outside our circle. In what was already a busy intersection, there were now more than a hundred people gathered. "None so far," he said.

Livingston's head snapped back. "How could that—"

Elizabeth cut him off. For all his savvy, the mayor's chief of staff could still manage to be a little too white and a little too Connecticut. "They were gang members," she said. "No one's coming forward."

"They wouldn't be ratting on anyone except a serial killer," said Livingston.

"Would you like me to get you a bullhorn so you can tell them that?" asked Elizabeth.

Everybody and his uncle were here, yet no one was ever going to admit to seeing anything. These were the rules of the street. Keep your mouth shut.

C'mon, people. *Can I get a witness?*

Next thing I knew, he was standing right next to me.

CHAPTER 61

"DID YOU know that Bob Dylan won eleven Grammys and was inducted into the Rock and Roll Hall of Fame in 1988?" he asked.

I playfully rubbed my chin. "Gee, I didn't know that," I said.

"I googled him," he told me. "Dylan's pretty cool."

"Yeah, but Miles Davis is still the coolest," I said. "Right?"

"That's for sure," he said.

"I take it you two know each other?" asked Elizabeth.

I turned back to see everyone—Elizabeth, the mayor, Livingston, and Saxon—all staring at me talking to a kid who was four foot nothing, including his Questlove afro.

Small world.

"Hey, you're the mayor!" said Miles, pointing.

"That's right; I am," said Deacon. "Who might you be?"

Miles stuck out his hand as if remembering what he'd been taught. "I'm Miles Winston," he announced. "It's very nice to meet you, sir."

I watched as Deacon shook Miles's hand with a broad smile. Maybe the mayor was truly charmed by the boy, or maybe it was nothing more than his political instincts kicking in. There were, after all, news cameras and photographers scattered all around us. Not to mention the crowd itself.

Livingston, on the other hand, was neither charmed nor on the ballot in November. "Hey, kid," he said, frowning. "You need to get back behind those barricades, okay?"

Livingston sounded like a complete tool, but it did make me wonder what Miles was doing all by himself. He shouldn't have been alone. The next second, he *knew* he shouldn't have been.

"Miles!" yelled his mother. *"Miles Winston!"*

I turned back to see Ms. Winston squeezing between two barricades, running toward us in a panic. With a quick hand wave, Saxon told one of the cops about to stop her that it was okay.

What followed was what surely happens at shopping malls and playgrounds every day when parents don't see their kids wandering off. Sudden relief tempered by the anger of having been scared to death. Ms. Winston handled it better than I expected, though. There was far more relief than anger.

"Look, Mom," said Miles, pointing again. "It's the mayor!"

Deacon remained all smiles as he pressed the flesh with Ms. Winston. Naturally, he asked if she was a registered voter.

But Livingston was thinking bigger. His smile stretched wider than his boss's. A minute earlier, he'd told Miles to scram. Now he wanted him and his mother to stay right where they were, especially after she mentioned that the two of them lived directly across the street.

"Ms. Winston, the city needs your help," said Livingston, jumping right into it. As soon as he invoked "the city," I knew what was coming next.

Could she possibly "consult" with her neighbors to see if anyone saw the shootings? All it would take was one brave individual to come forward, he explained. Simple as that.

If only.

In the battle between civic duty and self-preservation, my money is always on Darwin.

"I'll see what I can do," said Ms. Winston. She was only being polite, though. All she could really see was her young boy by her side. What she may or may not have owed "the city" paled immensely to what she owed Miles. First and foremost was being there for him.

But the world is a far less complicated place for a six-year-old.

"Are you guys talking about the guy with the gun?" asked Miles. "Because I saw him."

"You did?" asked Livingston.

Miles nodded. "Yeah. I was practicing my trumpet in front of the window in our apartment and—"

Ms. Winston all but slapped her hand over Miles's mouth. "No, he didn't," she said. "He didn't see anything." As fast as she had arrived, she grabbed his small hand and began walking away.

"Wait!" said Livingston. He was about to chase her down when I stepped in front of him, blocking his way. He glared at me. "What the hell do you think you're doing?"

"Being smarter than you," I said.

He tried to push his away around me. "Get out of my way," he said.

That didn't work out so well for him, as I quickly found his right clavicle with my thumb and forefinger, squeezing good and hard. The Chinese call it the rooster pinch because the remaining fingers look like a rooster's comb. I simply call it the way to stop a man cold in his tracks when kicking him in the balls isn't an option.

Either way, I suddenly had Livingston's undivided attention. He knew the only way the pain would stop was if he listened, so he did.

"There's a better way to do this," I said.

CHAPTER 62

"THAT WASN'T exactly on my bucket list," said Tracy, stepping out of the cruiser on the corner of 112th Street. It was his first time riding in a police car.

"Believe me, that won't be the last of your first-time-evers today," I said. "C'mon, let me introduce you to the mayor."

Tracy had tried to convince me over the phone that the subway would've been a faster means for him to get up to Harlem. He might have been right, but it wasn't my decision. Once I convinced Deacon, Livingston, and even Elizabeth that this was the right move, the travel plans were out of my hands. Saxon radioed for the car.

"So you're the woman's attorney?" asked Livingston.

I had introduced Tracy to Deacon and the commissioner in the back of a nearby diner commandeered by the mayor's staff. Elizabeth was next when Livingston rudely jumped the line on her. To know Tracy was to know that that didn't go unnoticed.

"Hi, Elizabeth. I'm Tracy," he said, ignoring Livingston.

Elizabeth shook Tracy's hand, barely suppressing a chuckle. As first impressions go, Tracy had knocked it out of the park. "It's nice to finally meet you," she said.

"As to your question, *Beau,* the answer is no," said Tracy. Leave it to him to already know who Livingston was…and to call him by his first name. "I'm not Ms. Winston's attorney. However, I do provide legal counsel to her through a legal aid center here in Harlem."

"Tomato, tom*ah*to," said Livingston.

"Actually, no," said Tracy. "There's only one way to pronounce attorney-client privilege, and that's not something I currently share with her."

Livingston turned to me, piqued. "Remind me again why you wanted him here, Reinhart?"

"He's here because Ms. Winston trusts him and because he's the only one who might be able to get her little boy to tell us what he saw," I said. "Do I need to explain it to you a third time?"

"No, you don't," said the mayor, shutting down Livingston. He turned to Tracy. "We appreciate your help, Mr. McKay."

"You're welcome," said Tracy. "I just can't promise anything."

"I understand," said Deacon. "Of course that would make you a lousy politician."

"So are we ready?" asked Saxon. He motioned to the front of the diner, the door partially visible behind a waitress taking an order.

"Yeah. Let's get this done," said Deacon.

Immediately Tracy gave me the Look. I hadn't mentioned his one condition to the group, the one thing he required in return for agreeing to do this. I figured we'd cross that bridge when we came to it.

We'd come to it.

"Where's everyone going?" asked Tracy.

Livingston was mastering the art of chiming in at the wrong time. "We're going with you, of course."

Tracy shook his head. "Perhaps Dylan didn't make it clear, but—"

"We can't let you do this on your own," insisted Livingston.

"Yeah—that wouldn't be a good idea," said Deacon.

"Why not?" asked Elizabeth. "In fact, it's probably the best idea. If Ms. Winston trusted any of us we'd already be talking to Miles right now."

"She has a point," said Saxon. "I think we all benefit if Mr. McKay goes at this alone."

Deacon gave the nod, and the commissioner raised his notepad, adjusting his glasses. He'd already made a call and gotten the address.

"That's okay. I already know where they live," said Tracy.

Twenty minutes later, he was back in the diner. As soon as I saw him come through the door I knew something was up.

"Well?" asked Deacon. "How did it go?"

It was as if Tracy didn't hear him. Instead he walked straight toward Saxon, extending his hand as if the two had never met.

"Commissioner Saxon, my name is Tracy McKay, and I've just witnessed a murder."

CHAPTER 63

"ACTUALLY, MAKE that four murders," said Tracy.

The strongest smell in the diner was no longer the burgers on the grill. It was everyone's brain working overtime.

Deacon waved the white flag first. "What the hell are you talking about?"

Tracy didn't flinch. "As you know, Mr. Mayor, I do volunteer work in the vicinity, and I was out for a walk when I saw a black car—the make unknown—pull up to the curb across the street. Someone inside the car then opened fire on the four young men walking on the sidewalk. The last thing I saw was the driver of the car get out and approach one of the victims lying on ground. He put something in his mouth, but I couldn't see exactly what it was."

"Can you describe the driver?" asked Elizabeth.

Deacon, Livingston, and even Saxon did a double take on her. *What the hell is happening here? What are we missing?*

A law degree, for starters. Or just some very quick thinking.

"Good question," I said, joining in with Elizabeth. "Was the driver wearing any particular item of clothing or markings?"

"As a matter of fact he was," said Tracy. "He had a black bandanna tied around his arm, outside of a gray hoodie."

Deacon and Livingston had officially caught up. Saxon, too. "Black bandanna," said the commissioner. "That's the Tombs."

"Let me guess—another new gang name I have to learn," said Deacon sarcastically.

The mayor knew all too well that keeping track of street gangs in the city was like keeping track of restaurant openings.

"The Tombs actually broke off from the Broad Day Shooters," said Saxon. "Apparently they didn't do enough shooting for their liking."

For better or worse, Saxon's job required that he keep track of *every* gang. As well as what it takes to prosecute and convict them. He turned back to Tracy.

"You can't do this, Mr. McKay," he said.

"Do what?" asked Tracy.

"Substitute yourself as a witness for someone

237

else. If this was a gang killing we can protect the boy and his mother," said Saxon.

It was actually fun watching Tracy give the Look to someone other than me. He simply stared at Saxon long enough to make the words redundant. *You can't protect them any better than I just did.*

"For fuck's sake, Hank, what are you going to do? Arrest him?" asked Deacon.

Saxon was resolute. "If this were to ever go to trial—"

"Do you mean if the gang member who shot four members of a rival gang actually lives long enough to make it to trial?" said Deacon. "Is that what you're worried about, Hank?"

There is no gambling like politics, said Benjamin Disraeli.

Deacon dismissed Saxon's concern as fast as he dismissed Saxon himself, his frustration boiling over. Livingston was a mere bystander, too. "So what in God's name just happened?" he asked Elizabeth and me. Mostly me.

"Remember the idea of taking the deck out of the Dealer's hand? Someone beat you to it," I said.

A gang saw an opportunity and grabbed it. Did one of them see or hear about the jack of spades before Lange's body was discovered? Maybe. Better than maybe, even. So he posed as a serial killer to take care of his own business. Members of a gang can live—and die—with the threat of retaliation from the street, but at least they won't have the police to worry about. Or so went their plan. After all, no witness would be foolish enough to come forward. You'd have to be sick in the head.

Or maybe just six years old.

Amazing. Tracy, without the slightest hesitation, was willing to do everything he could to protect Miles.

Your witness, Gateway Adoption Agency. Any more questions about Tracy being a suitable parent?

"One hell of an afternoon," muttered Deacon.

Grim nods followed from Livingston and Saxon. Even Elizabeth bowed her head a bit.

Not me, though. I was practically smiling. Tracy had done more good than he realized.

Deacon glared at me. "What the fuck are you so happy about?" he snapped. "We just went down a dead end."

"No," I said. "It's the exact opposite. It's the break we've been waiting for."

CHAPTER 64

TICK-TOCK...

His name was Jackie Palmer.

Back in the early 1970s, he was a member of the Black Spades, a gang that ruled the Bronx like no other before it...or after it. They were violent, extremely territorial, and built to last, with Palmer as one of their warlords.

But then Palmer got political.

Not run-for-city-council political. Instead he blew up an army recruiting station because of the way he thought the US government was exploiting African American soldiers in the Vietnam War. *That* kind of political.

Palmer had visited the recruiting station in the Bronx under the pretense of obtaining enlistment brochures. While there he asked if he could use the bathroom, where he allegedly planted a pipe bomb with a timer set to explode that evening after the station was closed. *Allegedly.*

What he didn't know was that the recruiting officer was using the supply room as a bedroom for the night because his apartment was being fumigated. The officer was killed in the blast.

There were no witnesses, but a log sheet was recovered from the wreckage showing that the officer had listed "Jack Palmer" as the sole visitor to the station that day. More incriminating were the bomb-making materials the police found in Palmer's apartment after they obtained a search warrant.

But none of that actually proved anything beyond a reasonable doubt, especially because this was before the days of sophisticated forensic evidence. Palmer never even admitted that he'd set foot in the station. Ultimately, no charges were filed.

One very committed detective, however, never let go of the case. Ten years later, courtesy of advanced CSI techniques, a hair sample from the station was shown to be a match with Palmer's. It "positively" placed him at the army recruiting station. With no statute of limitations on murder in the state of New York, Palmer was arrested and tried.

He was found not guilty.

The case against Palmer began unraveling when his attorney successfully challenged the admissibility of the hair sample based on a technicality—the temperature at which it had been stored over the years. Still, the prosecution continued, abetted by a jury that seemed ready to convict regardless. That's when it happened. Jackie Palmer came forward.

A different Jackie Palmer. But similar in many ways. He was black, roughly the same age, and lived in the Bronx. He claimed he was the Jack Palmer who had gone to the recruiting station that day. The reason he never came forward previously was that he feared he'd be charged with planting the bomb. He was terrified, he said. Of course, he was also lying.

No one could prove it, though, and that gave the defense just enough reasonable doubt to prevent a conviction. Palmer was a free man.

I remember reading about the trial in an article that discussed the various tiers of morality. In this case, someone was willing to obstruct justice in the name of avenging a perceived larger injustice. Vietnam, as it turned out. The Jack Palmer who took advantage of a common name and came forward had not only been a conscientious objector but also an outspoken critic of the war.

Funny how the mind works. Tracy was protecting little Miles Winston for all the right reasons. The poser in the Jackie Palmer trial was protecting the "real" Jack Palmer for all the *wrong* reasons. The similarity, though, was enough to trigger the thought in my head and make the connection.

The jack of spades is Jackie Palmer.

"Yeah? Who is it?" came his voice through the intercom outside the brownstone where he now lived, still in the Bronx.

"Detective Needham with the NYPD, Mr. Palmer," said Elizabeth. "My partner and I need to speak with you immediately."

That was the first time she'd called me that. Her partner.

Tick-tock . . .

We waited for that annoying yet still welcome sound of his buzzing us in. There was a time when Jackie Palmer would've probably told us to get the hell lost before ducking out via his fire escape. But that was decades ago. Jackie Palmer was nearing seventy now.

He wasn't ducking anything anymore. "Suit yourself," came his voice again.

Followed by the buzz.

CHAPTER 65

I WOULDN'T presume to read a man's soul. His mind is hard enough.

But the man standing in the foyer of his third-floor apartment was making it all too easy. He was going to hell, and he knew it. It was only a matter of time.

"I assume this is a sit-down conversation?" asked Palmer, not so much leading us into his living room as just assuming we would follow him.

He found his way into what was clearly his preferred armchair as Elizabeth and I sat down opposite him on a faded brown couch. His apartment faced the street and had a western exposure, the late afternoon sun filtering through half-open venetian blinds. There are those who might see God in the resulting streaks of light. Others might only see the dust particles floating in the air.

"Mr. Palmer, have you been watching the news

about the serial killer with the playing cards?" asked Elizabeth.

"The Dealer," he said. "News people havin' a field day with it."

Perhaps it was good that he was sitting down, because Elizabeth cut right to the chase. "We have reason to believe you might be his next target," she said.

Sitting down be damned. Palmer barely even blinked. "What reason is that?" he asked calmly.

"There's something those news people don't know yet," said Elizabeth. "It's a card that this so-called Dealer left behind on his last victim."

"Do you mean the joker? Because I saw that on the television earlier," he said.

"That's another thing that hasn't gone public yet," she said. "Whoever killed those four young men today wasn't the Dealer."

I watched Jackie Palmer's forehead crinkle in thought beneath his short-cropped gray hair. I tried my best to see the young man with the corn-rows who walked out of the courthouse after being found not guilty so many years ago. That picture was one of a handful featured in the article I'd read about him. He wasn't smiling then, and he wasn't smiling now.

"It was another gang, then, huh?" he said.

"Yes," said Elizabeth. "The card we're talking about is the jack of spades."

"You think that's supposed to be me, huh?" he asked.

"We do, Mr. Palmer," she said. "Does that concern you at all?"

"The Dealer is hardly the first person who's wanted to see me dead, Detective."

"Yes," said Elizabeth. "But he might be the last."

"What do you want from me?" he asked.

"Your cooperation," she said. "Help us catch this guy."

"You mean you want to use me as bait," he said.

Elizabeth wasn't about to sugarcoat it. "I'm afraid you're bait no matter what we want."

"Then let him come," he said. "I'll be ready for him."

"That's all we're really asking, Mr. Palmer. Let us be ready right along with you," she said. "We have officers who would—"

He waved a hand, stopping her. "You do whatever you want, but you do it outside this apartment. You understand?"

"We want to make sure we can protect you," said Elizabeth. "The best thing would be if you didn't leave your apartment, at least for a while."

Palmer leaned forward in his armchair, his finger jabbing the air. "Whoever this son of a bitch is, the last thing I'm going to do is be afraid of him, you hear? Because that's worse than being dead."

Jackie Palmer was living with the kind of guilt that doesn't swallow someone whole. Instead it nibbles away over time until there's nothing left except resignation. He couldn't care less about saving himself. But what about saving others?

Tick-tock…

It was time for another approach.

"Mr. Palmer, I can't speak for Detective Needham here, but to tell you the truth, I don't really give a shit whether you live or die," I said.

Of all things, he smiled. "Is that so?"

"Yes," I continued. "What I do care about is the next victim, the one who comes after you." I paused and held his stare. I was hoping that maybe the image of that innocent army recruiter had surfaced somewhere behind that crinkled forehead of his. "You can't save the dead, Mr. Palmer. But you can still save someone else from dying."

Five minutes later, Elizabeth and I were back in her sedan outside Palmer's brownstone.

"Nicely done," she said. "I'll tell the mayor, and we'll coordinate with Saxon for logistics—how many officers around the clock and where to station them in and out of the apartment." She rolled her eyes. "Ideally before Palmer changes his mind."

"Sounds like a plan," I was about to say when

my phone rang. Tracy's number popped up. He was calling from his cell.

Only it wasn't Tracy.

"Hello?"

"Hello, Dr. Reinhart," he said. "I knew I was right to choose you."

CHAPTER 66

I COULD feel the rage building and burning inside me. The fear. The panic.

No—I couldn't give in to it. All that stuff only gets in your way when you need to get things done.

I suddenly had a lot of things to get done.

"It's him," I mouthed first to Elizabeth, who immediately knew what she had to do. She bolted out of the car—and out of earshot—so she could call in a trace on the Dealer's location off my cell number. That was a gimme.

Now things got tricky.

Tick-tock…

I tightened my grip on the phone. "Where is he?" I asked.

"Do you mean Tracy?" he answered, although it took me an extra second to put the words together. He was using a voice modulator, the kind that changes both pitch and cadence on the fly.

One second he was Darth Vader. The next an alto in the Vienna Boys' Choir.

"*Where is he?*" I asked again.

"You know me better than that, Professor," he said. "I presume he's still back at that Starbucks looking for his phone. You can't put anything down in this city, not for a second."

"Say the words, and I'll believe you," I said. "Tell me he's safe, that you didn't harm him."

The sound of his laughter through the modulator was like that of the devil incarnate. "He's safe," he answered finally. "This isn't about the innocent."

"All your victims...explain it to me...they're so guilty they deserved to die?" I asked.

"What do you think, Professor?"

"I don't know," I said. "Lawyers ask questions they already know the answers to, but I don't."

Elizabeth caught my eye through the windshield. Her head was cocked, her phone wedged between her ear and shoulder. She was pinching her fingers, pulling her hands apart as if she were stretching taffy. It was the symbol they give a newscaster who has a minute to fill but only ten seconds of copy. In other words, keep him talking.

Tick-tock...

"Do you know what I think? I think you're a little ahead of schedule," said the Dealer.

"I caught a break," I said. "I got lucky."

"Luck is the by-product of preparation, Professor. You of all people know that," he said. "But yes, the gang members...trying to steal my act. They were gang members, weren't they?"

"Yes," I said. "Did you watch the news?"

"I'm watching everything," he answered.

Forget the modulator. There was no masking what he meant by "watching everything." He wasn't talking about his TV habits.

Shit.

I hit the Mute button on my phone, leaning over to punch the steering wheel. Elizabeth, her back to the car, practically jumped out of her skin at the sound of the horn. She turned to see me circling my finger in the air. To that same newscaster it would look as if I were saying "Wrap it up." To Elizabeth, it meant she could stop tracing the call. The Dealer was close by. So close that he was watching us. Maybe worse.

"Elizabeth!" I yelled, opening the door. I was frantically waving to her. "Get in the car!"

She was out in the open, exposed.

"No, no, no," came the Dealer's voice. My phone was still on mute. Wherever he was, he could see us. "I need you to get out of the car, too, Professor. There's something I want you both to see."

Said the spider to the fly.

I took the phone off mute, putting it on speaker

251

as Elizabeth returned. She got back behind the wheel, her face asking, *What gives?*

Tribeca 212. The lobby. The Dealer shooting at us from the mezzanine. "We're not about to be your target practice again," I said.

"If I wanted to kill you at the hotel I would have," he said. "And don't pretend you haven't already figured that out, Professor. You're no good to me dead. Now, both of you . . . I need you out of the car."

I looked at Elizabeth, my face doing the asking now.

Tick-tock . . .

What do you want to do?

CHAPTER 67

SOMETIMES YOU talk out a big decision, weigh the pros and cons, cover all the bases.

This wasn't one of those times.

Elizabeth and I both reached for our doors without so much as a word between us. A spoken word, at least. Maybe it was pure stupidity. But if the Dealer wasn't going to kill us, the curiosity was.

You're no good to me dead, I kept repeating in my mind.

Everything I knew about human behavior was telling me I could believe him, but there was no shaking the first rule of being human. We all make mistakes.

"Okay, we're outside the car," I announced, holding the phone up in front of my mouth as though it were a slice of pizza. Elizabeth was right alongside me in front of Palmer's brownstone. We were both slowly walking in a circle, our eyes moving along the rooftops.

"Take me off speakerphone," said the Dealer.

Elizabeth gave me a nod, as if it only made sense he would ask that. She was right. With a tap of my finger, I put the phone to my ear. "It's only me now."

"Good," he said.

"Can you see me?" I asked.

He ignored the question. He had his own. "Do you know why I chose you, Professor?"

Keep it simple, Dylan…

"Because there's a reason you're killing, and you want me to figure out why," I said.

"Have you yet?" he asked.

"I'm getting close," I answered. "You already know that, don't you?"

He ignored that question, too. "Ask me what you really want to know," he said.

"Fine," I answered. "I will. There's more, isn't there? You want me to figure out more than just the why."

"Right again, Professor," he said. "Time is running out, though."

"How so?" I asked. "You said I was ahead of schedule."

"Only for the murderer on the third floor," he said.

I turned to look up at Jackie Palmer's apartment. "In other words, we got to him before you did."

That goddamn laugh again through the modulator. I could barely keep the phone to my ear. "I wouldn't go that far," said the Dealer.

A tingling feeling shot up my spine. All at once, it was a premonition of something horrible about to happen and the inability to do anything to prevent it. Total helplessness.

"What do you mean?" I asked, if only to stall.

I couldn't even do that. It was one more question that would fall on deaf ears.

"Come to think of it," he said, "what I really should've told you is that you're right on time."

Tick-tock...

Boom!

CHAPTER 68

THE BLAST blew out the windows of Palmer's apartment, the fireballs shooting out like cannons. The sound, the shock, the sheer force of the explosion buckled my knees, my legs giving way as I fell to the pavement. Only at the last second was I able to reach out with my hands so that I didn't crack open my skull.

Somewhere along the way I caught a glimpse of Elizabeth doing the same, a split second that seemed to play out in slow motion—her legs staggering before she tumbled, her slim frame slamming against the ground amid the shards of glass that were raining down upon us.

For several seconds, all I heard was the echo of the blast, the sound pounding inside my head. I couldn't even hear myself asking Elizabeth if she was okay.

I yelled back to her. "*What?*"

She answered again, louder. My ears finally

kicked in. "I said I'm all right...I'm okay," she told me.

As she got to her feet I thought she was saying something more, only to realize it wasn't Elizabeth. There was another woman's voice I was hearing. It was faint. It was also familiar.

I turned, looking around me along the street. The voice was coming from my phone. *Huh?*

My phone. I'd dropped it while I was falling to the ground. The screen was shattered, but through the cracks I could see that the call hadn't ended. The line was still live.

"Thinking 'bout a life of crime..."

I looked up again at Palmer's apartment, the black smoke billowing out from every window, the place entirely engulfed in flames. His neighbors would live to tell about it, but Jackie himself wouldn't. He wasn't merely dead, he was *gone*...and there was nowhere to put the card for the next victim.

Except in a song.

The woman I was hearing was Juice Newton, and the song was "Playing with the Queen of Hearts."

"Knowing it ain't really smart..."

Elizabeth came over and listened. She asked a question, only it was as if my ears had stopped working again. I could barely hear her. I could barely hear the song. Instead it was the Dealer's words that were pounding inside my head. Our conversation. Something he had told me.

For the first time, he had made what seemed like a mistake. I was sure of it. Unfortunately, I was also sure of something else.

There was an inferno raging above my head, and people were spilling out onto the street in panic, crying out to God. The only way the metaphor would've been more obvious were if the devil himself had appeared and poked me with his pitchfork.

There was no doubt in my mind. None whatsoever.

The real hell was only just beginning.

BOOK FOUR

DOWN AND DIRTY AND VERY, VERY DEADLY

CHAPTER 69

THE GUY at the table next to us the following morning was eating pancakes and reading the *Gazette*. The front cover was staring right back at me. Taunting me, maybe.

Give it up for Grimes, though. He put it together all on his own regarding Jackie Palmer. There was no headline, just a giant jack of spades with a big X through it. Of course, Grimes had already called and left three messages for me trying to find out who was next.

"It's you," said Elizabeth.

"It's not me," I assured her.

She was hardly assured. "It *could* be you," she said. "At least admit that."

"Fine. It could be me," I said. "But it's not."

She sighed, exasperated. "You are so stubborn, Reinhart."

"No, what I am is right," I said.

"Stubborn *and* arrogant."

I smiled. "You say that like it's a bad thing."

"I'm glad you're amused," she scoffed. "The supposed psychology genius who doesn't even know he's in denial."

"*Supposed?*" I asked.

"Christ," muttered Tracy.

Elizabeth and I both turned to him. "What?" we asked in unison.

Tracy put down his mug. Other diners had food that was just as good, but the Rooster & Rabbit, two blocks from our apartment, poured the best coffee by far. "You two are like an old married couple," he said.

"Only we're not," Elizabeth shot back. "Do you know why? Because one of us happens to be—"

"I haven't told him yet," I said, cutting her off.

"Told me what?" asked Tracy.

It was the one detail I left out in telling him about the Dealer's phone call—on Tracy's phone, no less—outside Jackie Palmer's apartment before the explosion. A sin of omission, but for good reason. Simply put, it was bad enough that I was going to hear it from Elizabeth.

"The queen of hearts," I said.

"That was the card?" asked Tracy. "The next victim?"

"It wasn't actually a card," I said. "But yes."

I explained about the song as Elizabeth resumed eating the egg-white frittata the waiter had highly recommended. He'd also suggested the huevos rancheros, although I was fairly certain it was only because he liked the sound of his own voice saying "huevos rancheros."

"I think I auditioned with him once," Tracy whispered after the guy had taken our order and walked away.

"So there you have it," I said. "The Dealer is a Juice Newton fan, apparently."

"You're hardly a queen, at least as far as gay slang goes," said Tracy. "But taken with your last name...yeah, Dylan Reinhart could definitely be the queen of hearts."

"Only I'm not," I repeated.

"Why am I even debating this with you?" said Elizabeth. "I already arranged protection for you starting this afternoon. It's done."

There was no point in arguing with her. I may have lapped Elizabeth when it came to arrogance, but we were neck and neck in terms of stubbornness. Sometimes you fight. Sometimes you retreat.

Sometimes you strike a deal.

"Tell you what," I said. "Postpone the start of that protection until tomorrow, and I won't say another word about it."

"Why tomorrow?" she asked.

"Because there's something you and I need to do today," I said. "Just the two of us."

"Gee, thanks," said Tracy.

"I didn't mean it like—"

"I'm kidding," he said. "Besides, I've got my own plans, beginning with buying a new phone. That's still freaking me out, by the way—the fact that this psychopath was in the Starbucks with me."

"Yeah, but that was the break we were waiting for," I was about to say.

I didn't, though. Truth was, as much as I thought the Dealer had finally made a mistake, I couldn't know for certain yet. He still could've been playing me. Or at least trying to.

One way or the other, I was going to find out for sure. It's true what they say.

A man can never fully leave his past behind . . .

CHAPTER 70

IT WASN'T so much a blind spot as it was our laying down the shovel too early. In other words, we didn't dig deep enough.

Now we needed a little more than a shovel. More like a backhoe, really.

I knew just the guy.

"You've got to be kidding me," said Elizabeth. We had walked from the diner to the parking garage near my and Tracy's apartment.

"I'm hardly kidding," I answered, handing her a blindfold, which was really just the sleep mask I wear when flying. "In fact, what I am is absolutely crazy to think I can bring you along."

That softened her stance a bit, the mere possibility that I could change my mind. "I'll look ridiculous," she said.

I pointed at the spare helmet under my arm with the heavily tinted visor. "No one will even know."

She was out of arguments, so on went the

blindfold, on went the helmet, and on jumped Elizabeth to the back of my motorcycle. It didn't get any more Bruce Wayne than this.

Twelve miles and twenty minutes longer than it should've taken, courtesy of a closed lane on the George Washington Bridge—which Chris Christie, I hoped, had nothing to do with—the two of us were standing inside a steel door that was ten feet behind another steel door that was past the security gate to a warehouse for a medical supply company in Fort Lee, New Jersey, that nobody had ever heard of, primarily because it didn't actually exist.

"Who the bloody hell is that?" asked Julian with his British accent, pointing at Elizabeth with a finger on the hand that wasn't gripping his customary highball of whiskey. Back in the day, he was always a no-brainer for a birthday gift—just as long as it was single malt.

Elizabeth extended her hand. "I'm Detective Elizabeth Need—"

"Christ, darling, don't tell me your name!" said Julian. "I don't want to know who you are, and you definitely shouldn't know who I am."

"It's okay," I assured Julian. "She doesn't even know your zip code."

Julian Byrd, who single-handedly was keeping the word *curmudgeon* alive and well in the English language, managed a shrug. He wasn't actually mad that I had a plus one. If he had been, we never would've made it past the security gate.

"What is it with you and protocol, Reinhart?" asked Julian as he turned and led us back to his office.

"Yeah, I know," I said. "The thing is—"

"Yeah, I get it. This Dealer guy could stand trial, and your detective friend needs to cover her tracks and have her own version of events for when she testifies," said Julian, always seeing a few moves ahead. The world was Boris Spassky, and he would forever be Bobby Fischer. He glanced back over his shoulder at Elizabeth. "She's rather good-looking, isn't she?"

"You know that I'm actually here, right?" asked Elizabeth.

"Yeah, he knows," I said.

That was Julian, thoroughly British but still like the original Marlboro cigarette. No filter.

Throw in his crazy hair and even crazier beard, and he was either one of two things: Charles Manson's doppelgänger or what he actually was, the greatest hacker ever to work for MI6.

As well as for the CIA.

CHAPTER 71

"WHOA," SAID Elizabeth.

"Yeah, I get that a lot," said Julian as we entered his office. "Or at least from the few people who have actually been inside here."

It wasn't the massive terminals or the fact that Julian's giant "desk" was made from the wing of an old Fokker Eindecker, the first German fighter plane. No, what had Elizabeth's jaw nearly scraping the floor was the view. In an otherwise windowless room in a windowless warehouse, the four walls in Julian's office, as well as the ceiling, were one seamless projection screen capable of carrying a live feed from any Internet, satellite, or LAN-based camera that Julian chose to hack into. At the moment we were floating in space above the earth. It was insanely cool.

"Russian satellite?" I asked.

"Chinese, actually," he said. "A stealth beta

launch of their Tiangong space station. It's comical: their firewalls are like rice paper."

Julian sat down behind a double row of screens and a single keyboard. His chair was the only one in the room. Again, he almost never had company.

"Thanks for doing this," I said. "Especially on such short notice."

"It wasn't as short as you think," he said. "The Eagle gave me the heads-up that you might be calling. He now thinks this is related to one of your past assignments."

"It's not," I said.

"Are you sure?" Julian asked. "He's convinced."

"The Eagle still thinks we faked the moon landing," I said.

"Well, if there was ever a guy who would know," said Julian before making a few taps on his keyboard. *Poof*, we were no longer floating in space. Now the entire room was the rotunda of the National Archives Building, in DC. It was a live feed from one of the security cameras aimed at the Declaration of Independence and Bill of Rights. "So whose civil liberties will we be violating today?" he asked.

Julian plus whiskey always equaled a wicked sense of humor.

I glanced over at Elizabeth, who still seemed undecided as to how surprised she was supposed to act after Julian referenced my "past assignments."

"Relax," I told her. "I know you know."

"You do?" she asked. "Wait, what exactly do you think I know?"

"Nice try," I said. She was a born detective, seeing if she could get something more out of me.

"How would she know?" asked Julian. "You sure as hell didn't tell her."

"Apparently you're not the only hacker in the world," I said.

"No," said Julian. "Just the best." He meant it, too. Then he proved it.

CHAPTER 72

"HERE—THESE are all the victims so far," I said, handing Julian a list. Or so I tried to. He waved me off.

"I already created files on each and every one," he said. "The only thing missing is some brilliant insight as to what we're looking for."

That was my cue.

"*The Associated Press Stylebook and Briefing on Media Law,*" I began. "The *AP Stylebook,* for short."

Julian immediately raised a sarcastic finger. "One second," he said. He poured himself some more whiskey. "Okay, Columbo, now I'm ready."

I raised a finger, too. My middle one. That got a rare smile out of Julian. He loved busting my American chops.

I continued. "The *AP Stylebook* was first created in the mid-1950s as a language guide for newspapers, a way to establish uniformity of grammar, punctuation, and usage. It's been revised annually, but it's always been the bible for the news industry. Like any bible, it has its quirks, one of them being the use of the term *innocent* versus *not guilty*."

"I always wondered about that," said Elizabeth. "Papers always used to get it wrong."

"You're right, and they knew it, too," I said. "For decades, newspapers would always write 'innocent' instead of 'not guilty,' not because they didn't know the difference in the legal sense but because they were afraid of a disastrous typo."

"What do you mean?" asked Elizabeth.

"If a writer or an editor or a typesetter left off the word *not,* suddenly the paper would be declaring someone guilty instead of not guilty," I said.

"For real?" asked Julian. "This AP book says to use the word *innocent* simply to avoid that possibility?"

"For close to a half century, that's exactly what it said," I replied.

Julian took another swig. "Okay, but I'm going to run out of whiskey, Dylan." Translation: *What's the point?*

"The AP has since changed the rule. However, long before they did, there was a young reporter who refused to follow it. In fact, he made a big stink about it in the wake of the O. J. Simpson trial."

"You're kidding me," said Elizabeth. "Grimes?"

"Exactly," I said. "Back when he was just Allen Grimes, before Grimes on Crimes."

"How did you know that?" she asked.

"I didn't," I said. "The Dealer said something on the phone with me, though. He said, *This isn't about the innocent.*"

Julian nearly dropped his whiskey glass he was in such a hurry to return to his keyboard.

"Son of a bitch," he muttered. "That's it, isn't it?"

"Yes," I said. "I believe it is."

CHAPTER 73

I'D KNOWN Julian for ten years, approximately nine longer than necessary to understand exactly what he was doing at that very moment. Elizabeth, on the other hand, was still out in space. The dark side of the moon, in fact.

"What the hell is going on?" she asked.

"You and I looked at the criminal records of all the victims," I said. "Some had been arrested, but not all of them. One or two had been convicted of petty crimes, but again, not all of them. We didn't see a pattern, and we moved on."

"There is one?" she asked. "A pattern?"

"I'm almost sure of it," I said.

She raised an eyebrow. "Almost?"

"SARA will tell us," said Julian without looking up from his keyboard.

Poof, we were back on earth again. Julian's walls were now displaying direct feeds from the multiple screens on his desk, his entire office engaging in a game of *This Is Your Life* with each and every victim. Only this version of the game was unlike any other.

Elizabeth leaned over to me. "Who's Sara?" she whispered.

I thought it was an acronym the first time Julian mentioned the name. Short for "search all restricted accounts" or something like that. Instead SARA—the program—was named for Julian's older sister. "She was always such a bloody know-it-all when we were growing up," he had told me.

That was the program, all right. The ultimate know-it-all.

In fact there was a rumor when I first met Julian that Steve Jobs had somehow heard about it and named Siri as a tip of the hat to him. Of course, neither Julian nor Jobs ever had a word to say about that.

I turned to Elizabeth. "Just watch."

Julian's walls were churning through an endless stream of pages, so fast that Elizabeth didn't notice at first that this was more than simply a Google search on steroids. This was sealed court documents—city, county, state, and federal. This was unfiled depositions. This was the ultimate digital crowbar into the legal troubles of all the victims: Jared Louden, Bryce VonMiller, Rick Thorsen, Cynthia Chadd, Colton Lange, and Jackie Palmer.

Was it legal?

That depends on how you feel about Machiavelli. Or, for that matter, about serial killers. To paraphrase an old Chinese proverb, the enemy of evil must sometimes borrow from his foe.

"How does it feel to be back, Dyl?" asked Julian, finally looking up from his keyboard. By then, he was simply waiting for SARA to do her thing. We all were.

"Back?" I asked. "You mean in this office?"

Julian knew I was playing dumb. He also knew how to do a few impressions, although Al Pacino from *The Godfather: Part III* wasn't necessarily one of them. Not that that was about to stop him.

"Just when I thought I was out, they pull me back in!" he shouted.

"Always longing for the past," I said. "What is it with the British? I told you, whatever this is... it isn't *that*."

"But you miss *that,* don't you?" he asked. "I know you do."

"Ah... who's analyzing whom now?" I said.

"And that's a nondenial denial," he retorted.

I looked over at Elizabeth, sizing me up. Whatever she did or didn't know about my past, it was as if she were seeing me for the first time. "What are you looking at?" I asked, doing my worst Jack Nicholson imitation.

"You tell me," she said.

Suddenly the sound of Julian clapping filled the room. SARA had found something.

Or, rather, someone.

"Well, what do you know?" said Julian, staring at one of his monitors. "I do believe we have our answer."

CHAPTER 74

I WAITED until we were back over the George Washington Bridge, well into Manhattan, before telling Elizabeth she could lower the mask covering her eyes. It was in keeping with the general theme developing for the day. John 9:25: *Whereas I was blind, now I see.*

"Can't this damn thing go any faster?" she was soon yelling into my helmet.

Two things. First, complaining about the speed of a beautifully and painstakingly restored 1961 Triumph TR6 Trophy was—in my very biased opinion—like standing in front of the *Mona Lisa* at the Louvre and wondering why Leonardo didn't use a bigger canvas.

Second, we were already pushing seventy.

Make that eighty as we got onto the Henry Hudson Parkway. Next stop, the Bronx and Riverdale, the neighborhood that contains the northernmost point in New York City. We were headed for the Hudson Hill section, to be exact.

If Riverdale is the diamond of the Bronx, then Hudson Hill is the diamond you get at Tiffany's. About a mile past the Wave Hill House, where Mark Twain once lived, I pulled into the driveway of a sprawling Tudor home half covered in ivy.

"Do you mind taking your shoes off?" asked Arthur Kingsman, greeting us at the front door. "Its not a dirt thing—I just hate the sound of heels against my floors."

Elizabeth and I promptly removed our shoes.

If Kingsman's reputation for eccentricity preceded him, what he was wearing above his yellow wool socks all but confirmed it. Technically a red robe, it looked like the silken love child of a smoking jacket and a kimono. "I have tea. You want tea?" he offered.

"No thanks; we're good," said Elizabeth.

The words were polite. Her tone, though, was impatient. I couldn't blame her; I was feeling the same way. It was as if our minds were still back on my bike, hovering near the redline. This was happening fast, yet there was no shaking the feeling. Was it fast enough? *The Dealer's game—did we finally catch up?*

"Excuse the clutter," said Kingsman, leading us into his study. "You know, I can still hear my wife's voice telling me to tidy things up."

Fact: Kingsman's wife had died of breast cancer five years ago.

Somewhere underneath the stacks of files and books was the desk he took a seat behind while pointing us to a couch, the leather so worn and cracked it looked as if it were shedding. Not that Elizabeth noticed. We had barely sat down before she was rattling off the Dealer's victims.

"Do you recognize any of those names?" she asked.

Kingsman, a lean sixty-two with a shaggy head of gray hair, rolled his eyes behind his thick black glasses.

"This will go a lot quicker, Detective Needham, if you simply tell me why I should," he said. "For the record, you're not the only one capable of impatience."

And like that, he was no longer sitting at his desk. He was at the bench, and his study was now his courtroom.

The Honorable Arthur Kingsman. The rarest of breeds. A strict constitutionalist *liberal* judge. But that inherent contradiction—and his apolitical reputation, derived from it—had helped propel him from the New York State Supreme Court up to the US Court of Appeals for the Second Circuit. At one point, he was even rumored to be on the short list for the highest court in the land. The fact that he was a former air force pilot with combat history only helped his cause.

The reason he ultimately was never nominated to the US Supreme Court, however, was no mystery. Kingsman was a self-professed atheist. Legal scholars would point to that as being an advantage for a judge, a marker of his objectivity, but try telling that to a red-state senator up for reelection. Or, for that matter, to a blue-state senator.

"All those names I mentioned? They're all dead, Your Honor," said Elizabeth. "And at one time or another, they've all been in your courtroom."

CHAPTER 75

"I KNOW," said Kingsman.

"Wait—what?" said Elizabeth. "How could you—"

"I mean, I recognize the names," he said. "All of them except the woman's, that is. Can you say her name again?"

"Cynthia Chadd," said Elizabeth.

Kingsman shook his head. "I know the name of every person who has ever stood trial in one of my courtrooms," he said. "There's never been a Cynthia Chadd."

He was right. Unlike all the other victims, Chadd had never stood trial in front of Kingsman. She had, though, been in one of his courtrooms. She had testified for the defense in a hit-and-run case involving the death of an elderly man mowed down in a crosswalk. As for the defendant's name, the person she swore under oath she'd never met before? It was Rick Thorsen, the man shot to death with her in the hotel room at Tribeca 212 while in flagrante delicto.

Leave it to Julian—and SARA—to track down the witness list buried in the Manhattan DA's 128-bit-encryption file server.

Sure. It was borderline *Rain Man* that Kingsman had retained the names of every defendant who had come before him over a nearly thirty-year career on the bench. Even more hard to ⌐ ve, or so it seemed, was that he hadn't already made the connection between himself and the victims.

Elizabeth squinted at Kingsman. "You've been following the news about this serial killer, right?" she asked. "The Dealer?"

"*Following* would be too strong a word," he answered. "I've seen the headlines."

Usually that's a figure of speech. Not in Kingsman's case. He literally meant he'd seen the headlines and nothing more.

"Surely you've seen stories about the victims on TV," said Elizabeth.

"I don't own a television," said Kingsman. "We used to have one in the den that my wife would watch. I got rid of it when she passed. I do read the *Times* and the *Journal,* but only the headlines on the front and the pontifications in the back— the editorial pages."

I was listening to Kingsman the entire time, but something had caught my eye.

"What are you staring at, Professor Reinhart?" he asked finally.

"My book," I said.

"Your book?" He looked confused.

I pointed opposite the couch. "Second shelf on the right." I stood and walked across his office, then pulled the book from his bookcase, which was caked with dust. Ironically, the book itself was missing its dust jacket. I held up the spine so he could read the title, *Permission Theory,* along with my name. "That's me," I said.

"So it is," said Kingsman. He still looked confused.

"You haven't actually read the book, have you?" I asked.

"I didn't even know I owned it," he said. "What's it about?"

"Abnormal behavior," I answered.

The corners of his mouth tilted upward, a slight smile. "Abnormal behavior. I always found that term to be a bit redundant."

Good line. "Me, too," I said.

"So what is it?" he asked. "This permission theory of yours?"

"You'll have to take my class, Your Honor," I answered. "For now, let's just say it addresses the reasons why someone would be killing people who were indicted for serious crimes but ultimately found not guilty in your courtroom."

I was all prepared to continue. That was merely my opening statement. Hell, it wasn't even a question.

But Judge Arthur Kingsman still had the answer.

CHAPTER 76

"HELPLESSNESS," HE said. "The most dangerous people in the world are the ones who think they've run out of options."

"So they invent their own," I said. "They grant themselves permission."

Kingsman nodded. "The very nature of vigilante justice."

The cases were all legal layups. At least that's how they looked on paper. Reams of evidence and corroborating witness testimony for the prosecution and the Matterhorn of uphill battles for the defense.

Then again, not all defense attorneys are created equal. At a thousand dollars an hour, some aren't even really lawyers. They're magicians.

Jared Louden, victim zero on the Dealer's kill list, had been caught dead to rights bribing and extorting people in exchange for insider information on behalf of his hedge fund. The recordings made of Louden revealed him to be ruthless, malicious, and borderline pathological. But it wasn't the feds who secretly planted the bug in his office. It was an employee acting as a whistle-blower. His name was Bob.

Problem was, the feds didn't carefully read Bob's employment contract. Louden's defense team certainly did. During the trial, Judge Kingsman ruled that while Bob was "trying to do the right thing," he had indeed violated the morals clause of his employment contract with Louden's firm. Anything recorded on that bug was therefore inadmissible. Sorry, Bob. Nice try, feds.

And if it wasn't a high-priced lawyer pulling a legal rabbit out of a hat, it was a rookie cop making a rookie mistake. He left out a line from his Miranda warning to Bryce VonMiller after arresting the spoiled punk for selling Ecstasy on a playground. That's right. *A playground.*

Technicalities, loopholes, perversions of the law. They were the get-out-of-jail-free cards at one time or another for all the victims. Now, whether a few years later or many, the Dealer was making them pay. Did he know that Rick Thorsen was never carjacked, as he claimed—that he was the one who ran over that elderly man in the crosswalk with his BMW? Or that the woman who came forward as a witness—Cynthia Chadd—was actually his mistress?

He had to have known. Just as he had to have known that Colton Lange, while still in high school, had raped a girl at a party even though the rape kit from the hospital was ruled inadmissible by Kingsman. Once the lab technician stopped to go to the bathroom and left the kit unattended outside his stall, the chain of custody could no longer be verified.

So it went with all the trials, all the way back to Jackie Palmer and the negligent homicide indictment that came a decade later. The smoking-gun hair sample was disallowed, and yet another not-guilty verdict was rendered.

"I do what the law tells me to do," said Kingsman, slumping back in his chair. He removed his glasses, pinching the bridge of his nose. "It's not always what my conscience tells me, and sometimes it's not even what a jury tells me. I've overruled them before."

"Because you thought you were doing the right thing?" asked Elizabeth.

"What is the right thing?" asked Kingsman. "Is it what I think? What you think? What the judge in the next courtroom thinks? That's why we have laws in the first place, Detective, and no law can protect the innocent without occasionally helping the guilty. I offer no apology for that."

"We didn't come here for an apology," I said, sliding my book back onto the shelf. "We came here to stop a murder, and, if past is prologue, there's not a lot of time. What we want from you is your help."

"The queen of hearts, that's the next victim," said Elizabeth. "Assuming it's not you, Your Honor, then who is it? What was the case? *Who was on trial?*"

Kingsman thought for a few seconds.

"Here," he said finally. "This is the key to everything."

CHAPTER 77

"THERE'S NOTHING more I could find," said the man in the black turtleneck sitting across from Edso Deacon in the stretch limo driving through lower Manhattan, the tinted double-pane windows blocking out the bustle and noise of the city at night.

Nothing more he could find?

The mayor stared back at the man as if he didn't hear him, something he did a lot when he got answers he didn't like. This answer, in particular, he despised.

"Do you know where the expression *tit for tat* comes from?" asked Deacon, picking a piece of lint from the sleeve of his Kiton K-50 suit. "Some people think it's a shortened version of *this for that*. Others think it derives from the fencing term *tap for tap*, which would make sense from a standpoint of retaliation. Still others believe it to be less adversarial and more about equality. They point to the French culinary expression *tant pour tant,* which refers to a mix of equal parts of fine sugar and ground almonds. Which one makes the most sense to you?"

"I don't know," said the man.

Deacon nodded. "That's okay," he said. "Do you know why it's okay?" He leaned forward in his seat, clasping his hands over his knees as his jaw tightened. *"Because I didn't pay you to tell me that."*

"Mr. Mayor—"

"Shut up," said Deacon. "You said you could get more on Dylan Reinhart if I paid you more. So that's what I did."

"Do you want the money back?"

"I want what I fucking paid for!" screamed Deacon.

A lot of men would've reacted somewhere between wincing and wetting their pants after being yelled at by the mayor of the country's largest city, especially a mayor as wealthy and connected as Deacon. The man in the black turtleneck, however, barely blinked. He was untouchable, and they both knew it. Most former Mossad agents are. Once a member of the Israeli intelligence community, always a member—with all the book of Exodus protection that went with it. *An eye for eye, a tooth for tooth...*

"Do I have to explain it again?" the man asked calmly.

No, he didn't. Deacon heard him the first time.

Finding out that Dylan Reinhart had been CIA was just as much of a fluke as it was a result of brilliant hacking. The brilliant part was penetrating a beta test for a new software program that would allow the CIA to gather and cross-reference server activity from multiple Internet providers without detection.

The fluke part was the supposedly innocuous files inserted into the test. In what was a collection of deleted e-mails addressing such delicate matters of national security as the rules of an office football pool and directions to a 2016 holiday party at Mr. Nick's restaurant in Langley, there also somehow managed to be a highly classified pension-payout list for a handful of former field agents stationed in London.

Even the best coders aren't immune to a good old-fashioned fuckup.

"Are you sure you tried everything?" asked Deacon.

The man, who went by the name of Eli, nodded. "Everything and then some," he said. "We know that Reinhart was in the field and that his cover was the fellowship at Cambridge. As for what he did, any assignments, that's another can of beans, one that cannot be opened."

"*Worms,*" said Deacon. "Another can of worms—that's the expression."

"Whatever," said Eli. "That can can't be opened, either."

"So you say."

"Why is this information so important to you? Why must you know?"

"Because if Reinhart is who you say he is, there's hardly anything he can't also know about me," said Deacon.

Eli smiled, his teeth stained by years of nicotine and neglect. "You Americans and your mutually assured destruction," he said. "Everything is a Cold War to you."

No, you idiot. Everything is an election. That's what Deacon wanted to say. The only reason he and Eli, or whatever his real name was, were even sharing the same air was because Deacon had secretly funneled money to a key member of the Likud party for his election campaign to the Knesset. In return, Deacon was given access to the likes of Eli and an untraceable source of intelligence.

Tit for tat.

So much for that, though. Deacon pinched the skin of his forehead, as if that somehow could relieve the pressure. It couldn't.

He hadn't lied to Eli. Having dirt on Reinhart was a savvy political move, no matter how paranoid it was.

But it was what he hadn't told Eli. Deacon wasn't convinced that the link between Reinhart and the

Dealer didn't go beyond the professor's precious little book. Maybe, just maybe, it had something to do with Reinhart's CIA past.

All the mayor knew for sure was that he wasn't ruling anything out. Except, of course, his reelection if the killings continued.

CHAPTER 78

DR. AMY BENSEN slowly opened her eyes, her vision a hazy mix of light and shadow. She didn't know where she was or what had happened. The last thing she remembered after feeding her cat in the kitchen was the jolt of fear and the hand that covered her mouth before she could scream. Someone had broken into her apartment.

Oh, God, no. He's still here.

The lights and shadows were now shapes and movement. Actually, one shape and a single movement. Back and forth. Back and forth. A figure pacing before her at the foot of the bed. Like a Polaroid from hell, his face gradually came into focus. His eyes. His nose.

That smile.

She wanted to scream, but she was gagged. She wanted to run, but she was bound. She was stretched on her back, spread-eagled, each arm and leg tied to a post of the canopy bed she had bought in Paris a couple of years ago and had shipped back to Manhattan. The bed was a gift to herself after she'd been named the first female chief cardiologist at Bricknell Medical Center, in Brooklyn. Score one for the ladies.

"Wakey, wakey, Dr. Bensen," said the Dealer.

More details began to trickle back to her. She could feel the hand slapped over her mouth to stop her from screaming, followed by the other hand over her nose. Chloroform, for sure. That's how he knocked her out. That's how she ended up in her bed.

He's going to rape me.

She was sure of it. He'd already removed her blouse. Her bra as well. She was naked from the waist up. It was only a matter of time before he removed her skirt and underwear. He probably wanted her awake for that part...and every part of the nightmare that was sure to follow.

Dr. Bensen started to cry. She cried because she knew she couldn't scream. Because she knew she couldn't escape. Because the feeling was something she'd never truly felt in her entire accomplished life. Helplessness.

The Dealer walked to the side of the bed, staring curiously at the tears falling from the sides of her eyes. So many tears. He reached down, catching one on his index finger. For a few seconds, he simply gazed at the wetness.

"You never did cry in court, did you, Doctor?" he said. He then slowly licked the tear from his finger and smiled again.

That smile.

She had seen it before, hadn't she? She had seen *him* before. It was all coming back to her now. No mere trickle. A sudden wave. She was suddenly drowning in a memory she had tried so hard to forget.

"It was so long ago. That's what you tell yourself, isn't it?" said the Dealer. "That voice inside your head, so willing to assure you that you're a different person now, that all is forgiven. It's almost as if you've forgotten all about it." He leaned down, so close to her ear that she could feel the heat of his breath. It was like fire. "That's why I'm here, Doctor. Because you need reminding. *People need to be reminded.*"

As he turned and walked away from the bed, Dr. Amy Bensen realized that she was wrong. She wasn't about to be raped. She was about to be murdered. And the second he returned, the very moment she saw what was in his hands, she knew exactly how he was going to do it.

How fitting...

CHAPTER 79

"ANYTHING?" ASKED Elizabeth.

"No," I answered. "You?"

She shook her head, pushed her hair back behind her ears, and pulled out the next file. Between the two of us we'd already gone through ten boxes. There were twenty more to go. A long day was becoming an even longer night.

Judge Kingsman had called it the key to everything. It was. But only in the literal sense — so far. He'd handed us his key for a small locker at a self-storage facility in Yonkers, about twenty minutes north of his home. In the locker were thirty large boxes containing files of every case he'd presided over in the past thirty years. That was it. That was everything. There was nothing else Kingsman kept in the locker besides the files.

There was something not quite right about it all. I just couldn't figure out what.

Whatever it was, it wasn't obvious. The boxes

were organized by year, and the files within them were alphabetized according to the last name of the defendant. Within minutes, Elizabeth and I had easily found the files for each of the victims. They were right where they were supposed to be in their respective boxes.

So what is it? What's not right?

There was nothing out of the ordinary in terms of the labeling or the folders themselves. They were all the same color, that typical drab green.

Beyond the alphabetizing there was no system, no further means by which to differentiate one case from another. Murders were mixed in with assaults that were mixed in with drug smuggling, arson, and every conceivable form of racketeering. In the never-ending debate as to whether people are inherently good or evil, this was the mother lode of ammo for the evil argument.

"Needle in a haystack," groaned Elizabeth as she put the top back on a box and reached for another. She groaned again. Each box weighed a ton.

"We should be so lucky," I said. "At least with a needle in a haystack the needle exists."

That was the fear, of course—that we would reach the last box and be no closer to knowing the identity of the queen of hearts.

In the meantime, all we could do was guess. It was like a game, a brainteaser. We went back and forth. *Who's the queen of hearts?*

"The writer of a romance novel," I said.

"A prostitute," said Elizabeth.

"A drag queen."

"A descendant of royalty."

"A female heart surgeon."

"A female champion hearts player."

"No," I said. *"A female heart surgeon."*

Elizabeth looked up from the file in her hands to see me looking up from the one in mine. I had opened a new box and was about to go case by case, as with every other box, my thumb moving from tab to tab.

Only this case was right on top. The file was lying flat on top of all the others. I couldn't miss it.

That was the whole point.

CHAPTER 80

WHOOSH.

We were back in Manhattan, the Upper East Side.

"No way, not unless you've got a goddamn warrant," said the superintendent, standing in our path at two in the morning and trying his best to sound like a tough son of a bitch. The fact that he was fresh out of bed and wearing a fluffy blue bathrobe with little sailboats on it, however, wasn't exactly helping his cause.

Still, what were the odds? A building super who was going to law school at night. How much he enjoyed telling us that, too. Almost as much as Elizabeth enjoyed telling him that he should probably ask for his tuition money back.

There was only one thing we needed to get him to open the door of apartment 2402, and she practically had it pressed against his nose. Her badge.

"Besides, we're not trying to arrest Dr. Bensen, we're trying to protect her," Elizabeth added. *"Now, open the goddamn door."*

So much for our tough-talking soon-to-be law-school graduate. The super dug into the pocket of his fluffy blue bathrobe and began fumbling with an overcrowded key chain. Bensen's swanky high-rise building only looked like a hotel. There was no master key.

"Shit!" Elizabeth suddenly shouted. "Move!"

She'd heard the same loud crashing noise behind the door that we all did.

The super, slow with the keys, was even slower to move. Elizabeth promptly shoved him to the ground. She reached for her Glock, took one step back, and raised her foot, all in one smooth motion.

You want to break down a door? There's only one way to do it. Never with your shoulder. Never with a running start. You need to kick and kick hard, landing your heel a few inches to the left of the lock. Anywhere else and you might as well be kicking a concrete wall.

All that said, you still only have a coin flip of a chance.

"Do you plan on just watching?" asked Elizabeth after her first attempt failed.

"I thought women kicking down doors was like men asking for directions," I said, sidling up next to her. "Count of one, okay?"

"One," said Elizabeth.

Our technique hovered somewhere between Chuck Norris and the Rockettes, but the timing was spot-on, our heels landing simultaneously to the left of the lock. The wood splintered, and the door flew open. Instinctively I peeled off as Elizabeth crouched behind her Glock, shrinking herself as a target. She'd been trained well.

"Stay here," she said.

"No problem," I replied. She had a gun; I didn't.

Tell that to the super, though, who thought he could fall right in line behind her. *Have you never seen a single cop show, buddy?*

I grabbed him, yanking him out of the doorway. For the second time in less than a minute the guy was getting shoved to the ground. We were doing wonders for his self-esteem. At least he wasn't about to die stupid.

I waited as Elizabeth checked the apartment.

How do you gauge what someone means to you? Have her walk into danger when there's little you can do about it. Scary how much I could care about a person I'd only known for a short while. Actually, it wasn't scary at all. It was all too human.

"Clear," she finally said.

Although the way Elizabeth said it suggested there was a little more to it. That is, I was clear to come in, but there was still something to see. Something not good.

It's amazing how much one little word can tell you.

CHAPTER 81

"CLEAR."

How fitting…

I walked into Dr. Bensen's apartment through the foyer and into the living room, stepping over the shattered glass remains of what had surely been a vase. The flowers lumped on the marble floor amid the shards removed any possible doubt.

The flowers were also dead, I noticed.

"In here," Elizabeth called out.

I followed her voice down a short hallway to see her standing in front of an open bedroom door, culprit in hand. Actually, cradled in her arms was more like it. Dr. Bensen's cat was of course a Bombay. What other color but black could it have been?

We'd pounded on the door, and the cat freaked, ultimately knocking over the vase. That explained the crashing sound. It wasn't the Dealer. But even before Elizabeth turned and led me into the bedroom, I knew he'd been there. I could feel it. Days ago I would've laughed at the idea of being able to feel someone's presence. I would've made fun of myself, the full-on ridicule... professor with a PhD in psychology trips on a crystal ball and hits his head on a Ouija board.

Elizabeth put down the cat, saying nothing as we approached the bed. There was no blood, no gore to test the stomach and nerves. Yet that somehow made it even more chilling.

Dr. Amy Bensen was topless and tied up, but there was nothing sexual about it. There was also nothing to figure out in terms of how he killed her. One paddle under the right clavicle, the other paddle on the left rib cage.

Clear.

He shocked her over and over, jolt after jolt. So much so that the outlines of the paddles were practically singed on her chest, the skin crinkled and horribly warped. Portable defibrillators don't gyp you on the juice.

"How long?" I asked. "How long has she been dead? A couple of days?"

"At least," said Elizabeth. "Maybe more."

No wonder the cat was a bit panicky. It was starving. I quickly went to the kitchen and found its food in a cupboard next to the stove. I filled the water bowl, too.

"You would think someone would've noticed a missing doctor," I said, returning to the bedroom.

"Unless she was off for the weekend," said Elizabeth. "Also, she lived alone...no men's clothes in the closets, no wedding ring."

I hadn't noticed about the ring. I'd been too busy noticing what else she was missing.

CHAPTER 82

"THERE'S NO card," I said.

Elizabeth shook her head. "No. Not unless it's somewhere underneath her."

I knew the protocol. It was a crime scene. We weren't supposed to touch the body. Tempting as it was, we'd know soon enough.

"Did you call it in?" I asked.

She reached for her cell. "About to."

Twenty minutes later, Dr. Amy Bensen's apartment was only a few people short of what the fire marshal would have called maximum occupancy. Save for Elizabeth, it was all guys. As I sat off to the side in a corner of the bedroom, on a tufted chaise longue that was circa last-century Laura Ashley, I entertained myself by watching most of them steal furtive glances at Elizabeth as she chatted up a fellow detective. They all treated her like one of the boys, but make no mistake, they all wanted her like the prom queen.

All total, it took another hour for Dr. Bensen to be photographed, poked, prodded, and swabbed for evidence. When she was finally cleared to be moved, there was no playing card anywhere underneath her.

Why not? Why didn't you leave a card this time?

There was no way he was done killing. There was also something about the timing. Bensen's file had been pulled from its storage box and was sitting right on top. We couldn't miss it. Yet it was as if the Dealer knew that Bensen's body wouldn't be discovered right away. More than knew, in fact. It's what he wanted. *It's the way he planned it.*

I bolted up from the edge of the chaise, finding Elizabeth in the living room. She was off in the corner in an armchair, reading over her notes as the first responder. Her report would come later.

Later than she imagined.

"Judge Kingsman," I said.

"What about him?" she asked.

"We need to get back to his house," I said. "Right away."

Elizabeth didn't budge from her chair. She didn't even flinch. "It's four in the morning, Dylan," she said. "Are you saying he's the next victim? Because we'll call him and then—"

"No. We can't call him," I said.

"Why?"

"Because there's only a chance that he's the next victim."

There's no hiding fatigue at four o'clock in the morning. "For Christ's sake," snapped Elizabeth. "What are you talking about?"

I sat down in the other armchair, leaning forward. Only she could hear me. "There are two possibilities," I said. "The first is that Judge Kingsman is about to be killed."

"What's the second?"

I told her.

She didn't ask if I was sure. She didn't even ask me to explain. Elizabeth didn't say anything to me, in fact.

Instead she reached for her phone, dialing the dispatcher at the Fiftieth Precinct. She wanted a detail outside Kingsman's house, front and back. We were more than half an hour away, but the detail would take only ten minutes to get there, tops.

"No one goes in," Elizabeth said to the dispatcher. *"And no one goes out."*

Two possibilities.

Judge Arthur Kingsman was either a dead man or the Dealer.

CHAPTER 83

IT FELT like one of those sci-fi movies in which everyone else on the planet suddenly and mysteriously disappears.

We turned the corner near Kingsman's house, in Riverdale's Hudson Hill, the first hint of sunrise casting a yellowish glow over the entire street. Elizabeth had been keeping her hands warm in the pockets of my jacket during the ride, but she now took one out to tap my shoulder and point at my headlamp. She wanted me to cut the light.

Up ahead were the silhouettes of two cars parked at the bottom of Kingsman's driveway.

I knew what she was thinking underneath her helmet; she didn't have to say it. Why are there *two* cars?

There should've been only one in front. The other should've been on the street behind the house, covering the back.

Moreover, why were the cars parked directly

in front of the house? Too conspicuous. They should've been on the edge of the property or down the street a bit. All they needed was a decent view, not a front-row seat.

I cut the engine, waiting for Elizabeth to step off. It was hardly a wait. She was already swinging a leg before we even came to a stop.

Sure, it was the graveyard shift, but did it have to be a rookie detail? With a huff, Elizabeth removed her helmet and practically shoved it in my hands. Some greenies were about to get an earful.

No, they weren't. Elizabeth stopped ten feet from the first car. I caught up to her, and we were both looking at the same thing. An empty Honda Accord, lights off but the engine still running. Stranger still was that the front door on the driver's side was slightly open.

I was about to ask if the NYPD counted Hondas in their unmarked fleet. Apparently they didn't, because before I could ask, Elizabeth had drawn her Glock.

There was no doubt about the car behind the Accord, though. It was the same kind of sedan as Elizabeth drove. It was empty, too. The engine was off, all the doors closed.

"Tell me you carry a bug," I said.

That was a b-u-g, as in "back-up gun." My not having a weapon outside Dr. Bensen's apartment was one thing. This was another. Something was up, and we were as out in the open as it gets.

Elizabeth reached down to her right pant leg and removed the Glock version of a pocket pistol, the G42, from her shin holster.

"Don't make me regret this," she whispered, handing it to me. She was only half joking.

"Don't worry. I've only shot one other partner in the back," I whispered in return. I motioned with my hand. "After you."

The look on her face was almost as priceless as her slight hesitation. The irony, of course, was that there was no chivalry in this situation. I was technically a civilian, and she wasn't. There was no way she was going to let me lead.

But I had her back.

We walked up the driveway, the grumble of that Honda engine fading behind us. Every window in Kingsman's house was dark. There was no sign of anyone, inside or out. Maybe there were some early birds chirping, but all I could hear was the sound of my own heartbeat—that and the words of my first handler, a Frenchman, with whom I was stationed in London. It was his version of "Keep calm and don't panic." *"Le secret pour rester en vie? Ne jamais cesser de respirer."*

The secret to staying alive? Never stop breathing.

"This way," said Elizabeth.

Without discussion, she and I both knew where

we were heading. The back of the property. The front was a little too quiet for our liking. Way too quiet. My kingdom for some noise.

Elizabeth heard it first. We were halfway along the side of the house. Going on nothing but instinct, she plastered herself against the stucco of Kingsman's Tudor, her arm pulling me next to her. She pointed to her ears.

That's when I heard it, too. Dim but definitely there.

Voices. As in plural. It was at least two men talking. It might have been the patrolmen, but that wouldn't explain the Honda with the engine running. We needed to get closer to hear them better. Better yet, we needed to get a look.

Slowly we edged along the side of the house, the corner toward the back no more than ten feet away. We were as quiet as falling leaves.

So was the guy behind us.

CHAPTER 84

I ALMOST shot his head off. I mean, seriously, who clears his throat before yelling, "Freeze!"

A rookie, that's who.

I spun around so fast that the kid nearly tripped over his own feet. Luckily for him, I saw the uniform. All he saw were our street clothes and our guns. God knows what would've happened if Elizabeth hadn't been so swift with her badge.

"Whoa, whoa, whoa!" she screamed.

That brought another officer running over from the back of the house, in full sprint. With his buzz cut, he looked even younger than his partner. We were now the meat in a neophyte sandwich.

Quickly Elizabeth explained who we were and why we were there. The only reason they were there was because of her.

Their turn. Why the Honda out front? Why were they out of their cars and on the property?

"Follow me," said the buzz cut.

We followed him to a patio off the back of the house, where two more officers were standing—hovering, really—over another man sitting in one of four wrought-iron chairs, all of which probably had cushions on them a few months ago, during the summer. Or maybe not. The chairs and the patio itself had that overly neglected look. There were cracked bricks everywhere underfoot, along with a few spots that were missing bricks altogether. Judge Kingsman didn't strike me as a relax-on-the-patio sort of guy. Maybe his wife had been when she was alive.

Elizabeth and I both stared at the guy in the chair. He looked around my age, midthirties, with jet-black hair parted neatly to the side above a pair of black-frame glasses that were either hip or nerdy, depending on which borough you live in.

Intentionally or not, he was sitting dead center under a lone floodlight. He wasn't in handcuffs, but his body language was unmistakable. He wasn't there by choice.

"Who is he?" asked Elizabeth.

"No wallet or any ID on him, but he says his name is Elijah Timitz," said the buzz cut. He motioned to the guy. "Go ahead, tell them what you told me."

Dead silence. The guy simply sat there, staring back at us. There was no fear, but it wasn't cocky, either.

The buzz cut rolled his eyes. *Okay, pal, I'll tell 'em...*

"He says he works for the judge and was dropping off some files," he began. I could read his nameplate now, courtesy of the floodlight. The buzz cut was Officer J. Glausen. "He claims it's research for cases, and he led us to the back here to show us where he drops them off."

In unison, Elizabeth and I looked over at one of the other officers and the files tucked under his arm. Behind him was a footlocker-type box by the door to the house.

"Is it?" asked Elizabeth. "Research?" She didn't even bother asking Timitz directly.

"It's a bunch of notes and legal language," answered Glausen. "So maybe, yeah, it is. That's not the problem, though."

I got it before he said it. The problem was math. Everyone was armed, but there was still one gun too many. In other words, *everyone* was armed. Timitz had been carrying. The gun in Glausen's hand was in addition to the one in his holster.

"Do you have a license for that?" asked Elizabeth. Now she was talking directly to Timitz. He still wasn't answering. *Do you have a license to carry a firearm?* she repeated.

Finally, he spoke. Sort of. "I want my attorney present," he said.

Glausen snickered. "Do you know who asks for their lawyers? Guilty people," he said.

"Or maybe people who have an understanding of the justice system and how it works and sometimes doesn't work," I chimed in. "Perhaps someone who works for a judge?"

Elizabeth looked at me. She knew what I was doing. You catch more flies with honey.

Glausen, meanwhile, had no clue. Neither did any of the other officers, who had been standing around like mannequins.

"Yeah, and while we're at it, where is the judge?" asked Elizabeth. "Where's Kingsman?"

Glausen had no clue about that, either.

"Good question," he said. Cue the sarcasm. "Maybe the guy who works for him knows."

CHAPTER 85

"DID YOU call the home number?" asked Elizabeth. "The landline?"

"Yeah, we did that, too," said Glausen. "Twice."

They had knocked, they had banged, they had rung the doorbell repeatedly and checked all the doors of Kingsman's house to see if any of them was open. None was.

Elizabeth took off her jacket and began wrapping the sleeve around her fist. "Let's find the cheapest window to replace," she said.

"Or you could just use the key."

We all turned to Timitz.

"What?" asked Elizabeth.

"Judge Kingsman keeps a spare key underneath the middle flowerpot by the back door here," said Timitz, pointing.

"How do you know that?" asked Glausen.

But that was the wrong question. *Why are you*

telling us? That was the right one. Timitz was admitting he had access to Kingsman's house.

Glausen tried again. "How do you know there's a key?"

"I want my attorney present," answered Timitz. That figured.

Elizabeth unwrapped her jacket from around her fist. Apparently there was no need to break any windows. She also knew there was a difference between asking and telling.

"Don't just sit there: go get the key," she told Timitz. He didn't need his lawyer to do that.

Timitz got up, making his way over to a row of three flowerpots on the ground next to the door to the house. They were more like dirt pots, really. That's all they had in them.

Sure enough, there was the key under the middle one. Timitz grabbed it and walked over to Elizabeth, giving it to her. Glausen had a hand on his holster the entire time. Glock by my side, I was a bit twitchy myself.

Timitz returned to his chair as Elizabeth started orchestrating. Glausen and I were to come with her inside the house; the other officers were to stay outside and "keep Mr. Timitz company."

Five minutes later, we returned to the patio.

"Would you still like your attorney, Mr. Timitz?" asked Elizabeth.

He nodded. "Yes."

"Okay, then," she said, reaching for her phone. She held it out for him. "Give your attorney a call, and have him or her meet you at the Fiftieth Precinct in half an hour."

"Are you arresting me?" he asked.

"No," she said. "We'd like to ask you some further questions, and your cooperation would be appreciated. You would be coming with us voluntarily."

Timitz thought for a few seconds. "Okay, but I'd like to make the call from my own phone," he said. "It's in a coat in my car."

"The Honda out front," said Elizabeth. "Right?"

"Yes. It's also been running this entire time," he said.

"I'll take care of it," Glausen announced, heading for the front of the house. No one objected, including Timitz.

"So how long have you worked for Judge Kingsman?" I asked, filling the silence that followed. I wasn't sure Timitz would answer. He did.

"Almost ten years," he said.

"So you were with the judge back when he was on the New York State Supreme Court?"

"Yes," said Timitz.

"You're not a clerk, though, right?"

"I research cases for him, but I have no law training," he said. "Not in the traditional sense, at least."

"What's the nontraditional sense?" I asked.

"Being around a judge and his courtroom for ten straight years. Best law school there is."

"You're probably right about that," I said. "At the very least, you've learned the importance of having an attorney. Is he good, by the way? Your attorney?"

"I don't know," said Timitz. "I've never needed the guy before."

I wasn't sure if Glausen heard that as he came back around the corner of Kingsman's house. Either way, his timing was perfect.

In one hand was Timitz's cell phone. All eyes, however, were on his other hand.

Glausen was clutching a large knife, his shirtsleeve pulled down over his fingers to prevent getting any prints on it. There was some added pep in his step, and as he crossed over into the shine of the floodlight, the top half of the steel blade toward the handle practically glistened. It was clean as a whistle. Not the bottom half, though.

It was as dirty as dried blood.

"I repeat," said Glausen. "What kind of people ask for their lawyers?"

CHAPTER 86

"HE KNOWS we're watching him," I said.

"No; he thinks we're watching him," said Elizabeth. "He doesn't know for sure. No one can—that's the point."

I looked again at Timitz through the one-way mirror into the interrogation room at the Fiftieth Precinct. He was sitting, his arms folded on the metal table, completely expressionless.

"No," I said. "He *knows*."

If there was any room smaller than the interrogation room, it was the viewing room where Elizabeth and I stood on the other side of that one-way mirror. At least, that's the way it felt with the lights off.

The darkness also wasn't helping with what had become an unintended experiment in sleep deprivation. That dull ache in the joints had settled in, the eyes beginning to sting.

Elizabeth checked the time on her phone. It was

pushing 8:00 a.m. "Damn," she muttered. "Where the hell is this guy?"

"Is there a statute of limitations on waiting for an attorney?" I asked.

If there was, the one representing Timitz was cutting it close. Granted, Timitz had probably woken him up when he called from Kingsman's house, but that was more than an hour ago. Where was the guy coming from, Cleveland?

"We'll give him another five minutes," said Elizabeth.

"Then what?" I asked.

"I don't know," she said. "Ask me in five minutes."

Everything was falling into two categories now. What we knew and what we didn't. What we knew since arriving at the precinct was that Elijah Timitz was licensed to carry a concealed weapon in the state of New York. His name was in the database.

What we didn't know was the blood type on the knife found in his car.

The Fiftieth Precinct was hardly a forensics lab, but it could do your basic blood testing on the quick. Unfortunately, dried blood fell out of the realm of "basic" and required something called the absorption-elution technique. That took longer. Though maybe not as long as Timitz's attorney was taking.

"You want a refill?" I asked. There was an old Mr. Coffee down the hall.

"I couldn't even drink the first one," said Elizabeth.

She was right—the coffee was horrible. Sludge. Whoever made it should've been charged with depraved indifference to human consumption. But it was the only thing keeping me going.

"I'll be right back," I said.

I made my way down the hallway, passing Glausen's desk, where he was still working up his report on Timitz. His shift was almost over, and there were a few officers streaming in around him who looked decidedly fresher than anyone else. Not that Glausen was noticing. His head was down, his shoulders hunched. He was the body-language equivalent of a DO NOT DISTURB sign.

"Another victim, huh?" came a voice over my shoulder.

I turned to see one of those fresher-looking officers lining up behind me as I reached for the coffee. It took me a second. He was talking about the coffee.

"Yeah. I'm a glutton for punishment," I said, offering to fill his mug first.

"Thanks," he said. "Strangely enough, you get used to it."

He sidestepped over to a small fridge and grabbed a large carton of half-and-half. To free up a hand to pour it, he put down the newspaper tucked under his arm. It was the early edition of the *Gazette.*

Holy shit.

I grabbed the paper, lifting the front page closer to my eyes, if only to make sure I wasn't seeing things. I wasn't.

"Hey!" said the officer. "Where are you going? That's my paper!"

CHAPTER 87

ELIZABETH ALMOST killed us twice on the drive downtown, swerving in and out of traffic and blasting through intersections as if the streets of Manhattan were the backdrop to a video game.

"Nothing to it," she assured me, shouting over the siren of our borrowed patrol car. That was almost as funny as her telling the precinct captain that he could keep my motorcycle as collateral.

This is all because of you, Grimes. You're loving it, too, aren't you?

The headline above the picture of Judge Kingsman on the *Gazette*'s cover blared it in capital letters.

THE DEALER!

On the next page began the story. You could almost hear the back-and-forth between Grimes and his editor as they decided on the subhead, which might have packed an even bigger punch than the headline.

JUDGE, JURY & EXECUTIONER!
Arthur Kingsman had brought to life the ultimate revenge fantasy for a sitting judge who was sick and tired of letting the guilty go free because of loopholes in the law exploited by slick, high-priced lawyers.

Or so claimed Grimes. Or, more specifically, so claimed his unnamed source.

This source had evidence that Kingsman had hired a contract killer who, of all things, had his attempted murder charges dismissed by Kingsman years ago because of an illegal police search of his car's glove compartment. Grimes cited calls allegedly made by Kingsman to the contract killer from a pay phone inside the courthouse where he presided.

Having a surrogate commit the grisly murders? Using a pay phone to communicate with him? Kingsman was covering his tracks at every turn. Only that became the ultimate irony and the reason Grimes and the *Gazette* were so confident running with the story. Grimes's source had led him to the contract killer...

At the city morgue.

Three days ago, a man in his twenties named Reginald Hicks had been found stabbed to death in his apartment in the Bronx. Multiple tenants told detectives they had seen a man wearing a black fedora and a gray duffle coat in the building around the same time. All of them remembered the coat having very large toggle buttons, the same buttons on the same coat, along with the same black fedora, that Kingsman had been photographed wearing on numerous occasions.

Kingsman was covering his tracks at every turn, all right. Every last one. He had killed the guy who was doing all the killings for him. Reginald Hicks had managed to escape justice in Kingsman's courtroom. In the end, however, he wasn't able to escape Kingsman. He became one more victim of his revenge.

Elizabeth turned the corner onto Centre Street, the Thurgood Marshall United States Courthouse directly ahead.

"Damn. So much for getting here first," I said.

The front of the courthouse was a zoo of news trucks and reporters, all of them playing the same hunch we were. Grimes and the *Gazette* had treated the story as though they were carrying out the attack on Pearl Harbor—they gave no warning. Not to the police and certainly not to Kingsman. The odds were good that the judge went off to work unaware of it.

Of course, Elizabeth and I still didn't know where Kingsman had spent the night. *Is there a chance he actually did know in advance?*

We double-parked on the street, stepping out into the chaos. Courthouse guards were already

keeping anyone with a camera, microphone, and/
or perfectly coiffed hair off the steps and on the
sidewalk.

We had none of that—especially the hair, after
being up all night. But Elizabeth did have her
badge.

"Go ahead," said one of the guards.

No sooner did he move aside for us than one of
the reporters pointed and shouted, "There he is!"
as if he'd stepped out of some 1950s crime drama.
All at once, the entire press corps began rush-
ing madly up the steps. The guards never stood a
chance.

Kingsman, standing front and center on the
landing in front of the courthouse, was engulfed
within seconds.

The judge had a statement he wanted to make.

He wasn't the only one.

CHAPTER 88

"THIS WAY," said Elizabeth. "Over here."

I knew what she was thinking as I followed her up the rest of the steps, pushing past the media. They all needed to face Kingsman, but we didn't. When he was done with the reporters and turned around, the first people he saw—the first people he spoke to—absolutely had to be us. Best we positioned ourselves accordingly.

Not too close to him, though.

I've managed to learn a few things about a few things, but the one thing I apparently knew next to nothing about was the optics of an impromptu press conference.

If you want to look like you support the person doing the talking, you stand behind that person, where the cameras can see you. Otherwise you get the hell out of the shot.

Thankfully, Elizabeth had been there, done that. She yanked my arm seconds before every red dot on every camera lit up as they homed in on the judge. We were safely off to the side, out of frame.

"I'd like to comment on the so-called reporting in this morning's *Gazette,*" began Kingsman, slowly and calmly. "Then I'll be happy to take your questions, each and every one."

Kingsman wasn't wearing his robe. Nor was he behind the bench. But the judge was still the judge. He was laying the ground rules and instructing the jury. He knew as well as anybody—*better* than anybody, really—that the court of public opinion is more than just an expression. It's real.

It's also malleable. Like putty. Or a politician.

I stood next to Elizabeth, watching the horde of reporters collectively fall all over themselves so as not to miss a single word. Arms and shoulders bumping, they continued to jostle for position in the horseshoe that had formed around Kingsman. The space between him and the horde was disappearing fast. It was getting out of control.

"Please, everyone. There's no need for pushing and shoving," he said. That was far too polite, however, and he quickly realized it. Out wide went his arms, and up went his voice. *"Calm the hell down or I won't say another goddamn word."*

Much better.

All at once, the microphones and recorders fell

still. Each and every one. No—wait. All of them except one.

An arm was still moving, a body pushing through the crowd. I couldn't see his face, just the black recorder in his hand. Only it wasn't a recorder.

"Gun!"

I saw it, but I didn't yell it. You only yell it if you're Secret Service. It acts as a birdcall, telling all the other agents to collapse around the intended target.

It was someone else who yelled it, a reporter next to the shooter. He blurted it out before I could even take my first step, before I could try to—

Pop! Pop!

The first shot missed Kingsman, but the second didn't. His knees buckled, and his body collapsed at the top of the courthouse steps. I ran right past him, though. I had to. Everyone had run for cover except his killer. He was simply standing there, frozen. Except he wasn't a he.

The second I saw her face, I knew who she was.

She was vengeance.

CHAPTER 89

"LOWER THE gun!" I yelled.

I was running at her full speed, hurdling people still on the ground while trying not to tumble down the steps.

I'd been in her house. I'd smelled the bleach she'd used to clean her husband's blood off the floor. The blood was gone, but the stench of his murder would never fully go away in her mind, especially in its darkest corners.

She had read the *Gazette* and grabbed a cab, but not before first grabbing the 9mm Beretta that her husband had kept in his study. Jared Louden's wife was out for blood of her own.

"*Lower the gun!*" I yelled again, as loudly as I could.

It was aimed right at me, but that's not why I yelled. I hadn't even drawn the G42 that Elizabeth gave me, the bug she carried. Emily Louden was frozen. In shock. She couldn't pull that trigger again even if she wanted to.

No, I yelled because as long as she had that gun raised, at least one of the courthouse guards would reach for his—

Pop! Pop!

I could feel the bullets whiz by me, one followed by the other. They both struck Emily Louden in the chest, the navy-blue peacoat she was wearing exploding with two red spurts as she toppled back and collapsed.

She'd finally lowered her gun.

Immediately I felt another breeze as two guards sprinted past me, straight for Louden. I was the one now frozen. It was pandemonium outside the courthouse, some people still scrambling for cover, others calling 911, and still others seizing the moment—especially those newspeople with cameras. If it bleeds, it leads.

Some of the cameras were trained on Louden, the rest on Kingsman. I could see another guard hovering over the judge, radio in hand. I couldn't read his lips, but I could tell from his face that he was gauging Kingsman's chances. There might be a vacancy on the court.

This is crazy, huh, Elizabeth?

I spun back around, my eyes searching the top of the steps where we'd been standing. I looked left and right before turning a full three sixty, trying to spot her in the crowd. There were too many moving parts, a hornet's nest of people.

Elizabeth?

There was shouting, pointing, crying, consoling, and even one woman praying. Her hands, clasped tightly, were shaking.

Off in the distance, I could hear the sound of sirens. Kingsman and Emily Louden weren't moving. Perhaps they weren't even breathing.

But all I could feel was Elizabeth.

Something was wrong.

Terribly, terribly wrong...

CHAPTER 90

TWO PEOPLE shuffled to the left at the exact moment someone on the right leaned forward. For a split second, a space opened at the top of the steps, and I saw her profile. She was down, lying on her back, holding her chest. Her hand was covered in blood.

I raced up the steps, pushing people out of my way. Before I could even drop to my knees next to her I knew it was bad. The shot had hit her right below the collarbone, definitely piercing the lungs but, I hoped, not the heart. *I hoped.* I needed to see the entry wound to make sure.

"Who...who was it?" she asked. She could barely get out the words.

"Let's focus on you," I said.

I traded my hand for hers, keeping pressure on the wound while pulling back her blazer. Her white blouse underneath was soaked red.

"*Who?*" she repeated.

I told her only so she wouldn't keep trying to talk. "Louden's wife," I said.

Elizabeth blinked and managed a nod. I nodded back. Enough said. Senseless violence will make you scream to the heavens, but the crimes you can understand—no matter how wrong—just seem to settle over you like a tablecloth.

Elizabeth had been collateral damage, and she knew it.

"The ambulance is coming," I said. "We need to take a look, though."

Quickly I lifted my hand, using the hole in her blouse to tear it. Exactly what I didn't want to see was right there underneath it—a larger hole. Medicine has a lot of words and phrases that sound worse than what they're describing. They also have some that bluntly nail it to a T. *Sucking chest wound,* for instance.

The same people who had taught me how to kill had also taught me a few things about keeping someone alive. It wasn't quite med school, but it was a little more advanced than the Boy Scouts.

Elizabeth had worse than a collapsed lung. The severe shortness of breath, jugular vein distension...too much air had entered through the wound, leaking between the chest wall and her lung. She was in danger of what's called a tension pneumothorax, which also nailed it in terms of being as bad as it sounded. Next came shock. Then death.

Over my dead body.

I put my palm back on the entry wound, applying pressure. With my other hand I yanked off my belt. Ideally I'd have something sterile I could use. Next best thing was the back of my cell phone, because the case was stainless steel.

"I've got to lift your back for a second," I said, looping the belt around her chest to seal the phone in place over the wound. For what I was about to do next, I needed both hands free.

The sirens were louder; help was close. Not close enough, though.

The first ambulance to arrive would have a gurney to unload and stairs to negotiate. Wheels up or wheels down, gurneys and stairs don't mix. Most of all, the EMTs carrying it would have a decision to make as first responders.

Whom to treat first?

Unless I decided for them.

CHAPTER 91

I LOOKED over at the circle gathered around Judge Kingsman. I couldn't see him; there were too many people. Same for Emily Louden.

Making it even harder was the circle that had now formed around Elizabeth and me, including a cameraman and a few reporters.

I turned back to Elizabeth, her dark brown eyes staring up into mine. "Trust me," I said.

She had at least one more word left in her. "Always," she told me.

There was no time for a countdown. I scooped her up, cradling her in my arms. Don't move a shooting victim, the book says. Screw the book.

Run, Dylan. Run like hell...

Down on Centre Street in front of the courthouse, I could see the first of the ambulances approaching as I made my way down the steps. The pandemonium had spread. There were police lights flashing, sirens blaring, a cop waving frantically as he tried to part the heavy sea of cars, cabs, and trucks with their rubbernecking drivers. A news helicopter whirled overhead.

"Almost there," I told Elizabeth. "Hang on." But as I glanced down at her, she was even paler and barely breathing. Her lips were blue.

Faster, Dylan! Faster than you've ever run in your life...

I reached the bottom of the steps and sprinted into traffic, on a collision course with the grille of an ambulance. Stop or hit us—that was the choice.

It stopped. Out came the driver. He was pissed for a split second, or about as long as it took for him to look down and see Elizabeth.

"She's going into shock," I said.

"C'mon," he told me.

He led us to the back of the ambulance, where his partner had already bolted from his shotgun seat, popping open the doors from the inside. I handed her off, the two placing her on a gurney and immediately strapping it down. I climbed aboard.

"Out!" said the driver.

"But—"

He grabbed my arm, nodding at Elizabeth's

badge clipped to her slacks. "We got her," he said, handing me my belt and cell phone.

I hopped out, watching the doors close in front of me. I didn't want to argue, not if it meant wasting one more precious second.

I didn't know how many Elizabeth had left.

BOOK FIVE

SHOWDOWN

CHAPTER 92

I KEPT staring down at my shoes.

I had washed up in the bathroom near the surgical suite on the fifth floor of Manhattan South Hospital. My hands had been covered in Elizabeth's blood. My shirt and jacket were, too, but they had long since been tossed in the garbage in favor of a sweatshirt from the lobby gift shop. I ♥ NEW YORK, it read.

I wasn't so sure anymore.

I kept staring down at my shoes because I'd missed a spot, as it were. There was a drop of Elizabeth's blood on the toe of my right loafer, and all I could do was keep looking at it. The waiting room was packed, but I had blocked out the chorus of hushed conversations around me, various loved ones talking to one another if only to help pass the time and maybe, just maybe, not be consumed by the worries that would otherwise eat them alive.

As for me, I was getting devoured. *Will she make it? Please, please, let her survive.*

I suddenly got this weird sense. A vibe. I tried tuning back to the surrounding conversations, only they were gone. They'd stopped. The room was utterly silent save for one sound—a voice from the TV that hung on the far wall. I looked up, my head on a swivel, to see everyone staring at me. I then looked at the TV and saw why. The local news was showing me racing down the steps at the courthouse, Elizabeth in my arms.

"The shooter, identified as Emily Louden, was declared dead at the scene. Her intended target, Judge Arthur Kingsman, survived the shooting and is currently listed in stable condition. A second victim, shown here, is believed to have been hit by a stray bullet. She's been identified as Detective Elizabeth Needham of the NYPD, although there's been no official statement as to her condition. The man seen here carrying her to an ambulance is unknown."

I bounced some quick glances around the room as if to say, "Yeah, that's me." Most of the people went back to whatever it was they were doing—talking, reading, staring at their phones. The few who didn't stop staring, though, received a longer stare back from me, the kind with no ambiguity. *Mind your own effin' business.*

Back to my shoes.

Only for another minute. Another pair of shoes had walked right up to mine. Wingtips. "You look like shit," said Beau Livingston.

"If you're about to tell me that I need to get some sleep, save your breath," I told him.

"Okay, I won't tell you," he said. "Any word on Elizabeth?"

"Nothing," I said. "She's still in surgery."

"I saw what you did. You may have saved her life."

"We'll see."

He sat down in the empty seat to my left only to realize that about half a dozen people were within earshot. That was half a dozen too many.

"Come with me," he said.

The last thing I wanted to do was listen to Livingston, but he clearly had news about something.

I followed him out to the hallway, down to an area near a soda machine. We were alone; no one could hear us. Still, he whispered.

"Doctors won't allow us to question Kingsman yet," he said.

"You'll want to wait anyway."

"Why?"

"He's most likely sedated," I said. "Any judge, including him, would rule it inadmissible."

"Good point," said Livingston. He sighed. "Fuckin' Grimes and the *Gazette,* huh?"

"The story or the fact that they gave no one a heads-up?" I asked.

"Both," he said. "Could you imagine if they got it wrong?"

"What makes you so sure they got it right?" I asked.

CHAPTER 93

"THAT GUY you and Elizabeth brought in? Timitz? I got off the phone a few minutes ago with the captain of the Fiftieth," said Livingston.

"Did the lawyer ever show?" I asked.

"He did, but only after Timitz called him a second time, or so I was told. Not just any lawyer, either. It was Peter Xavier."

I followed the legal world about as closely as I did cricket matches in Mumbai, but Xavier was a name I knew. The guy was a killer defense attorney, as high-profile as they come. The joke I read about him once was that he had to have his suits custom made with a slit in the back to make room for his dorsal fin.

"Why did he need a guy like that?" I asked, although I didn't intend to say the words out loud. It was a reflex.

Nonetheless, Livingston had an answer.

"According to Xavier, Timitz was afraid he might be wrong about his boss."

"What do you mean wrong?"

"Timitz had told Xavier days ago that he suspected Judge Kingsman might be involved with the Dealer killings. He claimed he overheard Kingsman on a pay phone in the courthouse."

"Let me guess," I said. "Timitz was afraid to go to the police because he'd be risking his job if it turned out Kingsman was innocent."

"Exactly. Of course that doesn't explain the knife in Timitz's car," said Livingston. "Now ask me what does."

"It's not Timitz's car," I said. "It's Kingsman's."

Livingston looked shocked. "How the hell did you know that?"

"Lucky guess," I said.

"For years, Kingsman has let Timitz borrow the car on the weekends, a perk for his working on the case files," said Livingston.

"So Kingsman could've easily been the one to leave the knife in the car," I said. "Why even bother testing the blood on it, right?"

"The results came in an hour ago," he said. "It's AB negative, Jared Louden's blood type."

"The rarest of rare blood types, to boot," I said. "Imagine that."

Livingston cocked his head at me. "What are you saying?"

Nothing yet, Beau, at least not to you…

"Where's Timitz now?" I asked.

"Naturally Xavier said we had to arrest him or release him, one or the other. We couldn't arrest him. Still, the captain at the Fiftieth put four of his guys on him until we know for sure that Kingsman was the Dealer."

"How long ago was that?"

"Around forty-five minutes."

"Did Timitz know about Kingsman being shot?"

"While still at the precinct? I don't know," said Livingston. "Why? Do you want me to find out?"

"Don't bother," I said. "But bring Timitz back in."

"What do you mean?"

"I mean *bring him back in.*"

"I told you, Reinhart, we can't arrest him."

"I don't think you're going to have to worry about that," I said. "Just make the call."

CHAPTER 94

I WALKED back to the waiting room and began staring at my shoes again—and that drop of Elizabeth's blood. Ten minutes later, Livingston's wingtips appeared again.

"How did you know?" he asked.

"Same as before," I said. "Lucky guess."

"Bullshit." He sat down. He no longer cared who heard him. "Word just came in. Timitz had gone home and then out to a supermarket after leaving the precinct. One officer had the front entrance, another had the back. Two others followed him inside. Somewhere along the way they lost him."

"A supermarket?"

"He must have known he was being followed."

"Gee, you think?"

Livingston's phone beeped, and he looked at the screen. By the way his jaw tightened, I could tell it was a text from the mayor.

"He wants you back at City Hall pronto, right?" I asked. "He's demanding to know what's going on."

"Yeah," said Livingston, "and you're coming with me."

"The hell I am," I said. "I'm staying right here."

He knew he wasn't going to persuade me otherwise, not while Elizabeth was fighting for her life.

"Fine," he said. "I'll be coming back, then."

"Duly noted."

Livingston left in a huff. I actually smiled, if only because it made me think of how Elizabeth would've been smiling. She would've loved to have seen me piss him off like that.

What she wouldn't have loved, though, was the thought of my sitting here and doing nothing while Timitz was out there, whereabouts unknown. I could almost hear her voice, saying what I was thinking, putting it together.

Timitz didn't really call his lawyer from Kingsman's house, did he? He wanted to wait until we knew about Grimes's front-page story, and that could only mean one thing. He was Grimes's source.

I quickly stepped out to the hallway again, dialing Grimes's number at the *Gazette*. Three rings felt like an eternity.

"No, he's not in," said the young woman who answered his line. It was Grimes's assistant. I could tell she knew my name when I gave it to her.

"Are you sure he's not there?" I asked.

"Very sure," she said. "He said he's working from home today."

"You spoke to him? *He told you that?*"

"Yes, he called about half an hour ago," she said. "Why?"

CHAPTER 95

IN THE movies, a father working for the CIA would never want his son to follow in his footsteps. You could almost picture the heartfelt scene. A park bench or an old booth in a bar, the ink barely dry on the son's college diploma. There would be long stares, furrowed brows, and the perfectly scripted dialogue about the risks being too great.

Life ain't the movies.

At least not my father's life. Besides, he hates the movies. As he once told me, *"Who needs to watch some made-up crap when you can soak up the real-life stuff?"*

Not only did my father not have a problem with my working for the CIA, he also recommended me. There was one caveat, though. Words to live by. Literally.

"Sometimes, they'll have you do something crazy. Other times, they'll have you do something stupid. Just

don't ever let 'em make you do crazy and stupid at the same time."

I never did.

All these years later, though, I was suddenly like my dad and the movies. *Who needs the CIA when you can combine crazy and stupid all on your own?*

I took a deep breath and exhaled. Then I rang the doorbell.

Silence followed, but I knew he was on the other side of the door. With any luck, Grimes was still there, too. Still alive, that is.

"I came alone," I announced.

The silence that followed this time somehow sounded different. Sure enough, I next heard the snap of a dead bolt. The door opened.

Grimes simply stared at me, saying nothing at first. I stared back at him, noticing the down vest he was wearing. It was wired to the hilt with explosives. Give him credit: he managed to crack a joke about it.

"I saw it on the rack at Barneys and just had to have it," he said.

If only I could've laughed.

"Come in and close the door," said the voice behind Grimes. "Oh, and be sure to lock it."

I stepped inside as Grimes followed instructions, the dead bolt snapping back into place. In front of me, past the foyer, I saw Timitz sitting on one of the couches in the living room, a lit cigarette in one hand and a detonator in the other.

He held up the cigarette and smiled. "I know. These things will kill you, right?"

Grimes walked past me, sitting down in an armchair kitty-corner to Timitz. In front of the chair, on a glass coffee table, was an open laptop. *What are you writing, Grimes, and what's with all the scribbled pages spread out around you?*

"You should sit as well, Professor," said Timitz.

He was dressed in a black suit now with a white shirt open at the collar. He was freshly washed and scrubbed, a shine to his face. However he managed to elude the cops tailing him, he apparently never broke a sweat.

I walked the length of the living room, settling into the couch opposite his. All I knew was that I wanted to be facing him. And the detonator.

The thing was the size of a roll of quarters, with Timitz's thumb resting on top of the pressure release, a.k.a. the dead man's switch, which was surely linked to the vest via Bluetooth. All in all, easy to make if you know how. Thanks a lot, Internet.

There are two types of serial killers. Those who want to get caught and those who really want to get caught.

"You never intended to get away with this, did you?" I asked.

Timitz took a drag off his cigarette, ignoring the

question. "This is quite an apartment," he said, glancing around. "Don't you think?"

Grimes had clearly done well for himself. High ceilings, sleek furniture, gallery-quality artwork. The ultimate bachelor pad.

"It's very nice," I said.

Timitz smiled again. "Who says crime doesn't pay?"

I glanced over at Grimes as he forced a smile. His strategy was clear. Go along, get along…and maybe get to live.

"At least answer me this," I said, my eyes locked on Timitz and the detonator. "Have you been planning this moment all along?"

"It crossed my mind," said Timitz.

"More than crossed," I said. "I've learned you leave nothing to chance. Almost nothing, that is."

He knew exactly where I was heading.

"Yes, our grieving widow this morning," he said.

I nodded. "A wild card, right?"

"Yeah," said Timitz. He leaned forward, his thumb twitching on the detonator. *I hate wild cards.*

CHAPTER 96

MY MIND raced with thoughts of Timitz's childhood. Possible OCD, anger issues, a stunted internal conscience. None of it mattered, though. Not now. He was on a couch, but it was too late for therapy.

Still, there was a mind to pry. Answers to get.

"Judge Kingsman is only good to you alive, isn't he?" I asked.

"Of course," said Timitz.

"You want him healthy and on display, an innocent man jailed for all the guilty people he set free," I said.

"That wouldn't make him innocent, now, would it?"

"Exactly the point you wanted to make," I said.

"Well, if we're laying all our cards on the table," said Timitz, "I don't need a conviction. The indictment would be enough."

"But would it be the end?" I asked. "Would you be done killing?"

"Do I look like I'm done?" he asked. Timitz leaned back into the couch again, crossing his legs. He was calm. Too calm. "What happened this morning simply means we speed things up a bit. Clever of Allen here, though. The way he signaled you?"

"Not clever enough, apparently," I said.

"According to an interview in the *Observer* a few years back," said Timitz, "the infamous Allen Grimes never writes his column at home. He's always out and around the town somewhere. He brags about it, too, like it somehow makes him more of a New Yorker. Had you read the same interview, Professor?"

"No. I heard it straight from the source," I said.

Timitz smirked. "I rest my case." He turned to Grimes. We'd both been talking about him as if he weren't in the room. He wished. "Of course, there's a first time for everything, right? How's it looking so far, Allen?"

So that's what Grimes was writing. Timitz was using Grimes's column as a mouthpiece, a chance to tell the world his side of the story. It also explained the endless scribbled pages. Every inch of every paper spread around Grimes was covered with the musings and motives of a serial killer. The Dealer had his own manifesto.

Grimes tilted the screen of his laptop, gazing at what he'd written. Or was it transcribed? "I think it's what you want," he said.

I had a real bad feeling about where this was all heading. I could picture it, the scenes flickering in my head. Like a movie.

Grimes finishes the piece, hits Send to e-mail it to the *Gazette*, and Timitz thanks him for his time before bidding us both adieu. That damn detonator keeps our asses plastered to our seats right up until the moment that Timitz, along with Elvis, has left the building. At which point Timitz lifts his thumb, triggers the vest, and the only thing left of Grimes and me are some DNA samples.

At least Grimes would probably win a Pulitzer posthumously.

I could picture it, all right. I just couldn't believe it.

Maybe Grimes had served his purpose for Timitz, but my role still seemed underwritten. There had to be something more, something I was missing. Every instinct I had was telling me the same thing.

The Dealer still had something up his sleeve.

CHAPTER 97

TIMITZ STUBBED out his cigarette, using nothing but the glass of Grimes's coffee table as an ashtray. With his free hand he motioned inside his jacket. "How rude of me," he said. "Would you like a smoke, Professor?"

"That depends," I said. "Will it be my last?"

"I haven't decided yet," he answered.

"I think you have."

"You do, huh? Have I become that transparent now?"

Engagement. I could see it in his eyes, the way they lit up from anything or anyone that challenged him.

"Wasn't that the idea?" I asked. I leaned back against the couch, matching his pose. "Wasn't that what you wanted, to challenge me?"

"You say 'challenge,' I say 'use,'" he said.

"Either way, here I am," I said. "Why me, though? Why my book?"

"Don't you know?" asked Timitz.

"Let's just say I have a theory," I said. "But you don't agree with it."

"The opposite," said Timitz. "I think permission theory is an excellent approach to understanding abnormal behavior. In fact much of what I've done is modeled after it."

"A simple fan letter would've sufficed," I said.

"In a way, you'll get that, too," said Timitz. He turned to Grimes. "Did you send it yet?"

Grimes nodded.

There was something almost poetic about the faith Timitz placed in Grimes to e-mail what might be his very last column. Timitz didn't need to watch him hit that Send button or even read exactly how he'd distilled his manifesto. Grimes loved to drink and chase women. But he *lived* to write. It was only fitting that was how he'd spend his last remaining hours before dying.

As if on cue, Timitz leaned forward again. He held the detonator out in front of him. His words were all too familiar. "Can we ever really judge behavior simply by the behavior itself?"

"What else can you quote from the book?" I asked. "Go ahead—tell me that the differences between normal behavior and abnormal behavior have nothing to do with behavior but, rather, the circumstances in which they happen. Tell me all the exceptions to *Thou shalt not kill*. Tell me about wars and self-defense. Or capital punishment. Then tell me how killing us will help you prove your point."

"It's not my point; it's yours," said Timitz. "There'll be a lot written about me. That I was evil. That I was cruel and unjust. But you know what the truth is, and, in time, so will others. Because you know me, Professor. You've *already* written about me. For everything that I am, everything that I've done, the one thing I'm not is abnormal, and you know it. I'm the asterisk, the exception that proves the rule. *Crazy* is our security blanket, the word we use instead of the truth when the truth scares us even more. Justice isn't blind. *It's lazy.*"

Timitz locked his elbows, his arms shooting straight out in front him. His grip tightened on the detonator, every knuckle going white.

"Shall we count down together?" he asked.

CHAPTER 98

THE SERIAL killer who had thought of almost everything. Did he forget to frisk me?

Or did he choose not to?

I whipped my arm around, grabbing the grip of Elizabeth's G42, tucked into the back of my pants.

All I could see was the way Timitz was holding the detonator. It was out over the coffee table, ripe for the taking.

If you want to shoot to kill, you aim for the head or the heart. If you want to shoot to stun, you aim for the stomach.

I literally had one shot.

My arm came whipping back around as I found the trigger, squeezing it hard and fast a few times before dropping the gun. I lunged forward, my hands outstretched and reaching for his before any law of physics could kick in and kill us all.

He was shot, he was bleeding, but he hadn't let go—his thumb was still lodged on top of the dead man's switch as I slammed my palm down to keep it that way until I could pry it from him.

You gettin' this all down, Grimes?

Grimes?

He was gone. No—he was behind me. He'd scooped up the gun. "Don't!" I yelled.

I knew what he was thinking. *Shoot Timitz again.* He wanted to help, to do something, but Timitz and I were now one big moving target above that glass table, and I could practically hear Grimes's hand shaking.

I was bigger than Timitz. I was stronger. He was bleeding out and losing strength. It was only a matter of time. The only thing I needed to do was keep that thumb of his—

Huh?

Whatever fight Timitz had left in him drained out of his arms in an instant. He wasn't pulling or pushing anymore. He wasn't doing anything except surrendering.

"You win," he whispered.

I'd sooner lick an electric fence than trust a serial killer, but he was coordinating the transfer of the detonator, moving his thumb just enough underneath my grasp so I could take control of it without triggering the switch. Suddenly it was all mine.

You son of a bitch—are you kidding me?

It took only two seconds of holding it in my

hands to realize the detonator was fake, a fugazie. It had the weight of an empty Pez dispenser and was just as hollow.

Was there another trigger mechanism? Was this a decoy?

Timitz began to laugh. His chest was heaving, his lungs doling out their last breaths, and he was using them to laugh at us.

"Jesus Christ," said Grimes, taking a closer look at the vest Timitz had made him wear. There were wires galore, but that was it. The C-4 was as fake as the detonator. "It's painted Play-Doh."

Now you tell me, Grimes.

Timitz had blown up Jackie Palmer's apartment with Jackie in it. When it came to explosives, he knew what he was doing. So why did he do this?

"He wanted you here," said Grimes. "He wanted it to look like I was tipping you off. I'm sorry; I had no choice." He glanced at the vest again. "At least I didn't think I did."

"It's okay," I said. "Call 911."

That was nothing more than protocol, though. Timitz had no intention of hanging around until the EMTs arrived.

I watched as he fell back onto the couch, the cushions easing his fall but not the pain. He grimaced, his face contorted. Still, he continued to laugh.

Then, of all things, he began to sing. And, of all songs, it was "Take Me Out to the Ball Game."

He could barely get the words out.

"Buy me some peanuts and Cracker Jack. I don't care if I..."

The words stopped. There was no more singing. There was no more breathing. Tomorrow's front-page headline lay there motionless on the couch, his head slumped to the side.

HE'S THE REAL DEALER!

...AND HE'S DEAD.

CHAPTER 99

RULES ARE rules.

No one was allowed to see Elizabeth in the ICU at Manhattan South Hospital after she came out of surgery—not even her immediate family, even if they had arrived. Her sister was still en route from Boston, and her mother's flight from Seattle was almost three hours from landing.

The phrase often heard is "critical but stable condition." Elizabeth was in only one of those conditions. Critical. She had lost a massive amount of blood, her heart rate was too low, and she was barely conscious.

But she was alive.

"You should've told the nurse that you were her brother," said Tracy. He'd been waiting with me the past two hours, the first of which was spent repeatedly lifting his jaw off the floor as I told him everything that had happened.

"You heard the nurse—not even family," I said. "Hell, they didn't even let the mayor in."

Deacon had come and gone, as had Livingston again. I would never second-guess their concern for Elizabeth, but it was hard not to notice their ulterior motives. For Livingston and his boss, it was another photo op. The mayor arrived with flowers in hand and a prepared statement for the press. There were thoughts and prayers for Elizabeth up front before a quick pivot to the city's resilience. "Our streets are safer today, our mettle having been tested," he said.

Livingston probably had that line focus-grouped for the mayor in advance.

There were a couple of other visitors. I spoke to Robert briefly—Elizabeth's fellow detective— who seemingly knew more about her than anyone else. He reminded me that she and her father weren't on speaking terms. "Her mother's forgiven him for cheating, but Elizabeth hasn't," said Robert. "The girl really knows how to hold a grudge."

"This is crazy," said Tracy when it was only the two of us again in the waiting room. "You should be able to see her."

"It's okay," I said.

"No; it's really not. I'm sick of stupid rules for the sake of rules. It's always about what we can't do."

I rarely, if ever, put Tracy on the proverbial couch, but it was impossible not to see that he was projecting his disappointment over our adoption efforts onto this situation. In fact, from a certain angle, the nurse who told us that Elizabeth couldn't have any visitors sort of looked like Ms. Peckler from the Gateway Adoption Agency. She was even carrying around a clipboard.

It was obviously still bothering him. It bothered me, too. The only silver lining to chasing a serial killer, though, was that it took my mind off everything else.

"Excuse me," Tracy called out. The nurse happened to be standing in the hallway checking her clipboard. She came over, although she didn't seem too happy about it.

"Yes?" she asked.

"I know you said Detective Needham can't have visitors while still in the ICU," said Tracy, "and I know there's probably a good reason for the rule, but—"

"Good," said the nurse, cutting him off. "Then there's no reason to revisit the conversation, right?"

I looked at Tracy, who was blinking in disbelief. The words were forming on his tongue. He was loaded for bear.

Oh, shit, here we go again…

I was so busy bracing myself that I didn't notice

the other nurse who had come over. I could tell she was from inside the ICU. She had that look of experience, of having seen it all.

"Are you Dr. Reinhart?" she asked.

I nodded. "Yes."

"Detective Needham just regained full consciousness," she said. "You must be pretty special to her, because you're the first person she asked for."

"Can I see her?" I asked.

"Normally, you're not allowed to," she said before giving me a smile. "But what good is a rule if you can't make an exception to it?"

CHAPTER 100

ELIZABETH WAS bruised and bandaged and pale as a ghost. There were wires and tubes sticking out of her, a tangled mess. She took one look at me, though, and cracked a smile.

"Christ, I thought I was the one in bad shape," she said.

"Yeah, well, only one of us has gotten any sleep."

We both left the subtext unspoken. She almost didn't wake up.

"Are you in pain?" I asked.

"Only when I breathe." She smiled again, reaching for my hand. "Thank you...for everything."

"Nothing that you wouldn't have done for me," I said.

The story of what happened at Grimes's apartment could wait—or that was my thinking. I should've known better about Detective Elizabeth Needham. If she was breathing, she was working.

"I overheard two doctors talking about Timitz," she said. "Tell me everything."

I did. I told her everything, including the one thing I hadn't told anyone else yet. "When we were first at Kingsman's house, in his study," I said. "There was something about my book on his shelf."

"I remember there was no dust jacket," she said.

"There was no dust, period. The last time that bookshelf, let alone the study, got a cleaning was probably while Kingsman's wife was still alive. Mine was the only book not covered in dust, though," I said.

"Timitz put it there."

"As it turns out. We couldn't know it at the time."

"But you picked up on it," she said. "Then you heard Timitz had called his attorney a second time…"

"The book, the knife in Kingsman's car—Timitz was framing him. I still couldn't be sure, though. Then, before I went to Grimes's apartment, I made sure."

"How?"

"Julian," I said. "The storage facility where Kingsman keeps his files uses an online backup service on their security cameras. Julian was able to find Timitz going in and out of the building. He had a key."

"So Timitz pulled Dr. Bensen's file and made sure you couldn't miss it," said Elizabeth. "He was leading you to Kingsman all along."

"That's the part I still don't understand," I said. "Did he really need me? He had everything he wanted with Grimes—a guy to tell his story."

"Grimes was his pawn; you were his challenge," she said. "You made it interesting for him. He admitted as much."

"Maybe," I said. "For sure, Grimes is going to be a busy guy for a while."

Grimes had a story to write. A bunch of stories, actually. He also had amends to make. He'd been duped by Timitz into thinking Judge Kingsman was the Dealer. The mistake nearly cost Kingsman his life. If it had, it would've also cost Grimes his job, if not his entire bank account. Luckily for him, Kingsman hardly seemed like a guy who would file a civil suit. You could almost hear him citing the absence of malice.

Not only did Grimes now have the Dealer's manifesto, he also had his own eyewitness account of how the man who wrote it died. For the next couple of weeks, his paper would essentially be renamed the *Grimes Gazette*.

"You're going to use it, aren't you?" I asked him on the phone when he called me to check on Elizabeth.

Grimes knew what I meant. The nickname. "You

better believe it, Dr. Death," he said. "Don't worry. By the time I'm done you'll probably get a book deal out of it."

"For the record," I told him, "I think I'm done writing books for a while."

The last one was quite the troublemaker.

"All right, that's enough talking, you two," came the voice of another ICU nurse. She'd come over to take Elizabeth's blood pressure. "Our girl needs some rest."

I watched as the nurse looked me up and down, practically wincing. "Don't say it," I told her.

She said it anyway. "You could use some rest yourself, my friend. A shower wouldn't hurt, either."

Elizabeth laughed softly, as much as the pain would let her. It was easily the best sound in the world. She was out of the woods.

She was going to be okay.

CHAPTER 101

TRACY?

I returned to the waiting room. He was gone from his seat. He wasn't in the hallway, either.

I figured maybe he went to the bathroom or to get some coffee. Perhaps he wanted some privacy somewhere to make a call. It could've been anything. Then I thought about it for a moment and realized.

It could only be one thing.

I took the elevator down to the second floor, following the signs on the wall. They were pink and blue.

"There you are," I said.

I turned to see what Tracy was looking at. He had come to the maternity ward. The two of us were gazing through a large glass window at a roomful of newborns.

"I couldn't help myself," he said.

It was his tone. Each word sounded more anguished than the one before it.

"You've got to stop blaming yourself, Tracy."

"How can I? I ruined it for us."

"No, you didn't."

"I know you want to believe that," he said. "You're trying so hard to convince yourself it wasn't my fault."

"I don't need any convincing. I was there."

I turned so he could look at me. I wanted him to see my face, my eyes, to know that I was telling the truth. He kept staring straight ahead, though, and in the silence that followed I got the sense that I was missing something. This was about more than our adopting a baby. This was about us.

"You have feelings for her, don't you?" he asked.

"Don't be silly," I said.

"I'm not being silly," he said. "Be honest."

"Why would you think that?"

"I was there, too," he said. "I heard the nurse. Elizabeth wakes up, and you're her first thought."

"Tracy, look at me," I said. He finally did. "Of course I have feelings for her, but it's different. They're not the same feelings I have for you, that I'll always have for you."

He looked into my eyes. He could see the truth.

"I'm sorry. I guess I just needed to hear you say it."

"It's okay," I assured him.

He smiled. "She is pretty good-looking, I have to admit."

"Yeah. If I were straight I'd be all over her," I said.

"Yeah. Me, too," he said.

It felt good to laugh. It felt even better to hear Tracy laugh. He turned back to the window, pointing. "You see the one in the back row?"

I followed the line of his finger. "Second from the right?"

"Yes," he said. "Are you thinking what I'm thinking?"

A healthy baby boy—very healthy—was fast asleep in his bassinet, his chubby, round face all scrunched up. His little blue cap had slid off his head, revealing not a stitch of hair.

"Uncle Fester from *The Addams Family*," I said.

Tracy laughed again. "Totally, right?"

"Another classic TV show, by the way."

"How did I know you were going to say that?"

"Because you know me all too well."

"I do," said Tracy. "Don't I?"

"Yes," I said, taking his hand. "You do."

CHAPTER 102

I NEVER understood the expression "sleeping like a baby." All the babies I've ever known or heard about slept like alarm clocks, waking up their parents every few hours without fail.

"How did you sleep?" asked Tracy late the next morning.

"Like a log," I answered. Logs make much more sense. They lie there and don't move. That was me. Ten hours of blissful sleep, followed by a shave, a shower, some coffee, a bagel, and some more coffee.

Elizabeth had been moved out of the ICU. I checked in with her briefly. Her mother and sister were with her, and I told her I'd stop by later in the afternoon after I picked up my bike from the Fiftieth Precinct.

"Have you watched any of the news on TV?" she asked.

"No, not yet," I said.

"What about the *Gazette*? Have you seen it?"

"Do I want to?"

"I don't know, *Dr. Death*. Personally, I think your ego was too big to begin with," she said.

I hung up and checked out the online edition of the paper on my laptop. Grimes was true to his word on both counts. One, I had a new nickname whether I liked it or not. Two, he made me look good.

Of course, the better I looked, the better he looked. In fact the way he described "hunting down the Dealer," one would think that Elizabeth and I were attached to him at the hip. Even Brian Williams would've snickered at that.

To his credit, though, Grimes took sole responsibility for getting the story wrong about Kingsman. He could've hid behind the *Gazette* and its editors, but he stepped up and shouldered all the blame.

Multiple witnesses had seen a man wearing Kingsman's fedora and duffle coat—the one with the toggle buttons—in the building where Reginald Hicks lived. He was the supposed contract killer Kingsman had hired and subsequently murdered to cover his tracks.

It was Kingsman's fedora and coat, all right, only it was Timitz wearing them. He had taken them from Kingsman's home while the judge was away giving a lecture at the Pritzker School of Law at Northwestern University.

Perhaps more impressive than Grimes's mea culpa, however, was how quickly and accurately he was able to dissect the Dealer's background, linking it not only to his motivation but also to the means by which he carried out his murders. Grimes joked that when we first met he understood only half of my book. Truth was, he had it down cold.

Elijah Timitz was the troubled adopted son of Bill and Mallory Timitz from Buffalo, New York. Bill was a demolition contractor whose company specialized in felling major structures using targeted explosions. Mallory worked as a technician at a platelet and neutrophil immunology laboratory. In other words, Elijah Timitz grew up around blood and dynamite. He was smart and had high standardized test scores but was known as a loner. As for his propensity for guns and knives, Grimes noted that Timitz had participated in survival camps in upstate New York and paid membership dues at two different shooting ranges.

Grimes was even able to discover how Timitz could've known Jared Louden's rare AB negative blood type. As a research assistant for Judge Kingsman, Timitz had access to a police report of a DUI arrest in which Louden refused a Breathalyzer test in favor of having his blood drawn.

All in all, Grimes proved to be more of a journalist than people gave him credit for, myself included. He was thorough yet concise, writing in a style that was compelling without being overly burdened with hyperbole.

I couldn't know it at the time, but he only made one mistake. Actually, it was more like an omission.

Only minutes after I was done reading all Grimes's reporting in the *Gazette,* my phone rang. It was the landline.

I didn't recognize the number, but I answered anyway.

"Hello?"

It was Timitz.

CHAPTER 103

THE FEELING was more than déjà vu as I walked into the forensic biology laboratory on East 26th Street. It was dread.

"You need to see something," Dr. Ian Wexler had told me over the phone. "It's Timitz."

The Office of Chief Medical Examiner still reeked of antiseptic, but Wexler's attitude toward me had completely changed when I greeted him in his autopsy suite. He'd read what Grimes wrote in the *Gazette*. He didn't actually tell me that, nor did he have to. The fact that he dialed my number before calling the police said it all. Wexler was cutting out the middleman.

Apparently, Elijah Timitz had something else he wanted to share with me.

"It's on his inner forearm, a few inches up from the wrist," said Wexler, walking over to Timitz. I didn't know it was Timitz until he pulled back the sheet covering him. "The onset of lividity removed the swelling and redness, but the raised skin still gives it away. It's around two days old. Three tops."

I was looking at a tattoo on Timitz's arm. It was a black spade with an *A* in the middle of it. The ace of spades.

Had it been an old tattoo, the takeaway might have been different. Timitz liked cards, so—in keeping with permission theory—it only made sense that he would target his next victims by using cards. The fact that this was a new tattoo, and its location on his body, suggested something else entirely.

The Dealer was dead, but he wasn't done.

Is it really possible?

If Timitz truly had one more trick up his sleeve, then it would be one for the ages. A serial killer who managed to kill from the grave.

"Who else knows?" I asked.

"Only you so far," said Wexler. "Obviously, though, I'll need to put it in my report."

"Of course," I said.

Wexler gazed down at Timitz. "You know, I usually never cover anybody with a sheet in here," he said. "This guy, though? I can barely stand to look at him."

I understood. Yet looking at Timitz was suddenly all I could do. I stared at the bullet holes, shots that I had fired. The holes were black, the skin around them singed. I stared at Timitz's face, his almost serene expression. His eyes were closed, but it still felt as if he were staring right back, willing me on.

C'mon, Professor. You didn't think I'd simply go gently into that good night, did you?

This was his plan from the very beginning. He always intended to die for his cause. But this part didn't make sense.

He was hell-bent on exposing Judge Kingsman for being a pawn of an unjust legal system. Mission accomplished. Grimes wrote about it ad nauseam in the *Gazette*.

So why kill someone else? Who was the ace of spades?

Most of all, how could Timitz do it while lying here on this slab?

That's for you to figure out, Professor.
This is really why I chose you.

CHAPTER 104

TICK-TOCK…

With a picture of the tattoo on my cell phone, I was quickly in a cab again and heading north to the Fiftieth Precinct to retrieve my bike. The other destination was on my way. I was going to stop back at Kingsman's house, in Riverdale.

All things considered, the judge had gotten lucky. As Elizabeth could attest to, Emily Louden wasn't exactly a crack shot. The bullet that hit Kingsman got him cleanly in the arm. It was in and out and only flesh. No bone. He'd be in pain for a few days, but he had the luxury of going home without having to spend a night in the hospital.

"Greetings, Dr. Death," he said with a wry smile, standing in the paneled foyer of his Tudor home, wearing the same yellow socks and funky red robe he'd been wearing when we first met. With the blue sling supporting his arm, he had all the primary colors covered. "To what do I owe the house call?"

The Dr. Death wisecrack meant I didn't need to ask if he'd seen the *Gazette*. He was up to speed on everything Grimes had written.

There was no certainty at this point, only educated guesses and good old-fashioned reasoning. If Kingsman was the link to all the previous victims, he somehow had to be linked to the next one.

Only this was different. Why would Timitz wait until after he framed Kingsman if the ace of spades were simply another one of his cases?

Of course, logic isn't always the strong suit of serial killers.

For one reason and one reason only I didn't begin by showing Kingsman the photo of the tattoo or even mention it. Timitz turned out to be the Dealer, but that didn't explain where Kingsman had gone the night Timitz was at his house. It was nagging at me. I was curious.

When Kingsman hesitated after I asked him, I was *really* curious.

"I spent the night at the Harvard Club," he said. "I was spooked when you and Detective Needham came to talk to me. Even though I didn't think I was the queen of hearts, I live alone and didn't feel safe."

Fair enough. But the Harvard Club?

Kingsman wasn't a member. He couldn't be. He wasn't a Harvard graduate, nor had he ever taught there—the only two ways you would be allowed to spend the night in one of the club's guest rooms in Manhattan. Unless, of course, someone with enough clout pulled some strings.

"Beau Livingston, Mayor Deacon's chief of staff, went to Harvard," I said. "Did you know that?"

Kingsman's previous hesitation now seemed like a blip. This was a full-on freeze-up. The judge was hiding something.

"Yes, I did know that," said Kingsman finally. "Beau's the one who arranged my staying at the club."

"That was nice of Beau," I said.

"It was." Kingsman's tone shifted on a dime. It was as if he were reminding himself that this was his house and I was a guest, an uninvited one at that. "Is that what you've come to talk to me about?" he asked.

The subtext was clear as could be. *If it is, you won't be staying long, Dr. Death.*

"No. It's something else," I said, taking out my phone. One click brought up the picture. "I wanted to show you something."

Kingsman looked at the tattoo. I didn't even get the chance to tell him the arm belonged to Timitz.

"Oh, shit," he said.

He rolled up the right sleeve of his red robe, showing me the same tattoo.

"He wants you dead after all," I said.

"No," said Kingsman. "It's not me."

He told me why. Then he told me who. There was another ace of spades.

"Oh, shit," I said.

CHAPTER 105

THE BASIS for any murder: motive and means.

Kingsman had said enough for me to figure out the motive; now it was all about the means.

How does Timitz kill the mayor of New York City?

"Tell him it's urgent!" I yelled into my cell phone while breaking around half a dozen traffic laws at the same time. I was going ninety on a motorcycle without my helmet so I could talk on the phone while weaving in and out of traffic on the West Side Highway.

"I'm sorry. He's not available," said Deacon's assistant. I could barely hear her with the wind whipping past my ears.

"What about Livingston? Is he in his office?"

"What did you say your name was again?" she asked. "Reingold?"

For Christ's sake. "Dylan Reinhart!"

"Oh, of course . . . Dr. Reinhart," she said. Nice to

know she was up on current events. It's not like she worked at City Hall or anything.

Her knowledge of who I was at least got me what I needed—the mayor's whereabouts. Livingston was with him. Only I could still barely hear her.

"Say that again—where are they headed?" I asked.

In my mind, all I could see was the pain on Kingsman's face when I pressed him about his relationship with the mayor. He didn't want to tell me anything, but he had to. He always had his friend's back.

The two were among a handful of air force pilots who called themselves the Black Aces based on the black-ops missions they flew in Lebanon during the mid-1980s. Kingsman was one. Edward "Edso" Deacon was another. All of them had the same tattoo, and their bond was thicker than blood. After all, they had secrets they couldn't even share with their closest family members.

Decades later, long after their flying days were done, Kingsman and Deacon apparently racked up a few new secrets. Timitz had discovered what they were.

"That's all I can tell you," said Kingsman. He wasn't about to incriminate himself.

It was enough, though.

I shot between a Prius and a Range Rover, the

southbound traffic on the highway slowing to a crawl near midtown. Pressing my phone even harder against my ear, I was just able to make out what the mayor's assistant was saying. She, too, was practically yelling.

"...to Queens...throwing out the first pitch...Citi Field."

"How long has it been on his schedule?" I asked.

"I'm not exactly...at least a couple of..."

"Did you say days?"

"No," she said. *"Weeks."*

She was saying something more, but I'd stopped listening. I couldn't help it. The only thing in my head now was Timitz. He was dying on the couch in Grimes's apartment, dying and singing.

Take me out to the ball game...

I cranked my right wrist, maxing the throttle, the wheels on my bike jerking forward as I swung out to the narrow shoulder, blowing through the red light at the 42nd Street exit before darting in front of the oncoming traffic to cut across midtown, heading east for Flushing, Queens. Were there any more laws I could possibly break?

Hell, yeah.

I was just getting started.

CHAPTER 106

"JESUS CHRIST, mate, you sound like you're in a wind tunnel," said Julian.

It was actually the Midtown Tunnel. I was halfway through it, weaving in and out of both eastbound lanes like a guy with a death wish. Between my phone and the throttle, I didn't have a free hand to flip my middle finger to all the cars honking at me. "I need you to check something," I said.

"Check?" Julian said, laughing. He knew I meant "hack."

"Administrative payroll for the New York Mets," I said. "Elijah Timitz."

"You got it," he said. "One minute."

Julian's special talents aside—or maybe because of them—his next greatest asset was the ability to ignore human impulses. For example, anyone else would've asked, "What's going on?" or "Why do you need to know if the Dealer ever worked at Citi Field?"

If I was the one asking—that's all he needed to know. The details could come later over a bottle of very expensive whiskey, my treat.

Julian had asked for a minute. All he needed was half that.

"No," he said, coming back on. "No Timitz with the Mets."

"The entire payroll?"

"Unless he was an intern."

"No; that wouldn't make sense."

"Wait. There's something else I could try," he said.

"What?" I asked. But that was my human impulse. Stupid question.

"Got it," said Julian, another half minute later. "They farm out some of their overnight security, a company in Queens called Guardian. Timitz started there six months ago. Anything else?"

"Yeah," I said. "One more thing."

In 2006, Alexander Litvinenko, a former officer with the FSB, Russia's version of the CIA, died in London from acute radiation poisoning after being exposed to polonium-210. It didn't happen by accident. Whoever did it never wanted to be caught, and to this day he still hasn't been. Rest assured that the culprit wasn't a serial killer.

"If you wanted to kill someone from the grave— one man and one man only—and he's about to throw out the first pitch at Citi Field in ten minutes, how do you do it?" I asked Julian.

"Are we talking about Elijah Timitz, the son of a demolitions expert? If we are, you do it the same way I know that at this very moment you're on Northern Boulevard, exactly four-tenths of a mile from the stadium," said Julian. "Make that three-tenths now."

Then, with one more sentence, he explained exactly what he meant.

I hung up with Julian, shoving my phone away to get the maximum rpm from my bike, the first glimpse of Citi Field up ahead.

Forget that bottle of expensive whiskey, Julian. You, my friend, are getting a case and then some…

CHAPTER 107

"HEY, YOU can't park there!"

That was the first cop chasing me after I sprinted from my bike. The second was the one who saw me hurdle the turnstile into the stadium without breaking stride. Neither was fighting in his desired weight class, to put it mildly, but they were able to stay close on my heels because the people crowding the walkways, still making their way to their seats, were blocking my path. I was back to weaving in and out of traffic again, only now on foot.

Tick-tock...

I didn't need to check the time because I could hear the public-address announcer asking everyone to stand for the national anthem. I had two minutes at most to get to the mayor. Every year, you can bet the over-under in Vegas on the length of the national anthem performed at the Super Bowl. The average for the past ten years has been a minute and fifty-seven seconds.

As a Mets fan, I knew Citi Field pretty well. Even if I didn't, I'd still know where I was heading. Deacon would be coming out of the home dugout, along the first-base line, immediately after the anthem. Right up until then he'd probably still be taking his practice throws in the batting cages near the clubhouse.

President George W. Bush ruined it for every other politician, especially in New York, when he threw a perfect strike at Yankee Stadium before game 3 of the World Series after 9/11. He threw it from the mound and didn't cheat it by a foot.

There was no way Deacon would attempt anything different. He'd throw it from the mound, too.

"The bombs bursting in air..."

Whoever was singing the anthem was getting close to the end. I kept running and weaving, stealing glances at every section opening to see where I was in relation to the field. I had to time the turn just right.

Damn!

Up ahead, I could see two cops running toward me. Word was out—there was a crazy Mets fan on the loose. What they didn't know was that I was a New York Knicks fan as well.

Time for the pick and roll.

Slashing toward a concession stand, I drew the cops toward me, waiting until the last possible moment to spin around them, a condiments table running interference for me. Thank you mustard, ketchup, and sauerkraut.

"Stop him!" I kept hearing.

No one could, though, not yet. I passed another section opening, spying the end of the Mets dugout down by the field. On a dime I turned, blowing past the guy in charge of checking tickets to race down the steps.

"O'er the land of the free…"

I had a clean shot over the railing, catapulting myself over it and onto the field. No less than half a dozen police and security guards were on my tail down the aisle, with more coming at me from every angle.

The one who finally got me, though, was the cop in the dugout the second I tried to reach the tunnel to the clubhouse. He was definitely fighting in his weight class; there was no evading him.

"Gotcha, you son of a bitch," he said, slamming me down.

CHAPTER 108

"GET THE mayor!" I said. "Tell him it's Dylan Reinhart!"

The crowd roar drowned me out, though. The anthem had just ended.

I'd been all over the news, but no one was about to recognize me with my face smooshed hard against the concrete floor of the dugout. I was surrounded by arms and elbows, all of them angry and eager to keep me down. There was a heel digging into the back of my neck.

"The mayor!" I tried again. "He can't go out to the mound!"

The crowd was still too loud. The only voice that rose above it belonged to one of the cops hovering over me, who instructed the rest. "Get him the hell out of here!" he barked.

I got scooped up into a headlock, my feet barely touching the ground as they carried me through the tunnel leading into the bowels of the stadium.

The crowd noise dimmed, overtaken by the echoing voice of the public-address announcer asking everyone to welcome a special guest to throw out the ceremonial first pitch.

Immediately to my left, a door burst open. The mayor, surrounded by a posse of guards and staff, came walking out in a shiny blue Mets jacket as I passed by. I tried to call out to him only to get a thick, heavy hand from one of the cops slapped over my mouth.

From the corner of my eye, I saw my last chance. Livingston was bringing up the rear, busy looking at a folder. No way he was going to see me unless...

"Fuck!" the cop cried out, pulling away his hand in pain. I'd bitten the hell out of his finger.

"Livingston, it's Reinhart!" I yelled as loud as I could.

He couldn't see me, but he heard me. "Wait!" he said. "Stop!"

The cops stopped as Livingston walked over, confused. He knew enough, though, to tell them to let go of me so I could explain.

Only there was no time.

The crowd roared again—albeit with a smattering of boos mixed in—as Deacon exited the dugout. I could see over Livingston's shoulder as the mayor stopped for a moment to turn and wave, holding up a baseball in his other hand. Then he was gone...heading to the mound.

That made two of us.

Without a word of warning I shoved my way past Livingston, bolting back toward the dugout. I could hear the snapping sounds of hands on leather as the cops reached for their holsters, but there were too many people still lingering in the tunnel for a clean shot.

Springing into the dugout, I launched myself up the steps and onto the field, the mayor about to step over the chalk of the first-base line. I could hear the crowd gasp as I lunged in the air, tackling Deacon hard to the ground. He didn't know what had hit him—or who—as he rolled under my grasp, his first instinct being to get the hell away.

I wouldn't let him.

Every cop with every gun, every photographer with every lens—they all ran toward us.

Deacon was livid. "Reinhart, what the—"

"Give me your phone, Mr. Mayor," I said.

"My what?"

"Your phone. Give me your phone!"

Deacon hesitated, and the cops began to close in. Call it faith or call it curiosity, but he raised a hand for them to stand down. With his other hand he reached into his pants pocket, giving me his cell phone.

Assault and battery on the mayor of New York City in front of more than forty thousand people would normally require some explaining. But in the words of Mark Twain, actions speak louder than words.

Tonight, ladies and gentlemen, Dr. Death is throwing out the first pitch…

I turned and heaved the mayor's phone toward the pitcher's mound, directly at the rubber. It was a bit high and outside, but close enough to make my point.

Boom!

The mound exploded with the force of a grenade, everyone on the field taking cover. All they got on them, though, was some flying dirt.

Elijah Timitz, the man who would forever be known as the Dealer, had figured out a way to remotely detonate a bomb while being nowhere close to his intended target—in his case, as far away as hell.

"With GPS, your cell number can trigger anything," said Julian.

Ultimately, the reporters would all ask me the same question—how did I know?

The worst part was that I couldn't give credit where credit was due. Not that Julian Byrd would care one lick. Anonymity is the hacker's code, he was always fond of telling me.

How did I know?

"A little birdie told me" was all I'd say.

Then I wouldn't say anything more.

CHAPTER 109

"WHERE ARE you taking me?" asked Tracy.

We were in the backseat of a cab heading across Central Park to the Upper East Side. Tracy didn't recognize the address I gave the driver, nor should he have.

"You'll see," I said.

Earlier that morning I was far less coy with the mayor and his chief of staff. Edso Deacon, Beau Livingston, and I had a cozy little breakfast at City Hall. Deacon had eggs, Livingston had oatmeal, and I had all the leverage in the world.

Figuring out what Timitz had on Judge Kingsman and the mayor was as easy as following the money. It always is.

Kingsman wasn't crooked. It was more like bent. He was so blinded by his history with Deacon, the bond they shared, that he was willing to grant a mistrial in a case involving criminal negligence on a construction site operated by Deacon during his commercial real estate days. In return, Deacon—through a PAC and a couple of shell companies—essentially bankrolled two of Kingsman's reelection campaigns to the New York State Supreme Court.

Of course, it would've probably taken me months to piece all that together. Thanks to Timitz, it only took three days—UPS three-day shipping, to be exact. In keeping with the Dealer's knack for sending packages, I received all his evidence—timed perfectly, or so he had planned— after the mayor was supposed to have died at Citi Field.

"What are you going to do with it?" asked Deacon.

"The same thing you're going to do with whatever you dug up on me," I said. "Nothing."

Some people would argue that I had a civic duty to go public with the information. It's a fair argument. The problem is that life sometimes makes you choose between the lesser of two evils. Simply put, the people who would benefit from knowing my role in the CIA during my supposed fellowship at the University of Cambridge would make Deacon and company look like choirboys.

But that's a story or two for another time.

"Anything else?" asked the mayor.

He was all but assured reelection, thanks to his

surviving an assassination attempt, provided that the motives for the attempt never saw the light of day. He was doing everything in his power to make sure they didn't.

"Yes—one more thing," I said. "You're now going to tell me what Elizabeth had the integrity to keep to herself. Why did you originally have her transferred to your security detail?"

Life can often be messy and mystifying. As when an attractive young detective gets what looks like a promotion only to discover that she was assigned to the mayor in order to provide cover for an affair he was having. She could quit or go to the press, but either action would mean that she wouldn't get to do what she always wanted to do: serve and protect. So she stayed quiet, convinced ultimately that all the people she'd be able to help over time were far more important than one politician who couldn't keep it in his pants.

She was right.

The cabdriver pulled up to the brownstone on East 74th Street. I paid the fare as Tracy stepped out, still without a clue as to why we were there.

We walked up the steps, and I rang the doorbell. Seconds later, the door opened.

"Right on time," said Barbara Nash. "C'mon in."

The head of the Gateway Adoption Agency welcomed us into her home, a pair of golden retrievers with red bandannas around their necks happily greeting us right behind her. Behind them was Ms. Peckler. In her hand was an iced tea instead of a clipboard.

"I'm afraid we got off on the wrong foot," she said. "I'm sorry about that."

EPILOGUE

SPECIAL DELIVERY

CHAPTER 110

A FEW weeks before the big day, I thought I had a good idea how we would decide on her name.

First we would each write down our ten favorites. Then we would exchange lists to see if there was a name that both of us had chosen.

"What do you think?" I asked, pouring Tracy and myself some more coffee. I even brought two pens and a couple of sheets of paper with me to the kitchen table. "It makes sense, right?"

Tracy gave me the Look. Only this time, it felt a little different. There was a smile hiding behind it.

"I've got a better idea," he said.

Tracy grabbed a pen, quickly scribbling something before handing the paper back to me. He'd written only one name. Annabelle.

My mother's name.

Annabelle McKay-Reinhart arrived safely at JFK

airport, greeting us with a pair of big, beautiful hazel eyes and an extended yawn. It's a long trip for anyone from South Africa, let alone a two-month-old.

There were a few more papers to read and sign, which Barbara Nash took us through while Tracy and I took turns holding Annabelle. We did our best to pay attention, although at times all we could hear was the sound of our pounding hearts. We were awestruck and over-whelmed.

The escort from Gateway's affiliate in Germany, an angel of a woman, handed us a large envelope containing Annabelle's medical records, her birth certificate, information about the formula she was on, and a picture of her birth mother, as we requested. The envelope was red.

Who said red's never good?

"You have a beautiful and healthy baby girl. Congratulations," said the escort. "And if I do say so, she's quite the flirt, too. On the second leg of the flight, from Frankfurt, your daughter had a gentleman sitting next to us gushing over her the entire time."

"Did you hear that?" said Tracy. *"Our daughter."*

Yeah—life can be messy and mystifying, all right. But every once in a while you get a day that seems to make sense of it all.

Those are the days you remember most.

The days you cherish.

The days you hold in your arms with all the love that you could possibly have in your heart.

Isn't that right, Annabelle?

ABOUT THE AUTHORS

JAMES PATTERSON received the Literarian Award for Outstanding Service to the American Literary Community at the 2015 National Book Awards. He holds the Guinness World Record for the most #1 *New York Times* bestsellers, and his books have sold more than 350 million copies worldwide. A tireless champion of the power of books and reading, Patterson created a children's book imprint, JIMMY Patterson, whose mission is simple: "We want every kid who finishes a JIMMY Book to say, 'PLEASE GIVE ME ANOTHER BOOK.'" He has donated more than one million books to students and soldiers and funds over four hundred Teacher Education Scholarships at twenty-four colleges and universities. He has also donated millions to independent bookstores and school libraries. Patterson invests proceeds from the sales of JIMMY Patterson Books in pro-reading initiatives.

*   *   *

HOWARD ROUGHAN has cowritten several books with James Patterson and is the author of *The Promise of a Lie* and *The Up and Comer.* He lives in Florida with his wife and son.

BOOKS BY JAMES PATTERSON

FEATURING ALEX CROSS

Cross the Line • Cross Justice • Hope to Die • Cross
My Heart • Alex Cross, Run • Merry Christmas,
Alex Cross • Kill Alex Cross • Cross Fire • I, Alex
Cross • Alex Cross's Trial (with Richard DiLallo) •
Cross Country • Double Cross • Cross (also
published as Alex Cross) • Mary, Mary • London
Bridges • The Big Bad Wolf • Four Blind Mice •
Violets Are Blue • Roses Are Red • Pop Goes the
Weasel • Cat & Mouse • Jack & Jill • Kiss the Girls
• Along Came a Spider

THE WOMEN'S MURDER CLUB

16th Seduction (with Maxine Paetro) • 15th Affair
(with Maxine Paetro) • 14th Deadly Sin (with
Maxine Paetro) • Unlucky 13 (with Maxine
Paetro) • 12th of Never (with Maxine Paetro) •
11th Hour (with Maxine Paetro) • 10th
Anniversary (with Maxine Paetro) • The 9th
Judgment (with Maxine Paetro) • The 8th
Confession (with Maxine Paetro) • 7th Heaven
(with Maxine Paetro) • The 6th Target (with
Maxine Paetro) • The 5th Horseman (with Maxine
Paetro) • 4th of July (with Maxine Paetro) • 3rd

Degree (with Andrew Gross) • *2nd Chance* (with Andrew Gross) • *1st to Die*

FEATURING MICHAEL BENNETT

Bullseye (with Michael Ledwidge) • *Alert* (with Michael Ledwidge) • *Burn* (with Michael Ledwidge) • *Gone* (with Michael Ledwidge) • *I, Michael Bennett* (with Michael Ledwidge) • *Tick Tock* (with Michael Ledwidge) • *Worst Case* (with Michael Ledwidge) • *Run for Your Life* (with Michael Ledwidge) • *Step on a Crack* (with Michael Ledwidge)

THE PRIVATE NOVELS

Missing: A Private Novel (with Kathryn Fox) • *The Games* (with Mark Sullivan) • *Private Paris* (with Mark Sullivan) • *Private Vegas* (with Maxine Paetro) • *Private India: City on Fire* (with Ashwin Sanghi) • *Private Down Under* (with Michael White) • *Private L.A.* (with Mark Sullivan) • *Private Berlin* (with Mark Sullivan) • *Private London* (with Mark Pearson) • *Private Games* (with Mark Sullivan) • *Private: #1 Suspect* (with Maxine Paetro) • *Private* (with Maxine Paetro)

NYPD RED NOVELS

NYPD Red 4 (with Marshall Karp) • *NYPD Red 3* (with Marshall Karp) • *NYPD Red 2* (with Marshall Karp) • *NYPD Red* (with Marshall Karp)

SUMMER NOVELS

Second Honeymoon (with Howard Roughan) • *Now You See Her* (with Michael Ledwidge) • *Swimsuit* (with Maxine Paetro) • *Sail* (with Howard Roughan) • *Beach Road* (with Peter de Jonge) • *Lifeguard* (with Andrew Gross) • *Honeymoon* (with Howard Roughan) • *The Beach House* (with Peter de Jonge)

STAND-ALONE BOOKS

Penguins of America (with Jack Patterson and Florence Yue) • *Murder Games* (with Howard Roughan) • *Two from the Heart* (with Frank Constantini, Emily Raymond, and Brian Sitts) • *The Black Book* (with David Ellis) • *Humans, Bow Down* (with Emily Raymond, illustrated by Alexander Ovchinnikov) • *Never Never* (with Candice Fox) • *Woman of God* (with Maxine Paetro) • *Filthy Rich* (with John Connolly and Timothy Malloy) • *The Murder House* (with David Ellis) • *Truth or Die* (with Howard Roughan) •

Miracle at Augusta (with Peter de Jonge) • *Invisible* (with David Ellis) • *First Love* (with Emily Raymond) • *Mistress* (with David Ellis) • *Zoo* (with Michael Ledwidge) • *Guilty Wives* (with David Ellis) • *The Christmas Wedding* (with Richard DiLallo) • *Kill Me If You Can* (with Marshall Karp) • *Toys* (with Neil McMahon) • *Don't Blink* (with Howard Roughan) • *The Postcard Killers* (with Liza Marklund) • *The Murder of King Tut* (with Martin Dugard) • *Against Medical Advice* (with Hal Friedman) • *Sundays at Tiffany's* (with Gabrielle Charbonnet) • *You've Been Warned* (with Howard Roughan) • *The Quickie* (with Michael Ledwidge) • *Judge & Jury* (with Andrew Gross) • *Sam's Letters to Jennifer* • *The Lake House* • *The Jester* (with Andrew Gross) • *Suzanne's Diary for Nicholas* • *Cradle and All* • *When the Wind Blows* • *Miracle on the 17th Green* (with Peter de Jonge) • *Hide & Seek* • *The Midnight Club* • *Black Friday* (originally published as *Black Market*) • *See How They Run* • *Season of the Machete* • *The Thomas Berryman Number*

BOOK**SHOTS**

Detective Cross • *Private: Gold* (with Jassy Mackenzie) • *French Twist: A Detective Luc Moncrief Story* (with Richard DiLallo) • *Malicious: A Mitchum Story* (with James O.

Born) • *The House Husband* (with Duane Swierczynski) • *Hidden: A Mitchum Story* (with James O. Born) • *Come and Get Us* (with Shan Serafin) • *Private: The Royals* (with Rees Jones) • *Black & Blue* (with Candice Fox) • *The Christmas Mystery: A Detective Luc Moncrief Story* (with Richard DiLallo) • *Taking the Titanic* (with Scott Slaven) • *Killer Chef* (with Jeffrey J. Keyes) • *$10,000,000 Marriage Proposal* (with Hilary Liftin) • *French Kiss: A Detective Luc Moncrief Story* (with Richard DiLallo) • *Hunted* (with Andrew Holmes) • *113 Minutes* (with Max DiLallo) • *Chase* (with Michael Ledwidge) • *Let's Play Make-Believe* (with James O. Born) • *The Trial* (with Maxine Paetro) • *Little Black Dress* (with Emily Raymond) • *Cross Kill* • *Zoo 2* (with Max DiLallo)

FOR READERS OF ALL AGES

Maximum Ride

Maximum Ride Forever • *Nevermore: The Final Maximum Ride Adventure* • *Angel: A Maximum Ride Novel* • *Fang: A Maximum Ride Novel* • *Max: A Maximum Ride Novel* • *The Final Warning: A Maximum Ride Novel* • *Saving the World and Other Extreme Sports: A Maximum Ride Novel* • *School's*

Out—Forever: A Maximum Ride Novel • *The Angel Experiment: A Maximum Ride Novel*

Daniel X

Daniel X: Lights Out (with Chris Grabenstein) • *Daniel X: Armageddon* (with Chris Grabenstein) • *Daniel X: Game Over* (with Ned Rust) • *Daniel X: Demons and Druids* (with Adam Sadler) • *Daniel X: Watch the Skies* (with Ned Rust) • *The Dangerous Days of Daniel X* (with Michael Ledwidge)

Witch & Wizard

Witch & Wizard: The Lost (with Emily Raymond) • *Witch & Wizard: The Kiss* (with Jill Dembowski) • *Witch & Wizard: The Fire* (with Jill Dembowski) • *Witch & Wizard: The Gift* (with Ned Rust) • *Witch & Wizard* (with Gabrielle Charbonnet)

Middle School

Middle School: Escape to Australia (with Martin Chatterton, illustrated by Daniel Griffo) • *Middle School: Dog's Best Friend* (with Chris Tebbetts, illustrated by Jomike Tejido) • *Middle School: Just My Rotten Luck* (with Chris Tebbetts, illustrated by Laura Park) • *Middle School: Save Rafe!* (with Chris Tebbetts, illustrated by Laura Park) •

Middle School: Ultimate Showdown (with Julia Bergen, illustrated by Alec Longstreth) • *Middle School: How I Survived Bullies, Broccoli, and Snake Hill* (with Chris Tebbetts, illustrated by Laura Park) • *Middle School: My Brother Is a Big, Fat Liar* (with Lisa Papademetriou, illustrated by Neil Swaab) • *Middle School: Get Me Out of Here!* (with Chris Tebbetts, illustrated by Laura Park) • *Middle School, The Worst Years of My Life* (with Chris Tebbetts, illustrated by Laura Park)

Confessions

Confessions: The Murder of an Angel (with Maxine Paetro) • *Confessions: The Paris Mysteries* (with Maxine Paetro) • *Confessions: The Private School Murders* (with Maxine Paetro) • *Confessions of a Murder Suspect* (with Maxine Paetro)

I Funny

I Funny: School of Laughs (with Chris Grabenstein, illustrated by Jomike Tejido) • *I Funny TV* (with Chris Grabenstein, illustrated by Laura Park) • *I Totally Funniest: A Middle School Story* (with Chris Grabenstein, illustrated by Laura Park) • *I Even Funnier: A Middle School Story* (with Chris Grabenstein, illustrated by Laura Park) • *I Funny: A Middle School Story* (with Chris Grabenstein, illustrated by Laura Park)

Treasure Hunters

Treasure Hunters: Peril at the Top of the World (with Chris Grabenstein, illustrated by Juliana Neufeld) • *Treasure Hunters: Secret of the Forbidden City* (with Chris Grabenstein, illustrated by Juliana Neufeld) • *Treasure Hunters: Danger Down the Nile* (with Chris Grabenstein, illustrated by Juliana Neufeld) • *Treasure Hunters* (with Chris Grabenstein, illustrated by Juliana Neufeld)

House of Robots

Robot Revolution (with Chris Grabenstein, illustrated by Juliana Neufeld) • *Robots Go Wild!* (with Chris Grabenstein, illustrated by Juliana Neufeld) • *House of Robots* (with Chris Grabenstein, illustrated by Juliana Neufeld)

OTHER BOOKS FOR READERS OF ALL AGES

Crazy House (with Gabrielle Charbonnet) • *Word of Mouse* (with Chris Grabenstein, illustrated by Joe Sutphin) • *Give Please a Chance* (with Bill O'Reilly) • *Cradle and All* (teen edition) • *Jacky Ha-Ha* (with Chris Grabenstein, illustrated by Kerascoët) • *Public School Superhero* (with Chris Tebbetts, illustrated by Cory Thomas) • *Homeroom Diaries* (with Lisa Papademetriou, illustrated by Keino) • *Med Head* (with Hal

Friedman) • *santaKid* (illustrated by Michael Garland)

For previews and information about the author, visit JamesPatterson.com or find him on Facebook or at your app store.